G000166369

Published in Great Britain by

L.R. Price Publications Ltd, 2022

27 Old Gloucester Street,

London, WC1N 3AX

www.lrpricepublications.com

Cover artwork by LR Price Publications Ltd
Original image by misterd1948 Copyright © 2022

ISBN-: 9781915330123

# Crime Sheet

**Noel Spence**

## Split Decision

Edmond had his overnight bag ready and was waiting for the taxi to take him to the airport. He was quite looking forward to the journey: short flight from London to Glasgow, a pleasant trip on the West Highland Line from Queen Street to the little station at Taynuilt, and then a taxi to the Ardanaiseig Four Star luxury hotel. He had googled the hotel and it looked delightful, a genuinely authentic old country house of very generous proportions, and in a remote location on the edge of Loch Awe. It should be the ideal setting for his talk. The whole place looked like one big visual aid.

With about half an hour to spare before the taxi was due, Edmond idly checked his emails. There was one new message. He didn't recognise the display name of the sender. The message was a real surprise.

*Hello, Edmond. I hope you will remember me from school. I certainly remember you, even though it's about fifty years ago. I couldn't believe it when I saw in the local paper that Edmond Carroll was coming to speak at the Ardanaiseig. You see, I live only a few miles from the hotel. I'd love to meet up with you if your timetable allows it. Apart from the pleasure of seeing you after so many years, there's something I'd very much like to show*

*you. Did you hear of my good fortune?*
*I hope you get this message OK. I got*
*your contact address from your*
*website, so hopefully it's an up-to-date*
*one. Looking forward to hearing from*
*you.*
 *Regards,*
 *Max Wissler*

Yes, a real surprise indeed. Max Wissler. Edmond remembered the name all right, and with a bit of hard memory-searching he faintly remembered the person – a small boy with dark hair, a thin face, and glasses. Edmond wasn't one for Old Boys' Reunions and 'Class of Such a Year' get-togethers, that kind of thing, but this looked different. He checked his programme again. Lunch at 1pm, his talk at 3pm, and evening meal at six. That left the evening pretty much his own. At his age he didn't fancy a session in the bar, the way these things usually ended, so partly out of curiosity about what he would be shown, and largely to escape the liquid generosity of his hosts, Edmond emailed back that he would be very pleased to see Max any time from 8pm onwards. The mention of Max's good fortune stirred nothing in Edmond's memory, so he left that until they met.

 The trip was as trouble-free and relaxing as he had hoped it would be. For a man of Edmond's experience, it was strange that he had never lost the schoolboy's pleasure in 'looking out', just sitting at the window watching the sights and scenes roll by. He glanced briefly, very briefly, at the few notes he had scribbled down for his talk on *Scotland: History, Heritage and Hotels.* Edmond was a leading expert, or probably *the* leading expert, on the preservation and restoration of historic buildings, with the particular standpoint of converting and refurbishing them for the hotel industry. The PowerPoint presentation he would give would anticipate much of the opposition he might possibly encounter from those purists who would prefer a mossed-over derelict to a restored, active and viable tourist facility.

This talk, hosted and paid for by the Architectural Heritage Society of Scotland, was just one of several that Edmond had been asked to deliver since his retirement over a year ago. He was experienced enough to know that a distinguished Guest Speaker such as himself gave prestige and provenance to what was, in truth, something of a jolly. His audience wouldn't be expecting to learn anything new but would hope to hear personal anecdotes and reflections well-spiced with humour.

The hotel was everything, and more, that the brochures claimed. Set among woods beside the vast expanse of the loch, and cradled by imposing hills and slopes, it was reached by roads so narrow and tracks so bumpy that Edmond wondered how coaches could negotiate them, and what ensued when two coaches met face to face. His talk was extremely well received. He ended it with these words: 'Look around you, ladies and gentlemen, and what do you see? A pile of ancient stones in a forgotten heap, or a tourist facility sympathetic to past and place, proud of its present, and providing prosperity for the future? I rest my case.'

Just before eight, in the relative quiet of the Residents' Lounge, Edmond awaited the arrival of Max Wissler. He had no idea what to expect, but hoped it wouldn't be a dreary recital of all the names and people each could remember from half a century ago. He was tempted to ask the barman or one of the waiters what they knew of Mr. Wissler, but decided to wait and judge for himself. Edmond was about to order himself a drink when a waiter came over and informed him that a gentleman wanted to see him at Reception. Edmond followed him to the entrance hall.

The amazing thing was that Edmond would have recognised the frail little figure with the full head of white hair who came forward to meet him. It wasn't because he knew already that this was Max Wissler; if he had met this small man in the tweed suit by chance instead of by arrangement, he was sure he would have identified him. They shook hands, and Edmond invited him into the lounge for a drink.

'I'd prefer not, if you don't mind. I don't go into public places, as a rule. I was hoping we could chat at my place. It's only ten minutes away.'

'Fine. Do you want me to bring a bottle from the bar?'

Wissler smiled, 'No, not at all. I think I might have enough to do.'

Edmond was surprised to see the Volvo Estate car. Without quite knowing why, he had expected something less powerful, but then he remembered that it wasn't unusual for small men to drive big cars. 'Thanks for agreeing to see me, Edmond. I know you're a busy and important man. I've looked you up on the internet. You're a household name in certain circles – and a very successful one.' He eased the big car out of its space and towards the car park exit.

'What about you, Max? To be honest, I hadn't heard of you since I left school until I got your email this morning. What direction did you go in? What brought you up here?'

'A game of two halves, as the commentators say. First half a disaster, all downwards, second half a complete turnaround. You could have heard of me twenty years ago. You're talking to the first millionaire winner on the National Lottery. It was actually nearly one and a quarter million. I tried to keep it anonymous, the 'no publicity' thing, but you know what the press is like. I managed to escape the worst of it, kept it to a minimum, but for a few days they had me on the front pages and on the TV screens. Anyhow, it was a small price to pay. I've been on top of the world ever since.'

While they were talking, Max was handling the Volvo with practised efficiency along a road that bordered the dark waters of the loch. He sat with his head thrust forward, about a couple of feet from the windscreen, and peered at the road ahead, which seemed to Edmond to be getting even narrower as they went. Max explained that he lived on an island near the north end of Loch Awe. It was called Inishail and was among a group of islets in what he called the 'Lorn district', which meant nothing at all to his passenger. 'It's wooded, but there's plenty of grass too. The locals call it The Green Isle. That big bulk there, to your right, is Ben Cruachan.'

Just at that moment an animal such as Edmond had never seen before darted across the road about fifty yards ahead of them. It was black and brown with a long tail like a fox, but moved in a supple kind of way, like a weasel. Then it unaccountably turned and ran back the way it had come and disappeared into the undergrowth.

Max was spluttering with excitement. 'Do you know what you've just seen? A pine martin. That's the first one I've seen, and I've been here for twenty years. There are people that have lived here all their lives who've never seen one. They're about all right, but they're very shy. The luck of you, Edmond, here for one day from London, of all places, and you get to see what most local people haven't managed to see in maybe eighty years. Can you believe it, beginner's luck or what? It's a good omen, that's for sure. The luck has been with me ever since I won the lottery, and now I'm sharing it with an old school friend.'

He drove on for a few minutes shaking his head in wonder at their good fortune in seeing the elusive pine martin. Suddenly the narrow roadway, that had become little more than a path, broadened out into a wide stretch of smooth asphalt surface. The car came out from behind the wooded lakeside curtain and stopped in front of an iron gate that guarded a causeway leading directly over the water to the shape of a large island. Max pressed a button on a handset in the dash of the Volvo, and to Edmond's astonishment the black gate rose like a portcullis, and the car passed underneath and started across the causeway. He instinctively looked back and the gate was slowly descending to its closed position. Nothing was said. Max shortly resumed his tour guide role.

'Those ruins there, to the left, are the remains of a medieval parish church. There's an old graveyard beside them. I own the whole lot. I bought the island outright in late 1989. Got it for a song... and there's my house, right ahead. It hadn't been occupied since 1938 but was in remarkably good condition. No vandalism, no rain getting in.'

Edmond was truly astonished. What he was looking at was a true Scottish vernacular, a tower house, or fortified house as they were sometimes called, with the distinctive features intact – the heavy stone construction, thick walls, three floors, small windows, corner turrets. 'The closest thing to a castle I could get,' added Max, with a slight smile.

So, this was what Max had been referring to in his email, '*something I'd very much like to show you*'. Yes, and something Edmond would very much like to be shown. Max parked the car, and they went in through the front entrance, which had been very substantially widened. It was the one big alteration to the house exterior. The heavy wooden door opened automatically at the touch of another handset button, and Edmond smiled to himself at the notion of how defensive walls that could have resisted the heaviest of attacks could now be breached by the touch of a fingertip. A glance was enough to tell him that the interior had been converted to a very high specification. He was expecting to be shown round and invited to inspect the fine conversion, but instead Max offered him an armchair in front of the huge fireplace. He pressed a button beneath an elaborate mantelpiece corbel, and the 'log' burst into instant gas fire. Edmond allowed himself another quiet smile.

'You'll try a taste of the local 'vin de pays'?' asked Max, and produced a bottle of Laphroaig Islay Single Malt whisky. 'I'm not a great drinker, Edmond, but I enjoy a drop of this stuff now and again. When in Rome, and all that. Cheers.'

Edmond asked about the house: listed building, planning permission, architect, craftsmen, and so on. Apparently, the planning authority and local council were only too eager to assist the prospective buyer, especially when he promised that the materials and labour would all be sourced locally.

'You'd be surprised, Edmond, how many top-class tradesmen are available in a thinly populated area like this. I simply got the plans drawn up and approved, chose the team, and left them to it. 'Nae bother', as they would say hereabouts. My main interest was getting the place well insulated. The walls, floors, and roof are packed with the stuff. The causeway was only a line of rough stones, so it had to be done, and I got a high steel mesh fence installed right around the whole island. In case of a Viking invasion,' he added, with that same little half smile.

Edmond was waiting for the tour of the house to begin, but his host refilled their glasses.

It was odd that he seemed rather diffident about what must be his pride and joy. He swirled the whisky round in his glass, studied the effect, and said, 'You're the first guest, Edmond, the first visitor I've had in this house in twenty years. The local people call me a recluse, and 'daft in the heed'. Some of the older folk refer to me as the laird. I do my own cleaning and cooking, everything I want or need I order online, delivered to the gate. I go into Oban now and again and stock up the Volvo with other odds and ends. There's a local man who tidies the garden up a few times in the year, but he's never been in the house. What is it they say, 'An Englishman's house is his castle'?' Again, the little smile.

Edmond wasn't sure what to say, whether to show sympathy or approval. He chose to ask a neutral question. 'Why this part of the UK? It's very different from the south of England, from what you were used to, is it not?'

Max considered the question for a few moments. 'Are you a religious man, Edmond?'

The reply threw Edmond, but he gave as honest an answer as he could. 'Well, I'm not a worshipper or a churchgoer, but yes, I do believe that there is some kind of moral force out there, something at work, that holds things together. Call it God, if you wish. Put it this way, I've never bought into the evolution theory. I mean, how did we evolve to love music and beauty and art, to appreciate the natural world, for example? These aren't necessary for survival. There's more to us than just being the fittest to exist.'

Max slowly nodded his agreement. 'Let me take you back, Edmond, if I may, to that first half I mentioned earlier, or at least to the half time whistle. I was living, if that's the right word, in Brighton at the time, a down-and-out with more problems than you could even imagine. I was sitting on a bench crying. I wasn't begging, just crying. A woman came up to me, handed me a pound coin, said, 'Go and get yourself a cup of tea,' and walked away before I could even thank her. I looked up and the first thing I saw clearly through my tears was the National Lottery sign outside a small shop. I bought a Lucky Dip ticket, and a week later I was a millionaire. Had that woman not appeared from nowhere and given me that one single pound coin, instead of being a millionaire a week later, I'd have been in a pauper's grave. You see, I was sitting on that bench planning to take my own life. Chance, or fate, or what?

Two weeks later what happens? I'm in a private doctor's waiting room. I'm a very rich man in a very poor physical state after years and years of self neglect. I'm in for a complete overhaul. I pick up, at random, a glossy magazine from the table and open it with no interest at all in the contents. I can still remember the name of the magazine, *Country Life*. I had opened it somewhere near the middle, and what was looking out at me but this house we are now sitting in. Again, I'm asking myself, and you too, Edmond, chance or fate, or something bigger than both of these?'

Edmond was less impressed than he was expected to be. 'Why, were you looking for a tower house?' The answer sounded more sarcastic than Edmond had intended.

11

'No, but it gave me the idea, you see, pointed me in the right direction.'

'I see,' said Edmond, not seeing at all.

'It's certainly not what I had expected. I suppose it has its charms, and is undoubtedly of great historical and architectural interest, but I couldn't see myself living alone out here the way you do. I never saw you either, Max, as a modern frontiersman.'

'Ah, to explain that I'll have to go back to that first half I've been referring to, this time to the start, the kick-off. You should recognise the time and place, Edmond, for you were there. I'm talking about our dear Alma Mater and the class of '62. How much do you remember, I wonder? Do you remember Billy Wilkes, for example?'

Edmond laughed. 'Billy Wilkes? Basher Billy, as he liked to be known? Who could forget our charming school bully? I tasted his medicine more than a few times, but then who didn't, apart from his two sidekicks. Somebody in school told me that all bullies are cowards and if you fight back, they'll turn and run. Well, I was stupid enough to believe it and one day I hit Wilkes back. After he had recovered from his surprise, he nearly killed me.' Edmond laughed at the recollection. 'Remember that stupid song he used to sing before he punched me:

*Oh Carroll, you're such a stupid fool,*
*Carroll, I hate you, I'm gonna treat you cruel,*
*I'll hurt you, and I'll make you cry,*
*But if you tell on me, you will surely die.*

How's that, word-perfect after fifty years or more. Not bad, eh?'

Max was silent, his little face grim. He finished his drink and poured himself another. Edmond shook his head and held his hand over his glass. He could feel the whisky glowing inside him. Max took a mouthful and sat looking into the fire.

'Wilkes ruined my life, Edmond. I tell you, he ruined my life. Everything I became, everything I failed to be, every weakness I had, can be traced right back to him. I was his special target. He hated all the boarders, the spoilt little snobs that their parents didn't want, as he described us, but he hated me most. It was my name, you see, Wissler. Our languages teacher one day in class innocently mentioned that my surname was of German origin. That teacher had no idea the harm he did. From that day on I was the Kraut. Wilkes and his cronies gave me the Nazi salute and shouted Heil Hitler every time they had a chance, and chanted, 'Who won the war, who won the war, tell us Adolf Wissler, who won the war?'. Wilkes bullied me every day, pulling my hair, twisting my arm up my back, pulling my fingers back, thumping me in the stomach until I was crying and begging for mercy. He was careful never to leave bruises on me. My life was made a total misery.'

Edmond was genuinely taken aback, not simply on account of the extent of the bullying campaign, but because of Max's recounting of it. His voice had become shaky and his whole manner jittery, as if the words were expressing actual present pain and humiliation. 'Didn't you report him to the teachers, or to the Headmaster?'

'Of course I did, and to what avail? Things just got worse. Wilkes grabbed me a day or so later. 'So the little Kraut is a snitch, is he? Well, little Adolf, you're a dead little Kraut. We're gonna suffocate you in your sleep, and here's how we're gonna do it'. He clamped his hand over my mouth and held my nostrils shut until I nearly passed out. He left me choking for air on the ground, then came back and gave my hair a savage yank for good measure. I really believed him. I was afraid to go to sleep in the dorm each night and could only cry myself into a kind of half sleep. I've been afflicted with bouts of insomnia ever since.'

'This is terrible, Max. What about your parents? Surely they could have helped you, taken you away from the school?'

'My father was dead, and my poor mother had enough problems to deal with. Even as a boy I didn't want to add to her worries. School was a living hell for me, but I pretended it was all right. She would send me little parcels of goodies, and I had to surrender these to Wilkes to reduce my daily punishment. As you can imagine, my schoolwork suffered so badly that I quickly sank from near the top of the class in each subject to the bottom of the pack. Wilkes warned me that every time I answered a question correctly in class, he would later administer five punches in the stomach. I just sat and said nothing when I was asked for an answer, and the teachers soon came to regard me as a dullard. How could I have concentrated my mind on learning or studying when it was full to overflowing with fear of what I could expect to get every day from Wilkes? My mother had wanted me to be a doctor, but I left school with no qualifications of any sort. Any hope of a successful school career was finished.

He was a devil for inventing ways to terrify me. He picked up on my name in another way: 'Wissler? Wissler? OK, let's hear you whistle, Wissler. Give us a tune.' My mouth was so dry with fear that I couldn't whistle, no matter how hard I tried, and Wilkes would laugh at my efforts, and then pummel me savagely in the stomach for disobeying him. If I did manage to whistle, he would say he didn't like the tune, and would punch me just the same.

All the while he encouraged his fellow tormentors to practise their skills on me; they would empty bottles of ink into my schoolbag, tear pages out of my books, steal or hide my clothes when I was doing games or PE. There was nothing I could do. I used to yearn for the day when I left school and was away from their relentless persecution and bullying.

What a foolish belief, Edmond, that I could leave all this behind. Let me tell you some, only some, of the damage I carried with me. Apart from medical people and psychiatrists, you are the first person I have spoken to about any of this. For about twenty-five years I lived the life of a mental, physical, and nervous wreck. I developed a stammer, I wet the bed at nights and had to wear nappies like a child, I suffered a series of breakdowns, and made a number of pathetic suicide attempts. I became dependent on anti-depressants. I was in a permanent state of high anxiety. Oddly enough, unlike so many like me who were living in hostels and were unemployable, I never became an alcoholic or a druggie. Can you believe, I have never in my life had a relationship with a woman? I've never even been out with a woman, or had the courage to ask a woman for a date. I know you never married, Edmond, but that was probably by choice. I was too weak and frightened to make any choices.

OK, I spent many years, too many, in hospitals and hostels and Homes and clinics and the likes, or homeless on the street, while you went from success to success, but maybe we're not all that different: we're both single, we both went to the same school, we were both bullied by the same thug, and we're both now sitting at the same table on the island of Inishail. The draw of a lottery ticket changed everything for me, and that's why you're here. Makes you think, doesn't it?'

Max had got more and more agitated during his narration, his speech faster and his voice more emotional as he laid bare the sad truths of his early adult life. Edmond was starting to worry about the journey back to the hotel in the high-powered Volvo, with a very upset and probably slightly drunk man at the wheel. There were no steep drops that he could remember from the road down to the loch, but a whole series of twists and turns that could easily see them literally in deep water.

'I'm really sorry, Max, that you had to undergo so much, but I'm equally happy that luck has balanced things up for you. Thank you for a really different and interesting visit to your fine home. Now I've an early train to catch in the morning, so maybe we'd better think about hitting the road.'

'What!? Edmond, Edmond, you're not serious. I haven't shown you what your visit is all about.'

'It's OK, Max. I've seen enough to know you've done a great job. I've been on the go since early this morning, and to be honest, I'm just a little too tired to see round the rest of it. I'll come back again, I promise, and we can make a day of it.'

Max got up from the table in a state close to panic. 'You have to see this, Edmond. You can't not see it. It was meant to be. I promise you, it'll only take a few minutes, and you'll be so glad you did. Please just follow me, please. Just a few minutes.' He took a ring of keys from his pocket, selected one, and went over to a side door at the far end of the fire. Edmond felt partly pleased, partly disappointed, that the door wasn't opened by another button. They entered a short corridor, or perhaps tunnel might have been a better description, that ended with a second door. Max chose another key from the ring. His hands were shaking, with fear or excitement Edmond couldn't have said.

They went through into a larger room, very dimly lit. The first thing that struck Edmond was the terrible stench, unlike anything he had ever smelled before. It was like a blend of fetid cheese and rancid pus. Edmond almost retched, like he had done that day on the boat when his friend had pulled in the lobster pot with the rotten fish bait in it. Max seemed unaffected by the foulness and moved on into the room.

Edmond's eyes had partly adapted to the poor light, and he could see that the room was empty except for a large cage at the far wall. The walls were of rough stone, with none of the stud cladding that housed the insulation in the other rooms. His professional eye noted too that both floor and ceiling were of similar bare stone. These impressions were quickly forgotten, however, when his ear picked up a strange moaning or whimpering sound coming from the far end of the cage. In the murky light he could just about see something crouching in the corner of it. So Max was keeping an animal of some kind caged in this bare stone room. Whatever it was, the form rose unsteadily on its rear legs and came slouching towards the front of the cage. Edmond thought for a moment of an ape or some other primate, but when the slightly brighter light nearer the middle of the room showed the figure more clearly, he realised with a start that it was more humanoid than simian. The thing moved in a sloppy, floppy kind of manner. Suddenly, with a shock of horror that shook him to the core, Edmond recognised that it was wearing tattered clothing, that it was a man, unlike any man he had ever seen before, but a man just the same.

That first realisation, that image, would stay with Edmond the rest of his waking days; the long shaggy grey hair straggling down to the bony waist area, the beard that matched it in style and length, the curved yellowish finger nails, ragged and broken but over six inches in length, and, most of all, the filth on the face and on those parts of the body and limbs that showed through the numerous rents and holes in the clothing. Beneath the facial grime was a mess of scabs and ulcerous sores that pockmarked and stippled every inch of flesh that was free of hair. The being slumped a yard closer behind the bars, and Edmond saw that the feet were bare, with long twisted toenails that should have been the claws of some wild animal. It was making strange noises, like a human voice played backwards at too slow a speed. In the midst of his horror and revulsion Edmond heard Max speaking.

'Allow me, Edmond, to re-introduce you to our old school pal, Mr. William Wilkes, also known as Basher Billy. That noise is him crying. Two rules: don't get too close to those claws, he might not be as friendly as he used to be, and don't speak to him. I'm sure you're delighted to renew your acquaintance.'

'I think I'm going to be sick. It's the smell in here. Can we go back outside, please?'

'He's my remedy, my medication, my therapy, better than all the treatment I got from the so-called experts in twenty years. No more bed-wetting, no more depression or anxiety, no stammer, no insomnia. The game of two halves, Edmond, the game of two halves. He dominated the first, I'm in control of the second. It's all been planned. That woman who gave me the pound, she was sent to me. Maybe she didn't know it, but she was part of God's plan. He chose that lottery ticket for me, He showed me the way, the picture in the magazine. Your talk in the Ardanaiseig, that wasn't by chance, that is part of His plan. And the pine martin. Remember how it showed itself to us and then disappeared. That was a sign. He's showing me that I am doing His will in sharing my secret with you. None of it is my luck, or your luck, or beginner's luck, it's all been planned, the glory goes to Him. I'm His instrument of justice.'

Glory? That creature in the cage? Max was completely demented, deranged. Edmond couldn't bring himself to say one word of agreement or approval, but he was very much aware of his own situation, alone on a remote island with a madman. Who could know what he might do if he thought his guest was opposed to his and God's plans? Edmond chose to keep it neutral, to focus on the practicalities, the logistics.

'How on earth did you get him here? You surely didn't invite him?'

Max smiled. 'If you have the money, you can buy pretty much anything. There are people out there who will provide whatever service you want, at a price. He was delivered to me, all the way from Islington to Glasgow, sedated and trussed up like an oven ready chicken. Paid for in cash. Cost a pretty penny, but the best thing I've ever bought. Collected by me, in an estate car with false plates. I was disguised too, I should add. I drove him here in daylight, drugged in the back. Only two and a half hours, no hitches. Remember, I was still in my forties then, so I had no bother moving him in a wheelchair from the front door and dumping him into his present habitation. Those are the same clothes he was wearing when he arrived.' Apart from a slightly higher pitch of voice that suggested strained control of excitement bubbling underneath, Max recounted the details matter-of-factly.

'But what about the cage? You didn't get that locally, I would say.'

'No. Bought second-hand from a bankrupt circus in Italy. German made, self-assembly job. Located and shipped to Glasgow by the same kind of 'businessmen' who provided its occupant. I picked it up in a hire van and put it together. Lovely joins. Once the bars click into the frame, there's no chance of them coming apart. I had the toilet plumbed in already and built the cage around it. The toilet is the only furnishing he has.'

'What about power and water?' asked Edmond, anxious to keep the subject off the prisoner in the cage. 'You can't be on mains supply.'

'No trouble. Good generator, and water pumped from a spring well. Sorry about the smell down there, Edmond. I never thought of that. I never notice the smell, must be used to it. I'm sure you'd have liked to spend more time seeing him, Edmond, but never mind, I can tell you what you've missed.

The first few days were rich. I left him alone in the dark at the start, he hadn't a clue where he was. Then when I put on the light and he saw me, he ranted and raged and, wait for it, threatened me. Imagine, in his position he was threatening me. What did I say? Nothing, not a word. Here's the beauty of it. I told you how at school he forbade me to speak, to answer questions. Well, in twenty years I haven't said a word to him. He has begged me, pleaded with me, to talk to him or with him or at him, but I haven't said a single word. Not a sound. It has driven him mad.

But I'm rushing ahead. After he realised that shouting and raving were doing no good, he began to ask, and finally beg, for forgiveness. Then came the crying, the sobbing, the despair. He eventually lost all sense of time. I'd leave him sometimes, alone in total darkness, for a day or two, and the relief it was for him when I appeared. He would thank me for the light. I feed him bread and water every day. It's a tie, mind you, but I shouldn't complain, there's nowhere I'd rather be, or nothing I'd rather be doing. Maybe you've a dog or cat, Edmond, and you'll know what I mean.

I have to look after him, you see. As long as he is there, alive and suffering, then I'm well. I'm not sure he can talk properly now. For a few years I'd hear him singing and reciting nursery rhymes and, you'll like this, *whistling* to himself. But that has all stopped. His teeth have rotted, so maybe that's part of the reason. He's declined physically, of course. He used to try to exercise in the cage, keep himself fit doing press-ups and chin-ups, but he gave all that up about fifteen years ago. The muscles have all wasted, you'll have noticed, and movement is difficult. It's about twelve years, I'd say, since he last smashed his head against the bars to try to kill himself. I'm glad about that, what would I do if he died? To be honest, Edmond, I'm not absolutely sure how much of his mind is left, but as long as he's miserable and without hope, then I'm happy.'

Edmond listened to this terrible recital with a mixture of incredulity and incomprehension. How could this little man with the white hair and gentlemanly appearance be capable of such cruelty, and what was almost worse, how could he assume that Edmond would be party to it, virtually an accomplice? He recalled a film or story where a man had kept a portrait in his attic, and the more the painting aged and declined, the better it was for the man. Edmond's only wish now was to get safely back to the hotel and tell the authorities about the man in the cage, and the appalling goings-on in their small rural community.

'You've certainly done a thorough job, Max,' he managed. 'I'm sorry to say that I'm bushed right now, and I would appreciate it if I could get back and get my head on the pillow. Thank you for your hospitality and for showing me our old friend from the past.'

On the way back in the car he pretended to be asleep, to avoid further talk about the being in the cage. He couldn't think of it as the beefy, sneering Billy Wilkes of his memory. He kept one eye open to make sure the car wasn't going off the road. What amazed him as they shook hands and said their farewells, was that Max assumed implicitly that his secret would be safe with his friend; he made no mention at all of the importance of Edmond's keeping quiet about what he had been shown. Edmond's last words were, 'I hope to be seeing you again soon.'

The first things he did after Max had driven off were stay clear of the noisy company still enjoying themselves at the Function Room bar, and order a pot of strong tea to be brought to his room. He sat down, put his head in his hands, and genuinely asked himself if what he had been through in the past couple of hours or so had indeed happened, or were they a nightmare that he would awake from. Edmond was still burning with moral outrage at what was being done to a fellow human being, no matter how nasty a one he had been, but somehow in his cosy, secure bedroom, with the china cup of tea in his hands, the edge was off the feeling a little. He could have picked up the phone at his bedside, asked for an outside line, and dialled 999, but he hesitated. A very good friend, one whose advice he valued, had once told him, 'Before you put an angry letter in the mail, let it lie in a drawer overnight.' That advice sounded in his head now, and he decided to delay action until next morning.

Edmond may have been hoping for a night's sleep, but he certainly didn't get one. Uninvited, unwelcome thoughts circulated in his head all night. Yes, he was going to report next day to the authorities what he had seen on the island of Inishmail, but... *maybe Max was entitled to the justice that nobody else had been able to give him; maybe he should be left to play out the remainder of his second half, to reach full time unhindered; the poor man had laid bare his soul to him, and now he was going to betray him; his old acquaintance from school had trusted him entirely with his secret, and now he was about to squeal on him. A man's life had been saved, he had been given a second chance, so why should he now step in and destroy it; what good would it do the local people, or the hotel, or anybody, if this went public? Nobody would buy the tower house and the island would go to ruin; was he going to release the school bully and incarcerate the school victim? Had the man not suffered enough, the best years of his life destroyed, and the treachery of his so-called friend, Edmond Carroll, now about to finish the job...*

Edmond finished his breakfast the next morning, left a tip for the waiter, and went towards the Reception Desk. Five yards from the phone he still didn't know if he was going to ring for the police to arrest Max Wissler, or for the taxi man in Cladich to take him to the station.

## *A Bit of Bad Luck*

It was a good feeling, being the best, knowing he was the best. He allowed himself a little moment of self-satisfaction, checked he'd left nothing in the hotel room, and snapped shut the battered old brown suitcase.

That little moment was enough. He had never been one to dwell on his successes. Even when he'd been on the other side, working **for** H.M. Customs, he'd never joined fully in the backslapping celebrations among the rummage crews or anti-smuggling teams after a major seizure. Now, the classic gamekeeper turned poacher, he could feel the same quiet inner pride in avoiding detection as he had formerly felt in making it. As always, he kept the feeling to himself.

It wasn't just the risks in telling others of his superlative skills as a smuggler that kept him silent. He knew deep inside that any feelings of professional pride he might have were only sad little compensations for the true happiness he would never have again. Happiness, for him, had died the moment Denise had been murdered. Yes, murdered. *Tragic accident, terrible loss, cruel blow* – these all sidestepped the brutal truth, that the police car had deliberately mounted the pavement in its pursuit of the stolen car and smashed her warm soft body so hard against the cold stone of the bridge that he wasn't allowed to identify her for more than an hour, until the mortuary people had made her presentable.

He shuddered each time the memory of that day threatened to force itself into his mind. That was the cruellest thing of all, that he couldn't even enjoy memories of the good times Denise and he had known. He had trained himself to shut them out. For the sake of his own sanity, he did not dare allow himself memories of the person he had loved most in the world – they led inexorably to the terrible picture of her crushed form below a mortuary sheet, and the tormenting expression of mild surprise on her dead face.

It was something else, however, that had almost broken his reason, that had sent a whirling madness round and round in his head, in spite of the words of friends and colleagues, the work of doctors, counsellors, shrinks. It was the crass remark of that police officer in attendance at the identification that sent him to the verge of breakdown, and in due course reversed his entire life—*a bit of bad luck*. For weeks that phrase echoed inside his head, day after day, night after night, until it seemed that they were the only words that existed.

In desperation he had tried religion but could get from it none of the peace or comfort that some had supposed would be virtually guaranteed. What he did get, ironically, was a nudge in the direction of a new life, a life of crime, that was in time to stabilise his frantic mind through the therapy of hitting back.

He had noticed in his feverish rounds of the various churches and sects that many of the leaders, the pastors or priests, or whatever they were called, were little nondescript men who in any other walk of life would almost certainly have been ignored or ridiculed. In this profession they enjoyed a deference and respect that nobody thought to challenge or question. It was as though they were a special case, not subject to the realities that ordinary people faced every day.

The observation took hold. He recalled parties of nuns passing through Customs on their way from Lourdes or some such holy place. There had been no shortage of crude remarks and jokes passed privately among the Assistant Officers about what might be found under the nuns' habits, or who might have already been there, but he had never seen a nun subjected to a close personal search, nor her baggage seriously 'turned out'.

A course of action started to firm up: he could turn his understanding of its thinking, his knowledge of its practice, against H.M. Customs, against 'authority', and the way to do it was in the guise of a man of the cloth. He knew the idea was not a new one, that bogus clergymen had been rumbled before, but he would make deception an art form, he would take it to new heights. *A bit of bad luck?* No chance, luck wouldn't feature in his operations. Every precaution would be taken, every scenario would be anticipated, every challenge checkmated...

It would soon be ten years since the nightmare; in that period he had changed so utterly, in every respect, that he sometimes wondered who he was, and where and why, and if there ever had been a lovely, loving woman called Denise who had once been the best part of his life.

Irwin Davis was in a seriously grumpy mood. Quite apart from a throbbing wisdom tooth that his tongue refused to stop poking, and the row he'd had that morning with his wife after her old cat had peed inside one of his new shoes, there were larger matters behind the darkness of his face.

As H.M. Customs Surveyor he saw his work as a kind of trust, a charge, that denoted both character and ability. Declining detection or seizure figures in his Terminal, however slight, were, for Davis, a mark of personal weakness and failure. In spite of several recent successes that had seen a number of punters 'jobbed' and 'taken up the road' for cocaine and heroin charges, Davis's instinct told him that he was performing below his best; there was no evidence for this feeling, the statistics were relatively steady, but on previous occasions his instincts had proved to be correct.

He stared at his cup of cold coffee and shifted his mind into overview mode. Closing his eyes, he pictured the large slogan their instructor had made the trainees recite each morning: *The jails are full of people who thought they were smarter than H.M. Customs.* Yes, but the job had changed a great deal over his thirty years of service. The game had got tougher, the players dirtier, the stakes higher, the rules trickier.

True, he could still net a fair catch by the standard means, the known profile methods, the credibility checks. The overly nervous or confident passenger was still worth a turn out. So too was the scruffy passenger bound for the expensive destination, or the punter with too little money for his intended stay, but they were no longer the whole story. Now the smuggler could be the smart businesswoman, the travelling wedding guests, the pretty young mother, the grandmother going out to see her grandchildren.

Was it just a sign of his age, or was he right in thinking that new staff coming into the job were less dedicated than in his day? Their plans for the weekend, or interest in salary scales, were just as important to them as detecting unlicensed importation or evasion of revenue duties. Even informers today were of inferior stuff. Davis smiled, in spite of his gloomy thoughts. A few days earlier an informer had reported that a corner shop was selling cigarettes at 60p. When his story was checked out it emerged courgettes were on sale at 60p. Maybe informers should be asked to sit a reading test.

It was a lonely, humourless way of life he had chosen, a life of bare hotel rooms and colourless flats. How he used to enjoy coming home to share with Denise the incidents or gossip of the day. She had smiled to herself all evening at his account of the drug carrier caught by declaring he was on his way to take up a job as a barman in Pakistan – an Islamic 'dry' country. He had hurried home another day to tell her of the armed police reception for two men overheard to be arriving from Ireland with Armalite guns, but in fact travelling with nothing more dangerous than Carmelite nuns. She had laughed out loud over the passenger who, told he would have to go with his bag to the gate, had thrown his suitcase onto the belt, sat astride it, and ridden off through the curtains to the sorting area below.

Now, no matter how exciting or interesting his day might be, there was nobody he dared trust enough to tell it to. The only way to keep his secret was to tell nobody, literally nobody. A person sworn to secrecy will tell just one other person; that one other person in turn tells just one other, who then tells only one other, and so it goes until the secret is public knowledge. He remembered with a wry smile how a friend had once told him about an affair he was having, adding, 'Now, I don't want you to tell anybody, not even Denise. Promise.' What an innocent. Anybody who thinks for a minute that a husband will keep a piece of juicy news secret from his wife is too naïve for words. No, the only thing you can't tell is what you don't know.

A dog was barking below his hotel window. The racket reached him above the noise of people and traffic in the busy Bogotá street. Why did all these foreign towns and cities always have a dog barking somewhere, in the distance or right outside the window. Sometimes the barking would waken him from a dream in which a detector dog had been announcing a find. Strange, but even now, more than eight years since he'd switched sides, his dreams were still of those early days, or rather nights, the late-night baggage watch on the green channels, when he would search the holds and cabins of aircraft and ships, or carry out tarmac and dockside challenges.

He took the lift down to the hotel lobby, checked out, and, even though his flight was not due for take-off for three hours, took a taxi out to the El Dorado International Airport. He told the driver to drive slowly. He hated fast driving.

He caught a glimpse of his face in the driver's mirror. It was a face unrecognisable from the round, bearded one that used to belong to a man who worked as an Assistant Officer for H.M. Customs. This face was lean, grey, clean shaven, with a kind of gravitas in the lined forehead and in the serious eyes behind the gold-rimmed spectacles. The hair, once thick and strong, was now a thin distinguished white, combed back revealing a widow's peak and neatly trimmed above the clerical collar.

He had destroyed all photographs of himself and of his former life, and could scarcely believe that he had once been a 'heavy' fifteen stone. Three of these had vanished virtually overnight during his illness after Denise's death, and his subsequent new lifestyle had reduced him further to the present 150 pounds filling his neat dark suit.

The priest persona was used only for 'work'. For the rest of the time, he presented a very different appearance. Crouched inside a donkey jacket and wearing a beanie over straggly grey hair, he showed an unshaven face and coarse moustache. He enjoyed the contrast in his two roles. It was a kind of game, but never a game of chance. The gains he made, which were considerable, were his reward for winning the game, but it was the playing of it that mattered. He controlled the play; he didn't need luck. Why gamble when he could load the dice in his own favour. He kept away, for example, from his former place of employment. His disguise was good, but why put it to the unnecessary test of customs men who had known him in his former life.

He patted the suitcase beside him on the shabby leather seat. It was a relic from the fifties, chosen deliberately to underline his unworldliness. He would sometimes catch snide remarks from the Customs Officers about 'demob' and 'old Blighty' as they gave it a cursory check. Inside were more targets for the wits: old-fashioned underpants, the type that used to be known as trunks, backed up by long johns; a large face flannel enclosing a bar of Lifebuoy soap; Aertex singlets; a pair of suspenders to support the long black socks; a pair of broad, elastic garters to hold up the sleeves of the white clerical shirts; a clothes brush worn almost smooth by years of honest service; a shaving brush with an equally busy history.

Together with these carefully chosen items was the cassock and various trappings of the priest, and a selection of religious leaflets, pamphlets, and booklets. The centrepiece of the suitcase's contents was a large, well-used Bible, its leather covers almost as worn as the seat it now sat on. This was his money maker, his livelihood.

Just after he had started work as an AO, he had been asked to turn out the baggage of an elderly clergyman, and at the time had felt a little uncomfortable as he poked among the contents of the old fellow's bag, especially flicking through his Bible and ecclesiastical books. It was the same kind of feeling he still got when pulling out in a hurry to overtake an ambulance or funeral procession. Talking about it afterwards to hardened searchers he was surprised to learn that they could feel that same sense of impropriety.

'I'm not a religious man,' one of them had said, 'but I try to respect a man who is.'

He had remembered those words as with infinite patience he doctored the Bible, slicing its thin pages with a surgeon's scalpel and with a surgeon's skill. It was 'the oldest trick in the book' quite literally, but the care he took in distributing the little incised boxes at precisely calculated distances and positions throughout the Bible occupied him for the best part of a week. The result was a book that could be loosely skimmed through, with no evidence at all of the series of cavities hidden between its pages. So expertly were the pages sealed that a casual flick through them produced the wholly natural appearance of the leaves of a book turning over in random sections.

Nothing was left to chance. He had weighed the Bible before operating on it and was methodical in ensuring that the gemstones or gold tola bars he implanted in its secret niches did not make it noticeably heavier than it should have been. At no time did his Good Book's pages carry drugs; dogs didn't make any allowances for men in round white collars.

The airport lounge was relatively slack. He chose a seat in a corner and hid behind a newspaper. A priest was an invitation. On one occasion someone had taken a fatal heart attack just before boarding and he had been summoned to administer the last rites. It was a measure of his preparations for his new career that he had envisaged just such a situation and was able to act it out with 'professional' assurance, before slipping away through the crowd.

On another occasion he had the misfortune to have beside him on the plane a chirpy young curate, or some such apprentice, who was all set for intercontinental conversation. He had put a quick stop to that nonsense. From the gold nib of his old-style fountain pen flowed the words: *I'm terribly sorry, but at present I'm forbidden to speak. I'm on my way to have an operation for my throat cancer.* The curate squeezed himself into the far side of his seat. Cancer's not contagious, but...

Davis took his cup down to the staff kitchen. On the way back he looked in at the Staff Room. An officer and three assistant officers were playing poker before their watch started. They were in the process of recovering from a burst of laughing.

'What's amusing you lot?'

The officer was pleased to get the question. 'I've just been telling them about what happened yesterday. It's true, I swear it's true. I was helping an American Captain to fill in his crew declaration, and he was asking me about the tobacco products column. I told him to list any tobacco or fags he had on board and, I swear it's true, he wrote down, 'The Chief Steward, but I'm not certain.' I swear it's true.'

All four greeted the punchline with renewed merriment, and Davis conceded an amused nod.

'I swear something else is true,' he said. 'I've been looking at the figures. We've challenged more punters and turned out more baggage in the past month than any other Terminal, and we're still at the bottom of the table for arrests and seizures. Now, what does that tell you?'

One of the AO's looked up from shielding his hand. 'Maybe it's telling us we're the best. Maybe we should be top of the table, the deterrent table. Maybe our reputation's doing the business.'

Davis wanted to say something witty and withering in reply but couldn't deliver. The card game resumed. It annoyed him to see their apparent lack of concern. His thoughts turned bitter. Perhaps they were right in their outlook, and he was the one with things out of focus. Maybe the truth was that their work was no different than their game of poker. Both depended to a very large extent on luck: pulling the right card, picking the right passenger. Was there any difference? Maybe all their training and planning came right down to that, the luck of the draw, the throw of the dice, and he was having a bad run. Were all his training and knowledge and experience, the established procedures and methods, worth no more than the chance choice of a card?

Davis felt his mind slide from dark to black; he found himself thinking about having the cat put down.

The flight was as boring as the countless others he had made in his work. A little rebellious part of him occasionally hoped for a hijacking or some kind of drama on board, but he knew such thoughts were dangerously unprofessional.

He politely declined the drink the hostess offered him. As a teenager, in another life centuries ago, he had thought of air hostesses as having one of the most glamorous jobs in the world; now he pitied them, wheeling their trolleys endlessly up and down narrow aisles, issuing safety advice nobody listened to, sorting out the needs and mistakes of incredibly stupid people, and all the time having to smile and be pleasant. It would be better being a waitress in a corner café.

He liked the Colombian run. It was a popular target for drug searches which relied quite a bit on the dogs for detections. It wasn't a route that Customs associated with the smuggling of commercial gemstones. In reply to the familiar, 'Where have you travelled from today?' he would try to include biblical or 'churchy' words, if possible, in his replies. They were a guaranteed turn-off. A *Convocation* or *Synod* or *Ecclesiastical Council* would produce almost instant glazing of the eyes.

He checked his passport. Perfect, undetectable. He should know. He got a new one each year from the best forger in the business. It was worth the two grand. Too many entry stamps, especially of dicey countries, drew attention.

That was why he was the best – he could second guess the opposition. How he despised the raw, desperate amateurs, the swallowers and stuffers, the couple who split up to go through controls separately.

For Irwin Davis brooding was a positive thing, the first stage in a process that led to decisions, whether right ones or wrong ones. He emptied his cup and strode purposefully back down to the Staff Room, arriving just as the poker game was finishing.

'Wait a minute, Arthurs,' he intervened as the deck was being put in its box. 'Let me cut the pack.' He got the four of clubs.

'Ah, the devil's bedposts,' remarked Arthurs, who was a walking encyclopaedia of just such useless facts. 'Unlucky for some.'

'OK. That's it. Number 4. When you lot go on duty, I want you to turn out, and I mean turn out, every fourth passenger coming through. I don't care if it's the queen or the pope or your own mother, I want them checked over, right down to the gold in their teeth.' There were a few murmurs from the team. 'I don't care how long it takes. The public think we do random stops anyway, so for today let's prove them right. Turn out every fourth punter as if you know for sure he's carrying the Crown Jewels.'

His old suitcase was one of the first out at baggage reclaim. As always, after hours in a planeload of humanity, he looked forward to the privacy and independence of his own car in the Long Stay Car Park. Fortunately, there were only three other passengers in front of him as he entered the Customs Control area.

## *Penalty*

The entire penalty episode was one of those out-of-himself things that had happened to Ken a couple of times before, not unlike sequences on the screen where sound becomes blurred and everything goes into slow motion. He watched No. 9 place the ball on the spot and walk back a few paces with the footballer's slightly bow-legged cockiness. A distant whistle blew somewhere in his head. Ken knew he had to dive to his left, as though he had seen or done it before. There was no surprise to feel his outstretched left hand make contact with the ball. Then, like a diver coming up through the surface, he felt normality burst upon him. Jubilant teammates were leaping on his back, and as he collapsed under their weight, he dimly heard the whistle that put them into the final.

A pre-recorded *Thanks, but I'm driving* message would have been useful. It seemed that everyone wanted to buy Ken a drink after the match, but he confined himself to a single pint.

Once the congratulations had receded, Maurice finally got a word in, 'Typical. I miss a sitter at one end and five minutes later you pull off the save of the season at the other. It's time you found a mate who's a winner like yourself instead of a loser, big time, like me.'

Ken laughed. 'Stop moanin'. Think how the guy who missed the penalty must be feelin'.'

Suddenly Maurice was unusually serious. 'Well done, Ken. I don't mean just the penalty save. You're my good mate, my best mate, my only mate, whether you're saving penalties or not. Are you ready for another pint?'

'No, honestly thanks, Maurice. Can't take the chance. A Sales Rep needs a driving licence.'

'Yeah, you're right. Well, here's to you.' His pint disappeared at an impossible rate.

They were about halfway home, through a drizzle that had already started when they came out of the club. Neither had spoken for a time. The car reeked of muscle rub from their kit in the back seat.

'What?' Ken suddenly asked.

'What? What d'you mean 'What'?'

'What is it? You've been watchin' me since we left the ground. What's wrong with you? Have you taken a fancy to me or somethin'?'

Maurice pounced on the opening. 'What's wrong with me? That's a good one. What's wrong with me, and you sittin' there like a man under a death sentence.' He turned off the car radio. 'And you were the same back there in the bar. Man of the Match, probably Player of the Year, and you looked as if you'd sold the game. And you're askin' what's wrong with me? What is it, Ken, what's botherin' you?'

Ken rubbed the windscreen with the back of his hand. 'Nothin'.'

'C'mon, Ken, this is Maurice your mate you're talkin' to. I'm not stupid, y'know. I know there's somethin' worryin' you. There's somethin' on your mind.'

Ken looked ahead into the rainy road, his face confirming the allegation. Suddenly he wrenched the wheel and swung into the big empty Social Services Building car park. He parked right in the middle and switched off the ignition.

'OK, I woulda told you anyway, so why not now?' Then he sat back in the seat and said nothing.

'This looks heavy,' said Maurice. 'Have you got cancer or somethin'?'

Ken released a long intake of breath and turned so they were face to face. 'Maurice, we've been good mates now since the day I joined the club, and that's nearly six months ago, so you know what I'm gonna tell you is the truth, that none of it's my fault, even though you're hearin' only my side of the story.' He paused.

'Go on,' urged Maurice, 'what is it?'

'OK, here goes. It's Nicola. You know I like her and all that, she's a nice girl, but she's your girl and that's fine with me.'

Maurice looked puzzled. 'So what're you tryin' to say?'

Ken picked a piece of Blu-Tack off the dash and rolled it into a ball between finger and thumb. 'Remember last Tuesday the three of us were meetin' in The Half Moon and you were late? Well, I bought Nicola a drink while we were waitin' and next thing she... she starts comin' on strong with me, real strong, out of the blue, all of a sudden. She said it was me she fancied, always had been, and she was only usin' you to see me. I

41

didn't know what to do. There she is tellin' me all the things we could be doin' together if we left before you arrived.'

Maurice listened in silence, watching Ken closely.

'It's the truth, Maurice, I swear. I gave her no encouragement, none at all, there was none of it my fault, but it's been worryin' me ever since. I got up to go and right then you came in. You must've noticed the atmosphere was a bit tense. That's why I went home as soon as you arrived, even though you were expectin' me to stay.'

The drizzle had increased to a steady rain and for a moment or two its beating on the roof was the only sound in the car. Then Maurice gave an odd little laugh and said, 'It's all right, Ken, I know all about it.'

'What! She told you about it? I suppose she blamed me?'

Maurice repeated the little laugh. 'No, she didn't need to tell me about it. I asked her to do it. She was followin' my script.' He peeled a stick of chewing gum, bent it in two, and popped it in his mouth, while Ken sat waiting for the punchline. None came. Ken tried a little laugh just the same.

'Your script? I didn't know you were into comedy sketches, with me as the stooge.'

'It's not a joke, Ken. As a matter of fact, it's deadly serious. I asked her to do it, we rehearsed it together. It was a test. I was testin' you.'

'You were what?' Ken felt his voice rising.

42

'Testin' you. You remember a few weeks ago you found my wallet in the car with nearly a hundred quid in it? That was a test too. I knew you were a bit short of readies at the time. You passed that one too with flying colours.'

A redness was creeping into Ken's neck and over his face, but his tone was more confusion than anger. 'Maurice, what the hell's goin' on here? What's all this testin' stuff? You're not serious about any of this?'

Maurice looked him straight in the eye. 'Remember that time we slipped outa' the Indian restaurant without payin'? That was another test: I wanted to see if you'd take a chance, break the law.'

The hope of a prank ending gone, Ken's anger burst out in the volley of threat and abuse that comes with betrayal of friendship. Maurice sat calmly through it, expecting it, prepared for it. 'OK, Ken, but just let me tell you why, surely you want to know why. You don't think I'd do all that without a good reason, just to test your friendship? If you're still not happy when I tell you why, throw me out in the rain, and you can drive over me too, if you want.'

Curiosity prevailed over rage. 'You better make this good, Maurice. I don't like bein' made a fool of. I expect my friends to trust me.'

The rain eased briefly at that moment as if to allow Maurice the stage. He wound down his window and spat out the gum. When he spoke it was with an earnestness that he had never shown before in their half year of friendship.

'Ken, I need somebody I can really trust, trust with my life, and I'm not exaggeratin'. I'm gonna' tell you somethin', somethin' I've never told anybody else. You're the first because you're my mate and I know I can trust you all the way. You've proved it.'

'OK, but there was no need for all the testin' stunts.'

'Fair enough, sorry, but I had to be sure, completely sure.' He hesitated. 'Y'see, Ken, a year ago I killed somebody, a girl I was shacked up with. No, no, it was an accident, a pure accident, but it looked bad, or it woulda looked bad if I'd been found out.'

Ken had tensed at the confession, but he asked in fairly even tones what had happened.

'Her name was Kathy, and she was a few years older than me. Long story short, I was workin' my ass off for my finals, tryin' to make up for three wasted years. Kathy couldn't, or wouldn't, understand how important it was for me. She wanted me out with her on the town every night, instead of sittin' in studyin'. We were havin' rows about it all the time. She started goin' out with a coupl'a very dicey friends of hers, and comin' home late, drunk and aggressive, you know the score.'

'Yeah, an everyday story of city folk.'

Maurice massaged his temples for a minute, rubbed his eyes, and continued. 'Well, that night she came in about half eleven and started up as usual, callin' me all the worst names she could think of. I ignored her and that made her worse. I had all my notes and work in a pile, all in order, and she grabbed them off the table and scattered them all over the room.

I lost my temper, first time ever, and slapped her once, just once, not even all that hard, just a slap, and the nightmare began. Y'know in the old crime films how the victim trips and falls backwards and always manages to hit his head on a convenient fireplace? Well, Kathy must have read the script, for that's exactly what happened, just like in the movies, except this was real and she was lyin' there on the floor, dead, with a kind of froth at the side of her mouth.' He paused, squirming in horror at the recollection.

'Why didn't you just tell the police what happened? It was an accident, after all.'

'I've asked myself that question every day since. Maybe I should have, no, I definitely should have, but at that moment all I could see were finals missed, a trial, imprisonment, my life ruined, all the things that are supposed to happefn to other people. Maybe it was just panic, I don't know. My mind was in such a state for weeks after it that I never did sit my finals, so there was no advantage there.'

'So what did you do?'

Maurice drew a series of circles and squares on the steamy windscreen, reluctant to recite the details. 'There's no way of tellin' you what I did, Ken, without comin' across as a bad bit of work; all I can say is I was really desperate.' He stopped. 'All right, here it is. I rolled her up in a big piece of polythene a carpet had come in, hired a van next day, and somehow got her into it that night. Lookin' back now, I don't know how I went through with it – it was like I was somebody else. You couldn't imagine,

Ken, what it was like to find myself in that situation, doin' those things.'

Ken helped him out. 'It is hard to imagine. It must have been a nightmare. But what on earth did you do with the body?'

Maurice closed his eyes as he recalled his actions. 'I took her out to an old, abandoned quarry we used to play in as kids. I dumped her over the edge. She was small and slim, or I never could have managed it. The place is all shut off and grown over.' He paused. 'She's never been found. I reported her missin' next day after I had cleared everything up and got rid of a lot of her stuff to make it appear she had maybe been plannin' to move out. The police suspected me, of course. They questioned me over and over, upside down, inside out. There was one real nasty one, with flat eyes sort of half hooded. He was like that actor Peter Lorre from the old films, if you know him. Every time I looked up, he was starin' right at me with a sneery smile on, as if he didn't even believe my name when I gave it.

Anyhow, they turned the flat inside out, took stuff away, even went through my bin, but they couldn't find anything. I knew they were watchin' me, followin' me. I was gettin' paranoiac, thinkin' the flat was bugged, the phone was tapped, and never knowin' when the doorbell would ring and they'd be there to start the same questions all over again. At last, with no body and no evidence, they gave up, and I moved here a year ago to get away from the whole thing.'

Ken sat in silence for a few moments, weighing up what he'd just heard. 'It's a terrible story, Maurice, but how do I come into it? What's all this got to do with me?'

He'd hardly finished the question when Maurice was speaking, like a barrister who has spent necessary time constructing his case and has now reached the critical height of the argument.

'Because I need you, Ken, need your help, and I know I can depend on it. Y'see, next year they're goin' to turn that whole area into some kinda fun park or recreation centre or somethin'. I happened to read about it. They're sure to find the body in the quarry and the whole thing will start up all over again. They'll open a murder enquiry, that's a cert. I couldn't go through all that a second time. No, I have to move it, Ken, but it's definitely a two-man job. Don't worry about what happens then, I've it all sorted, but the quarry bit is where I need you. You'll be 'aiding and abetting', all that kinda shit, but I know you'll not let me down, that I can trust my best mate.'

The road was little better than a track, with long, straggly, whitish grass on either side and clusters of rushes trespassing most of the way. They sat in silence, Maurice at the wheel of the Transit van, his mind on the job ahead. Both men were in dark clothes. Everything needed for the work was in the back of the van. The weather was in their favour, murky and, most importantly, dry.

The quarry workings had stopped in the 1970's and nature had very quickly reclaimed possession. Access to the quarry from below was now virtually impossible, so dense was the scrub.

The road curved round in a spiral near the top of the quarry opening.

'A kid fell down it while I was still at high school,' remarked Maurice, as he wriggled the van through a gauntlet of scratching whin bushes. 'Broke his neck. They closed the whole place off after that. A few of us used to get in just to prove we could, but the place was soggy and dirty, and we soon gave up on it. I'd say the only way in now is from the top.'

'Wonder what sort of condition the body'll be in,' said Ken, cutting across the commentary. 'Will there be just a skeleton?'

Maurice kept his legs straight and his boots pressed hard against the rock face as Ken fed him down. His torchlight showed the rock wall smeared with green and dotted with grey and yellow growths.

'OK, steady, steady,' he called up to Ken. It was odd to be sending up his instructions in a kind of very loud stage whisper; although they were miles from anyone, Maurice felt constrained not to shout up at normal volume. The rope was tight and strong and good, and his boot soles gripped sure. He remembered the abseiling classes at summer school; incredibly, in spite of where he was and what lay ahead, Maurice felt a kind of athlete's satisfaction in his own competence and fitness for the descent.

'Ken, that'll do, I'm down,' and, forty feet above, the dark figure outlined against the charcoal sky straightened and disappeared. Maurice's fear had been that, for whatever reason, the body would be missing, or impossible to find, or pulled apart by foxes or other scavengers. He could hardly believe it when his torchlight's very first scan caught the dull grey gleam of polythene. The body, like a large, crudely wrapped package, was snagged in a broad bush growing at an angle from a bank at the base of the drop.

He could see the tape and the blue nylon cord. What a good job he'd made in trussing the little bitch up. How strong he had felt squeezing her scrawny neck until her feeble wriggling and flapping had stopped. The slyness of her, searching through his things until she found the precious packet that represented his livelihood for at least six months.

'*So this is how you've been looking for work every day? This is why you dropped out. You bastard. I know now where your money's been coming from. You're supplying freshers with their weekend party bags, their little packets of fun. You're the lowest form of life.*'

What did he care about her screechings, her hysteria? He started caring when she threw the priceless pack of white powder on the open coal fire; he cared enough to give a sob of rage and squeeze the pathetic life out of her.

It was hard work dislodging the crumpled bundle from the tree, but no harder than he'd supposed. As he struggled to secure the rope round the slimy polythene, a fold split open and something tangled in his hair. The wrinkled, rotten flesh, greenish black, had once been an arm.

Maurice pulled himself the last few feet to the top. The night was cool but sweat dripped freely from his hair and face. He threw himself down, exhausted but triumphant. It had actually been simpler than he could have hoped for – Ken had pulled the body up without too much trouble, and, when the rope had come back down, Maurice had simply done the descent in reverse. Perfect.

'We did it, Ken, we did it. Not easy, but we did it,' he panted.

As Maurice raised his tired head, he became aware of several dim shapes standing in a half circle in the darkness. He looked up to his mate for an answer. It came: 'Maurice David Creelman, I am Detective Constable Kenneth Banks of Merton CID and I am arresting you in connection with the death of Katherine Aileen Magowan on May 22nd, 1999. I have to inform you                              that...'

## Guardian Angel

Panic started to rise in her throat. She tried her coat pockets again. It definitely wasn't there. Her purse was missing. It was gone. But how? She hadn't dropped it. She was sure of that, because she had put it carefully in the pocket of the coat before hanging it up. Another hopeless, desperate check in the pockets. Empty.

Her purse had been stolen! It was the only explanation. But how was that possible? Her eyes had been off the coat only as long as it took her to try on the new one in front of the mirror, less than a minute. There was one possible way. Someone from outside could have slid a hand inside the cubicle curtain, felt the purse in the coat, and in an instant slipped it out of the pocket.

Marianne took a deep breath and whipped open the curtain. Apart from a couple of middle-aged women approaching with a red dress, the area was clear, the other changing cubicles empty and their curtains drawn back. A wave of fear washed over her. Everything was in the purse, not just her money, credit cards, debit cards, cheque card, but items of personal identity, keys, even her bus ticket.

In a strange kind of way, the theft was not a surprise. It was like a kind of culmination of the sense of anxiety and apprehension that had been growing in Marianne from the moment she stepped off the bus in the city centre. She had felt jittery, on edge, as if waiting for something bad to happen.

How could the main shopping area have changed so much, declined so rapidly? The pleasant streets and public flower basket displays had given way to pavements cluttered with traders' stalls selling bling, cheap lighters, batteries, computer accessories, and fake designer clothes. The traders themselves looked like criminal types and their hoarse street vendor cries sounded aggressive, even threatening.

There seemed to be beggars everywhere, and people selling Big Issue magazines, and others wanting her to be interviewed for surveys, and spitting, swearing hoodies marauding in groups, intimidating in number and manner. In short, there was, for Marianne, a distinct air of menace in the city; she felt vulnerable until she was safely inside Bloomers' long-established family store. She missed David, not because he would have offered much protection or security, but simply for the company, an arm to hold on to.

Ironic then that it was in Bloomers' old-fashioned, upper-class premises that the thief or thieves had struck. Marianne found a security man and told him what had happened. He led her down a back corridor to the office where she gave him the details and he logged the incident in a book.

'I'll call the police if you wish, miss, but it could take a bit of time and, to be honest, there's not a lot they can do. These people know where it's safe to operate. We used to have that area covered by the cameras, but some of the women customers complained until they got them removed. Best I can do is have a word with the store detectives and maybe they'll hit on some of the regular lifters.'

Marianne was obliged to borrow her bus fare home from the store. She literally did not have one penny on her person. She was close to tears on the journey. It wasn't just the inconvenience the theft entailed that upset her, nor the potential financial loss; it was the feeling of being a victim, of having been preyed upon by some heartless, worthless criminal who couldn't care less what humiliation or anxiety she would suffer.

A wider worry settled on her. Everywhere she looked society seemed to be in decline. Antisocial behaviour was rife, and authority seemed unable or unwilling to do anything about it. The graffiti scrawled on the seats of the bus said it all. How were helpless, law-abiding and civilised citizens like herself going to find justice, or ultimately survival, against the swarming forces of violence, yobbishness, and lawlessness. They were so weak, so threatened. Victims.

Marianne retrieved the spare front door key from under the oil tank. Once safely inside she wanted to curl up on the couch and feel sorry for herself, but first there was the necessary business of phoning the bank and credit card companies to cancel her cards. She thought about ringing the police but couldn't bear the prospect of their invading her home with their silly notebooks and routine questions.

She was just starting her second cup of coffee when the phone made her jump. It was a woman's voice on the line. 'Hello, Miss Taylor? This is Bloomers.'

'Yes?' Marianne's voice was shaking.

'We think we may have found your purse. We need you to come down to identify it.'

'It's dark red, with a brass…'

'I'm sorry, but you'll have to identify it in person. Can you come to the office? We're open late, until eight o'clock this evening, if that makes things easier for you.'

'No, no, I'll come now. I'm on my way. Thank you very much.' Marianne discovered she had been holding her breath and gave a long slow sigh of relief.

The bus ride into the city centre was in slow motion as Marianne's mind raced ahead. She tried to envisage the outcome. What was it the woman had said, that they'd found the purse? Did she mean just that, an empty purse? Surely not, she wouldn't have been asked to go to identify just an empty purse. She had heard stories just the same, of stolen bags and purses being found a short time after the theft, dumped in toilets or litter bins, emptied of all their contents.

Maybe the thief had just taken the money and left the rest, or maybe, as the security man had suggested, the store detectives had been able to catch a well-known offender with the purse in his or her possession. It was more likely to be a woman, Marianne figured. A man would have been too conspicuous in the ladies' changing room area. She hoped she wouldn't have to meet the thief face to face, if they had caught her. She wouldn't know how to react. Would it be the store or the police, or Marianne herself who would decide whether to press charges or not?

A more agreeable thought eased her mind. Perhaps some decent, honest person had found the discarded purse and handed it in. It was reassuring to think that there were still good-hearted people out there who would do the proper thing.

The central shopping area was even more crowded than before, if that were possible, with lone musicians at every corner collecting coins in their instrument cases and hats. Marianne wriggled through the noise and bustle and smells of fast food to Bloomers' grand old Edwardian building, its bright red SALE posters in the windows at odds with the worn, dignified stonework. The lady behind the desk had nails to match the window signage. She was in her fifties and there was a kindly tone in her 'Can I help you?'.

'Yes, I'm Marianne Taylor. Maybe you remember me? I saw you earlier when I was in with one of the security men. I had my purse stolen from the ladies' changing rooms.'

'Ah, yes, here it is,' replied the lady, referring to the entry she had turned to in the book. 'I'm sorry about this. It's happening more and more often, sad to say.'

'But you've found it. You rang me to come in and identify it.'

The lady looked puzzled. 'I'm sorry?'

'You rang me, or somebody did, from Bloomers, less than an hour ago. She asked me to come in here to the office, to identify my purse. I don't think it was you, the voice was different.'

'I'm really sorry, but I didn't ring you… and if I didn't, nobody did. There's nobody else on today, and there hasn't been a purse left in. I'm certain about that. Are you OK?'

Marianne felt a rush of blood to her face at the same time as a cold shock robbed her of breath and sent a shiver of fear right through her. She had to grab the desk to steady herself. She felt giddy, sick.

She had been tricked. It was the thief who had rung her, the thief who now had her address and house keys, the thief who right at this moment was probably plundering her lovely home. She thought she was going to faint.

The lady brought her a glass of water. What to do? Should she ring a neighbour? No good, the old couple she was friendly with would be useless. The police? But what if she was wrong, if it was just a malicious call that had been made, and nobody was burgling her house? Wasting police time, isn't that what they called it? Her brother? But he lived right on the other side of the city, he would need at least an hour to get there. No, she had to get back home as quickly as possible and see for herself.

The kind lady called her a taxi. Marianne couldn't remember much about getting into it but found herself sitting in the back giving the driver her address and telling him to hurry because her house might be getting robbed.

'Have you called the police?' he asked over his shoulder.

'No, I'm not sure if it's being done or not. It probably is, but maybe not.'

The driver shook his head. He couldn't smell drink off her, but you couldn't tell what they were on nowadays. Either that, or a bit loopy.

Marianne's lip was quivering. How could anyone be so cruel, so evil? Even if they were not burgling her house, how could they make such a nasty phone call, raising her hopes and then destroying them? What pleasure or satisfaction could anyone get from doing these things to a stranger? She was about to give way to the relief of sobbing, but caught the driver's eye in his mirror and managed to control herself.

'There's a plastic bag in the back there, missus, if you're goin' to be sick.'

As soon as Marianne opened her door, even before she had seen the evidence, she knew somebody had been in her house. She *felt* something different in the room. Nothing looked wrong in the lounge, but as soon as she opened the bedroom door the truth was all too clear. Every drawer had been emptied upside down on the floor, and she knew without checking that all her jewellery and valuables were gone. A terrible sickness, like some insufferable grief, took hold of her as she stared at the depredation in her own lovely private bedroom.

She knew now what victims of housebreaking meant when they said they felt like they had been personally violated. She had often heard how burglars would trash the house they had entered, vandalise it out of sheer wanton badness. She tried to comfort herself that at least she had been spared that cruelty. Something warm and wet fell on her wrist. A teardrop. A teardrop of self-pity, but also of helpless rage.

Marianne knew not to touch anything. She went back into the lounge to phone the police and was just about to dial when someone knocked at the front door, two distinct raps: that grinning taxi driver had said he would wait outside to see if everything was all right. She opened the door.

She may have screamed, she couldn't be sure. Framed in the doorway, and seeming to fill all its space, was the huge form of a man, a man she recognised instantly, the terrifying individual who lived in the bungalow right opposite. A hundred thoughts rushed in a second through Marianne's panic-stricken mind. Was it he who had burgled her house? Was he behind the theft of her purse? Was he here now to finish the job, to eliminate her as a witness? Cochran. His name reached her through her terror. She was sure she was going to pass out.

'Marianne, are you OK?'

He was speaking to her. He knew her name. Her head reeled in shock. Marianne had seen him a number of times working in his front garden but had never spoken to him. She had noticed him watching her on several occasions from across the street as she went to and from work, and once she thought he had called a greeting of some sort, but he was such a frightening looking person that she ignored him and hurried inside. The neighbours claimed he was a former SAS man who had fought in Iraq and Afghanistan. His savagely cropped hair, facial scarring and heavily tattooed arms lent weight to their claim. Cochran was the kind of man she had gone out of her way all her life to avoid, and now here he was in her house, and he knew her name!

'Marianne, please don't be afraid. I'm not going to hurt you. I would never do that. I have brought something back for you.'

Marianne discovered that she had sunk back onto the couch and had her hands over her tightly closed eyes. She opened them expecting to see a gun, or worse still, a knife, but instead saw a face, a damaged face, that was registering sympathy and solicitude.

'These are all yours,' and he held something towards her in two large hands. Marianne recognised them at once, her purse, its contents, and her missing jewellery. She was too scared and confused to reply, but her face must have relaxed enough to show relief and possibly a diminution of terror. Perhaps it was the quality of his speech that diluted her fear. She may have expected, if anything, a drill sergeant's parade ground bark, but this voice was refined, educated.

'I'll leave them here on this table for you. They're safe now.'

'How... where did you get these?' she managed.

'It doesn't matter about that now. Marianne, there's something else you need to see. It means crossing to my house. Will you do that?

I promise you, you will be totally safe. You've nothing to fear, from me or from anybody else.'

Why should she trust him? How could she trust anybody? Maybe this whole thing was a set-up he had contrived to lure her over to his place. She had already shown herself to be naïve and gullible. All her experiences of men had proved that none of them could be trusted. Why should this brutalised-looking character from across the street be on the side of the angels?

Marianne nodded. She believed him. Incredibly, in the middle of her distress and confusion, still shaking and bewildered, she believed him.

They were outside his garage. Marianne looked back to her own house while he unlocked the up-and-over door. From this different viewpoint the familiar avenue and dwelling looked suddenly unfamiliar, strange. Misgivings almost overcame her resolve, and she would have tried to run back home, but just then the door sprang up. Cochran shepherded her inside and pulled the door down into place. Marianne found she was looking at a scene such as she hadn't ever witnessed before, not even in crime films.

Trussed up in grotesque fashion on the concrete floor were two people, a man and a woman, both in their late teens or early twenties. Each was lying on one side with the hands tied behind the back and the feet tied together. The head was pulled back as far as it could go, and the knees were bent so that the heels were almost resting on the buttocks. What wrenched head and feet towards each other was a makeshift rope of clothesline noosed round the neck and stretched taut down the back to join the bound feet, with the hands also connected to this rope. Any straightening of the legs or movement of the hands would tighten the noose round the throat. It was an arrangement that guaranteed minimum chance of escape, and maximum discomfort.

'These are the sewer rats who burgled your house and stole your property. How did they get your house keys?'

Marianne explained about the stolen purse and bogus phone call, inspecting the perpetrators as she did so. Both were typical hoodies, wearing the regulation cheap track suits, or 'trackies', with the hoods that gave the owners their generic name. The man's face was badly beaten, and blood was trickling out of his ear. He lay still, in sullen silence.

'So it was you, then, who tricked this lady with the phone call,' said Cochran, leaning down close to the woman. 'I suppose it was you who stole her purse in the first place?'

She kept a defiant silence, but fear was written all over her thin, white face. Cochran placed his foot on her throat and applied a little pressure.

'Yis, it was me, mister. Lemme go and I won't do it no more. Honest.'

Marianne wondered how this lowlife could have fabricated the official-sounding phone call that had deceived her so easily. She felt sick. Cochran noticed her distress and suggested they go into the house to discuss the situation further. The garage had a side door which he unlocked, and they entered his house at the back. He gave

Marianne a glass of water and she accepted his invitation to sit down in the front room. It was clean, tidy, nicely furnished. She sipped the water and felt a little more composed.

'I want to thank you, Mr. Cochran, for everything you've done for me. How did you know I needed help?'

'It's Ken.' He paused, judging the moment. 'I've been watching over you.'

'What? What do you mean?' Marianne felt uneasy. She tried to remember if she always closed her bedroom curtains at night.

'Marianne, there's a lot of bad people out there. Very bad people. A girl like you, living on her own, is a soft target. She needs looking after, protecting. That's what I've been doing.'

Suddenly some things started to make sense to her. Small things that had puzzled her. She recalled the time her bin had blown over in the storm and spilled its contents over the driveway, but next morning it was upright again with everything back inside.

So that was why he had accosted David! On their very first date David had arrived white and trembling at her door. He had been parked outside, probably combing his hair, when 'some Neanderthal' had knocked the driver's window and proceeded to give him the third degree.

'I wasn't going to argue with a psycho like that,' David had pouted. 'How do you exist, with Conan the Barbarian right across the street from you?'

In spite of everything that had happened, and her present situation, Marianne could hardly resist a smile. The gap between David and this man Cochran was wider than the Grand Canyon.

'Thank you,' she said. 'I suppose after what's happened today, I could do with some looking after. How did you know I was in trouble?'

'Well, I saw you leaving and a couple of minutes later a car pulled up, down the avenue, about thirty yards. They must have phoned you from the next street. She got out and knocked your door, and inside a minute he joined her, they found the right key and went in. I checked to make sure there wasn't a third one, a look-out, still in the car. They sometimes do that.

I waited until they came out, about fifteen minutes later, carrying a shopping bag. I then went out and 'collected' them and brought them over to the garage for a 'chat'. They had stolen the car, of course. After I had 'secured' them, I checked it out. Some mobile phones and other stolen items. They planned to burn the car as soon as they had finished here and steal themselves another one.'

Marianne marvelled at the easy, assured way he recounted the details. How helpless she, and most other people, would have been in the same situation.

'Tea or coffee?' he asked, and he went off to fix the coffee. Marianne looked round the room. There were several pictures of Ken Cochran and other soldiers in what looked like desert locations. She studied the freestanding framed photograph on the coffee table beside her. Colonel Ken Cochran. So this battle-scarred, tattooed neighbour had been a colonel. He

certainly didn't look like any colonels she had
ever seen in the war films on TV.

Suddenly the strangeness of what was
happening struck her. If anyone had told her a
few hours ago that she would be sitting in the
house opposite her own being served coffee by its
fearsome occupant, she would have diagnosed
dementia.

'What happens now?' she asked over
the coffee cup.

Cochran rolled himself a cigarette and lit
it before replying. 'You've got three options, as I
see it. The simple one might seem to be calling
the police and letting them take over. You want
my opinion on that one?'

She nodded. 'Please.'

'Big mistake. First of all, the police will
try to talk you out of legal proceedings. You've
got your stuff back, nobody's been hurt, and it's a
waste of time and money – not to mention the
paperwork, just for putting scum like this away
for a few months, if they even get that. They've
probably got a criminal record as long as your
arm. They'll be back on the streets doing the
same things as soon as they're out.

What's more important is what would
happen to you. Your name and address would be
shared around, popular currency, a well-off girl
living by herself in a good area. Easy pickings.
Criminals like this will do the same house time
and again, regardless of what security measures
the householder may take. If these two did get
banged up, their mates would probably take
revenge, on you, your property, or both. Don't

think for one moment that the police could protect you. They're overwhelmed as it is.'

Marianne felt fear just listening to his appraisal. She didn't doubt for a moment that every word he said was true. He finished his cigarette and resumed.

'Option two is to let them go and try to get back to normality. Not a chance. Don't expect natural human responses from the pair out in the garage. Scumbags like these don't know what gratitude is, or decency, or compassion, or any of the ordinary emotions. They would laugh at you for your softness if you let them go, and regard it as an invitation to come back for another go.

These are the rats brave young men are fighting and dying for in Afghanistan. While soldiers are tackling terrorism abroad in the name of freedom, these dregs are free all right, free to roam the streets and terrorise the decent people at home.

Next time they'll be more careful when they pay you a visit. They won't bother me. The point is, Marianne, I couldn't be sure I'd catch them every time, and who knows how they'd treat you.'

He took the coffee cups back to the kitchen and rinsed them under the tap. Marianne sat still, a kind of dread in her that life was never going to be the same, and all because she had gone to buy a new coat. It wasn't fair. Why her? She wiped a tear away before he returned. He sat in the chair in front of her. She raised her head and looked steadily at him. In that rough, ravaged, masculine face she saw something totally unexpected, tenderness.

'What about the third option?' she asked. There was a long pause before he replied.

'The third one is the easiest and the most complicated. There are a lot of strings attached. It's the one I would want, but the decision is yours. You would need to think long and hard about everything involved in it, and ask yourself if it's what you want. I think you should go back over to your own house and examine what it would mean for you. You don't have to give me your answer right away, or face to face. Here's a card with my phone number, if that would be easier for you, but please, Marianne, think what comes with it. It's a commitment. You need to be sure. Like me.'

Marianne had grown more nervous with every word. She couldn't speak. He waited a moment, then continued. 'Option three is to leave everything to me. I will vanish them. Completely. No more bother from them or their kind, ever. All you have to do is say the word and I'll do it.'

'*Vanish*' them. She knew what that meant all right. She had already seen the effects of his 'chat' on the face of the man tied up on his garage floor.

Marianne was back in her own familiar surroundings, but instead of feeling safe she had never felt so shaky in her life. There seemed, according to Cochran, only one way to secure her future, and that was to become an accessory to murder, or at least to turn a blind eye to it. She had no doubt that he could, and would, do what he said if she gave him the go-ahead. How many people had this man killed already in the field of war – why would these two cause him a second thought?

And what would that mean for her? To be always under his control, his influence, for as long as he wanted? That terrible knowledge would be the secret that would bind them together in some unholy alliance until maybe he would choose to '*vanish*' her too. She shuddered.

But wait, he had not needed to get involved at all. He could have left her and the criminals to their own devices, kept himself out of the picture altogether. Why hadn't he? Because he was 'watching over her'. He had done everything <u>for her</u>. The tenderness in his voice and face came back to her. She shuddered again, this time with shame.

Marianne looked around her room, at all the things that were near and dear to her, and suddenly they were of no value at all. Her eye fell on the photograph of David, his handsome face studiously casual in its set, not a blemish, let alone a scar, to upset the image.

At that moment something very strange happened, something that Marianne could never afterwards find the right words to describe. It seemed that a kind of light or ray of clarity spread over and through her consciousness, a personal epiphany in which everything in her life was illuminated and evaluated. Looking back later at the experience she found an analogy in the notion that at the moment of death, a man's whole life will flash before him.     '

She saw herself as in a vision, a moment of preternatural, heightened self-awareness: thirty-four years of age, and half of those years wasted in chasing after the kind of good-looking men who would always love themselves more than they could ever love her, or anyone else for that matter. She saw herself alone, fearful, increasingly isolated and desperate in a coarse, unfeeling world. She saw a man, a strong and good man, who would selflessly be in her life to love and protect her so that she would never again feel helpless, weak, vulnerable.

Already she was different. Stronger. She found the card that this man had given her. With a completely steady hand she dialled the number, and with an equally steady voice she said, 'Do it.'

## *Leopard*

When I was in my late teens, I was witness to an incident that affected me greatly. A car parked on a sloping gradient in a national forestry car park suddenly started to roll forward, just a few yards from where I was standing. By the time I had taken in what was happening the car had picked up speed and was careering down towards the shop, public toilets area and administration block. My cry of warning was feeble and probably heard by nobody but myself. The inevitable happened as I stood frozen in apprehension. A woman walked out from behind a parked van right into the path of the runaway car. She may have seen it, I couldn't be sure, but there was no time to avoid the collision, and I watched in horror as her body was tossed to one side and the car crashed full force into the front of the office block. People were screaming. I felt sick and my heart was thumping. I found out later that the victim survived the impact but suffered life-changing injuries.

What stayed with me long after the accident was that terrible feeling of total helplessness, of seeing something terrible occurring but being absolutely powerless to prevent it. Many years later I experienced again that feeling of having to watch from the sidelines as someone's life was seriously damaged. There were some big differences, however. This time the injury was not physical, and resulted not from one sudden event, but over a protracted period – the major difference was that this was no accident, no chance misfortune that couldn't have been prevented.

When Louise and I moved to the outskirts of town shortly after we married, we quickly got to know the man in the detached house next to us. Eric Kemper was a bachelor in his fifties, a quiet, kindly man, normal, even nondescript, except in one vital respect, his hobby. Hobby. What a paltry word to describe an unmitigated obsession, an all-consuming interest that completely dominated his existence. Eric Kemper bred, reared, and showed wire-haired fox terriers. These dogs were why he lived and breathed, they were the meaning in his life, in evidence right from the knocker on his door and the ornaments on his mantelpiece through to an entire half acre of back garden devoted exclusively to dog kennels, dog houses, dog runs, dog fences, dog compounds, and dog boxes.

We soon discovered that Eric was one of the top breeders and experts in the land, known far and near for his pedigree, and offered staggering sire fees for the services of his champion terriers. Eric's name was the seal of quality, his dogs' names the guarantee of provenance. When we glanced through the vast array of doggy magazines that littered his house, there was Eric's picture in virtually every one, as often as not on the front cover. He was in huge demand nationwide as a judge at the various shows and was known for his fairness and total integrity. Every room in the Kemper house was stuffed with trophies, awards, plaques, photos of winners... In short, Eric Kemper was a legend in the world of the wire-haired fox terrier fraternity. My job as a reporter for the town's main newspaper involved irregular hours and an unpredictable working week, but when opportunity permitted, I really enjoyed a visit to 'The Treatment Room', as Eric called the large wooden shed at the back of the house where he did all the nursing and nurturing and grooming of his precious dogs. He would place a terrier on the bench, tighten the little overhanging leather noose around its neck to give the appropriate posture, and go to work with a mixture of professional detachment and paternal pride, choosing the proper comb, brush or trimming knife with the care of a surgeon, and giving a running commentary on the history, hopes and needs of the patient undergoing the operation. I soon came to understand the importance of ear carriage, tight-fitting mouth, level topline, alert expression and the like, but in truth the dogs all looked the same to me and I was pleased just to be able to distinguish the males from the females.

In the course of these trips to The Treatment Room I came to know Eric Kemper very well, and to like him very much. Compared to the people I normally met in my daily round he seemed rather unworldly, even naïve, with none of the usual ambitions or material values that characterised my colleagues and companions. For Eric, the goals that mattered were Best of Breed, Best in Group, and Best in Show. Never once did he make mention of his daytime occupation, and I finally had to ask him what he did for a living, which was some indeterminate administrative job in the local council.

Life in the district of Fernton was leisurely and harmonious but, as if to give balance and contrast, there was one serious blot on the landscape. The Bensons. The very name was enough to cause shivers in the milder members of our community. About five years earlier when old Arthur Townsend died, his estate, including No. 97 Fernton Avenue, went to his sole living relation, a nephew from up north somewhere, a certain Tom Benson; our neighbourhood had been bequeathed its balance and contrast, all under one roof. The arrival of the Benson tribe provoked locals to comparisons that included flocks of starlings and biblical plagues of locusts. Certainly they were great in number. The proud boast of the Head of the tribe, Tom himself, was that he had never done a day's work and never would do a day's work.

As for the children, nobody could ever say with certainty exactly how many they numbered. One story had it that on a particular evening the Benson parents had corralled them all and packed them off to bed, only to discover half an hour or so later that they had one extra, a neighbour's child who had by chance been passing and had been swept up in the great round-up. Whatever their number, the Benson offspring, from toddler to teenager, all shared the same white faces, lank hair, and hungry eyes.

Things changed in Fernton almost from day one of the Benson invasion. No longer could garden sheds be unlocked, doors and windows lie open, milk sit on doorsteps. In double-quick time

Fernton had a house with dirty windows, a jungle of uncut grass and spiky bushes, and pavements scrawled with chalk marks, with untrimmed hedges straggling over them. Such was the reputation of 97 Fernton Avenue that it featured in the local witticism that Fernton folk were trying to ban smoking in order to get rid of Benson and hedges.

One evening Eric told me he had taken on a helper. I was a little surprised. He had always seemed happily independent and had never indicated the need for any kind of assistance, but that surprise soon gave way to something worse when I learned the identity of this assistant.

'Yes, I put an ad in the newsagent's window for a dog walker. I'm finding that I can't take them all out by myself in an evening. This young lad applied and he's just the ticket. He's interested in the dogs and he's helping me exercise them and feed them, and do a few other bits and pieces. Lucky to get somebody who's interested, and he lives locally. There's a big family of them, I think.'

A warning bell sounded immediately. 'What's his name? Maybe I know him.'

'Joe. Joe Benson. He's a good lad. Smart for a fifteen-year-old, and quick to learn. He'll be here shortly.'

Who knows, maybe at this point I could and should have made some cautionary noises, but what could I have said about someone I'd never met, and what would it have achieved? I contained my misgivings and told myself that maybe this Joe would be fine, that I shouldn't judge the apple by the tree. After all, hadn't he replied to Eric's advertisement in the first place, which implied a willingness to work.

My first meeting with young Joe Benson put paid to these hopes immediately. I took an instant dislike to him, and not just because he embodied perfectly all the distinctive Benson features; a lank fringe swept down over his eyes, and I imagined a cave of secrets hidden behind that waterfall of dark hair. It was the strange mix of furtiveness and defiance in his manner, however, that concerned me more. Eric introduced Joe to me, and throughout the meeting seemed to be showing him off, almost in the way a proud father would have done. I could see Joe *listening* all the time, and quietly studying me as one would assess an enemy, but every time I turned my eyes on him, he was just turning his away. As Eric and he left to walk the dogs and I stepped into my own driveway next door I had the odd feeling that I was abandoning my friend, leaving him at the mercy of someone much too streetwise for his trusting nature.

I conveyed my concerns to Louise, of course, and she listened intently before her response. 'He's only a boy, Simon. You're talking as if he's some kind of seasoned criminal. Would you think this way if his name wasn't Benson? Are you sure, Simon Cameron, that there's not a little bit of snobbishness going on here?'

I bristled and prepared to defend myself against the charge until I saw that she was only teasing me. Her words stuck, just the same, and I asked myself if perhaps I was prejudiced against the boy because of his family background. I resolved to be fairer, more open-minded, in subsequent meetings. The problem was that every time I met him, I saw more to dislike, and became more convinced that my original judgement was correct. I noticed, for example, how he would memorise and repeat comments Eric had made some days earlier, passing them off as his own. Eric recognised none of this, and looked pleased when Joe made the remarks. The word that came to me every time I saw Joe or thought about him was *sly*. It seemed to somehow match both his nature and appearance.

If items had started to go missing, if Eric had inexplicably 'mislaid' things, I would definitely have made him aware of my uneasiness about his young assistant, but instead all I heard were reports of his fondness for the dogs, and a progress in caring for them that now allowed him to help groom them – something I could never have imagined Eric entrusting to another expert, let alone to a fifteen-year-old boy. In the face of all these positives, how churlish, even cynical, would I have appeared in expressing doubts about young Joe Benson. Yet the sceptic in me trusted my own suspicions. Deep inside I was definitely a 'leopard doesn't change his spots' man. In the courtroom each week when I was covering local crime for The Tribune I would see the same faces, the same offenders again and again, each time vowing they had '*turned a corner*', '*made a fresh start*', '*hoped to wipe the slate clean*', '*needed a chance to turn over a new leaf*' ...

Louise was much more liberal in outlook. 'Give the boy a chance, Simon, and

don't forget, Eric's doing what he wants to do,
nobody's forcing him. Maybe the man's lonely.
He has no family of his own. The boy's probably
filling an emotional gap for him, he's probably
the closest Eric will ever get to having a son of
his own. In any case, I've always believed that
someone who's kind to animals can't be a bad
person.'

The entire sequence that followed slowly picked
up speed. Momentum was certainly gained when
Eric started taking Joe with him to various dog
shows across the country, sometimes to show his
own terriers, sometimes to judge other people's.
These trips often involved overnight stays. I was
seeing less and less of my neighbour, and asked
no questions when we did share a conversation. I
preferred it that way. Too much information
might well have tempted me into critical
comment.

Further acceleration resulted from a big
mistake on Eric's part. He gave Joe one of his
dogs, a pup of impeccable pedigree, sired by a
Cruft's champion from a bitch with a string of
Best in Show wins. Along with the gift of the dog
came a fully equipped shed, erected on the
Benson property. Eric encouraged his protégé to
'ready the pup for showing', while he took care
of the necessary paperwork, registration and
such, to enable Joe to enter his young dog for
competition. The problem with competition is
that it can easily become rivalry, and rivalry
keeps close company with resentment and
recrimination. As I found out later from Eric,
long after the trolley had come off the rails, this

was the formula that took effect here. Joe entered his dog in two shows in succession, and Eric entered a second-string terrier just to keep his hand in. In both competitions the judges commended Joe's dog for its physical qualities and potential, but marked it down for poor handling and presentation, while Eric's inferior terrier won Best of Breed on the strength of its excellent set-up.

Eric was embarrassed by his wins and blamed himself for having entered a dog at all, but, in his defence, his offer to help Joe prepare and present his entry had been declined. Whatever the rights and wrongs of the matter, the outcome was sudden and startling. Joe terminated all contact with his mentor, benefactor and friend, and the 'experiment' was over. Part of me wanted to congratulate Eric on his good fortune, but he was clearly so upset by the turn of events that I avoided even the tiniest hint of '*I could have told you so*'. My hope was that Eric had emerged from the whole thing, as they say, a sadder but wiser man.

About six weeks after the fracture, when everything had been more or less restored to its former state, I came home from work and Louise handed me a note which she had found pushed through the letter box. It was from Eric, requesting me, if at all possible, to call and see him. I went next door immediately and found him in a perplexed state.

'Thanks for coming round so quickly, Simon. Take a look at that,' and he handed me an official looking letter on headed paper.

It was a letter from one of the so-called 'No Win No Fee' Legal Firms that appear on afternoon television. They appeal to unemployed viewers to dig deep into their experiences and try to unearth grounds for a claim against anyone and everyone, individuals, companies, sports clubs, public bodies, the government, churches, hospitals, everybody. This particular lawyer was acting on behalf of his client, Joseph Benson, who was suffering trauma following a near accident when he was a passenger in a vehicle driven by Eric Gerald Kemper. The letter went on to give details of the date, time and circumstances of the incident, and outlined the effects on Joseph Benson, which included nightmares, high anxiety, panic attacks, loss of confidence, and a number of other pseudo-psychological conditions. Mr. Kemper was invited to respond to the letter and cautioned that failure to do so would be to invite legal action in the civil court, a course which his client would be willing to waive on payment of three thousand pounds.

'What's this about, Eric?' I asked. 'Was there any near accident?'

He shook his head, as much in dismay as in reply. 'The only thing was so minor that I had to think hard to remember it. We were coming back from a show, and I slightly misjudged an exit and clipped the kerb, but there was absolutely no danger, no collision, no other vehicle. I just drove on. Trauma? The whole thing is ridiculous. I'm surprised Joe even knew it had happened. It's nonsense, Simon. I can't believe this is happening, that Joe has done this.'

It was a time for action, not reflection. 'I'm going to hold on to this letter, Eric, and tomorrow I'll give it to a friend of mine, a real legal eagle who despises these No Win, No Fee merchants. He'll make short work of this, I promise you. I've seen him in action before, and it's scary. If you want to see a true terrier at work, you should see him. You do nothing, just sit tight. Don't get in touch with Benson or your solicitor or anyone. We'll put a stop to this for you. That's a promise.'

I've made it a rule in my life never to make empty promises, and this one was no exception. Next day my friend entered the fray, and a couple of phone calls later it was all over as a contest. I was able to tell Eric that very same evening that he would be hearing no more from the No Win, No Fee bandits. His relief was palpable, his gratitude heartfelt. If he thought his troubles were at an end, however, he was shortly to find they were only beginning.

It was about three weeks later. The World Snooker final was on that evening, and I was settled on the couch looking forward to a few hours of relaxed, uninterrupted viewing, so when the door bell rang just into the first frame I dispatched Louise to take care of it. She was back in a moment.

'It's Eric. He says it's important.'

I knew it was important. This was the first time he had ever announced himself at our door. His practice, whenever he wanted to make contact, was to leave a note through the letter box before we got home from work. I whispered to

Louise to record the snooker and went to the door. I didn't get time for a greeting or to ask what was wrong.

'Simon, something terrible has happened. Really terrible. I can't take it in. I can't deal with it.' Eric was shaking and looked like he was in shock. I got him into the front room and into a chair, poured a quick whisky, and thrust it at him neat. His hand was trembling as he mechanically took it.

'Take your time, Eric, and when you're ready tell me what has happened, but first of all get a mouthful of that into you.' I knew Eric wasn't a drinker but figured that the kick of it would steady him. He was far from steady in voice or nerves when I got the story from him, but I was able to nurse it out of him and piece it together. It wasn't a pretty tale.

Eric had had a visit from Ma and Pa Benson, two outraged parents seeking justice for a son who had been sexually abused by a predatory paedophile, a man who had groomed him and cruelly defiled him. These were not the terms the Bensons had used, nor even the terms Eric recounted to me, but the language that I knew would be presented in court and would scream from the tabloids. Clearly Eric was shocked by the coarseness of the Bensons' accusations. I doubt if he even understood a lot of them, but he knew he was accused of 'interfering' with Joe, and was reeling from the allegations and the violence of the Bensons' verbal onslaught. The upshot of it was that they were demanding justice for their child and were on the brink of going to the police, but out of concern for their boy and what he would have to go through in a public courtroom, they were prepared to be compensated out of court, and felt that a sum of ten thousand pounds would go some way towards the justice the lad deserved.

Painful as it was both for me and for Eric, I decided to be devil's advocate and question him prosecution style. What I would dearly have liked to do was to direct him to press charges of blackmail and extortion against the Bensons, but I had too much experience of the legal system to recommend that. Instead, I questioned him closely about all his dealings with Joe Benson, right from the original advertisement to the point of their severance. The more I asked, the more hopeless it looked for Eric. An unmarried man advertises for help he doesn't really need and employs a young boy from a deprived background. He is kind to him and buys him the kind of gifts that would turn the head of a poor underprivileged lad. I learned that Eric had overpaid Benson and bought him shirts and pullovers and a watch, simply because he liked him and wanted to be nice to him. I believed this totally, and anyone who knew Eric well would have done the same, but this would be icing on the cake for a prosecutor. In my experience of courts, they didn't much believe in kindness and goodness. Every good act Eric had done, every kindness he had shown, would be another nail in his coffin. Even the gift of the prize pup would be part of the grooming process, the seduction.

Then man and boy start going away together, the idea coming from the adult. Next thing they are staying overnight, not just in the same hotel, but in the same room, in single beds. I pressed Eric on this. It wasn't for financial saving he had done this, but out of concern for Joe. He was worried that the boy might be lonely and afraid on his own in a strange room away from home. Again, I believed this completely. I knew it was true because I knew Eric, but how many men and women on a jury would do the same if the case went to Crown Court? The prosecutor would tear Eric to shreds, mock his story, make mince meat of him. Then the eventual separation. The poor abused boy has suffered enough, he can take no more, the nightmares are terrifying him, keeping the terrible truth secret is destroying him, until finally he opens his soul to his distraught parents and the monster is brought to face justice.

The popular press would have a field day with the case, especially since Eric Kemper was outwardly a highly respected, even revered, figure in the doggy world, a judge known for his honesty and straight dealing. I envisaged the play that would be made on 'grooming', the salacious reports about *Sicko's Treatment Room Secrets* and the scandal that would have the well-heeled Fernton citizens *Barking Mad*. How ready the public would be to believe the allegations of a lowlife and discredit the protestations of innocence from someone of higher social position. Add to this the contrast in court between the rehearsed deceptions of Benson and the genuine stumbling confusion of Eric, and the case for the defence would be utterly without hope.

Eric was in a state of nervous exhaustion. Having to answer the questions from me, his friend, in a friendly, private environment, had just about drained him. How on earth would he cope with the savagery of a top prosecuting lawyer in a public court, especially in an atmosphere of scepticism and hostility.

'How am I going to face those terrible people again, Simon? They're coming back tomorrow evening at six o'clock and I dread seeing them. Their language is foul. I've never heard a woman use that kind of language before. It's terrifying. What am I going to do? If I don't agree with what they want, they're going straight to the police. What am I going to do? Should I go to the police myself?'

I looked down at this innocent cradling his drink, his knees together, bewildered, at a loss, and all too likely to end up in prison. I shuddered at the prospect of Eric's likely future, in the company of rapists and paedophiles and the worst kind of serial sex offenders, despised and probably brutalised by the 'straight' prisoners.

That was the evening I made the hardest decision of my life. I made Eric finish his whisky, poured him another, took one myself, and told him what probably broke my heart as much as it did his.

'Eric, I want you to listen to this, hard as that might be to do. You can't win this thing. Even if it goes to court and you are found innocent, which I don't honestly think would happen, your life will be ruined. Mud sticks, and even if you were acquitted there are many who would see it as an injustice, as the privileged guilty winning out over the innocent poor. You'd always be doubted, even by friends who claim to believe in you. In any case, I think the odds are totally stacked against you. I know you are wholly innocent, but the circumstances make you *look* guilty, and that is what will convict you. It breaks me up to say this, Eric, but deal with the Bensons. See if you can reduce what they are asking for, but deal with them. I repeat, Eric, you can't win in this. You could never cope with the gossip and abuse and vilification that are sure to follow you.'

I never did find out if he managed to reduce the tariff, but I think he probably didn't even try. It hurt me more than I can say, but my good friend and neighbour Eric Kemper put his house and dogs up for sale, and inside a month was gone from Fernton. We still get a Christmas card from him each year, but we have no return address to reciprocate. The only cold comfort I got from the whole sad affair came a few months later when Joseph Benson was sentenced to two years in juvenile detention for setting fire to a shed and burning alive seven wire-haired fox terriers that belonged to a rival breeder and competitor in a neighbouring town. At least I could say that this particular leopard was still wearing the same spots.

## *Going Privately*

'I'm sorry, sir, but we don't allow the papers to be read in the aisles.'

'I'm sorry, I...' Alistair Youle was already apologising before he had seen the speaker. Normally he would have simply folded the newspaper, set it back in the rack and walked away, but now he found himself saying, 'I couldn't get a local paper in the hotel to see if there are any good shows on, and that's what I was doing when...' the words trailed off very lamely.

What had prompted this poor attempt at an unnecessary explanation was the discovery, when he lowered the paper, that he was face to face with an unusually attractive woman, clearly the manager of the bookstore he had wandered into. She was in her late twenties or early thirties and, unlike the rest of the staff in their corporate uniforms, was wearing a slash-neck striped shift dress that showed off her figure to very good effect. Her dark hair was trimmed very short all over and clung around her face in an elfin style that enhanced large dark eyes and a very pretty Brigitte Bardot mouth. Had she been one of the other staff, Alastair would have, no doubt, been a hundred yards down the street by now, instead of standing feeling, and probably looking, decidedly foolish.

She was about to move away but hesitated, and then said carefully, 'Sorry about this, sir, but it's shop policy. People were coming in here to spend half an hour or more reading the dailies and blocking the aisles, and never buying a paper, so we had to introduce a ban. I wouldn't want you to think we're an unfriendly store, or town, especially if you're a visitor. Please take the paper with you, compliments of the house.'

While she was speaking, she was getting prettier and prettier in Alistair's eyes, eyes which had also clocked that there was no ring on her ring finger. He thanked her for the offer, took a deep breath, and threw the dice. 'Look, I'm here on business which has finished early. I'm going back in the morning, and I've an evening to spend here without knowing anywhere or anyone. I need direction and directions. Could we possibly have a coffee after you finish, and maybe you could give me the benefit of your local knowledge?'

She studied him closely, her pouty mouth in a half smile. It was the smile of someone used to chat-up lines and pick-up ploys. 'Where are you staying?' she finally asked.

'In the town centre,' said Alastair, careful not to name the hotel.

'OK. You'll have no trouble finding Stalford Street, then. There's a nice little coffee shop called The Bluebird. Here's what I'm going to do. I'll meet you there at half five for ten minutes or so. You're either a smooth operator or a nice guy who's feeling a bit lost and alone. I'm guessing it's the second one.'

'You've guessed it right. Thanks. I'm Alan, by the way.' The lie was instant, instinctive. He had learned to stick to a name that started like his own. At first, he had used so many false names that he was sometimes in danger of not remembering the right one.

'I'm Danielle.'

'Oh,' with a quick laugh, 'that's something. My middle name's Daniel.' Another lie. 'I'll put this paper back. Shouldn't need it now.'

She smiled again, and moved over a couple of aisles to speak to one of her staff.

Danielle came into the coffee shop at half five on the dot. Alistair was pleased. No little waiting games. She was wearing a long tie-belt camel coat. He stood up and offered her a seat before taking his own place again, with his back to the window.

'Thanks for coming. To be honest, I knew you would. You look the type who means what she says.'

Danielle laughed. 'Oh, so I'm a type, then, am I? I'm not sure if I like that or not.'

'Type or no type, I have to say this, you look a bit different out of the work situation. Less scary.' He was good at this. He knew that women like to hear about themselves.

She laughed again. 'Scary? That's a new one. I've never been called that before. So, that's me summed up then, a scary type. That's a good impression I've made.'

They were off and running, Alastair adept in his part of the slightly gauche, forthright male, too transparent and literal to carry hidden undercurrents. 'Do I detect a trace of a foreign accent somewhere?' he asked after the cappuccinos were brought over to the table.

'You've a good ear. My father was French, my mother American. In fact, I was born just outside Paris and spent my first seven years there, until dad was killed in a car accident and mum brought me to England. She died two years ago, cancer, and I moved down here.'

'Sorry.' Steering back on track, Alistair added, in that plain-spoken manner that he could see she liked, 'No wedding ring decorating that finger.'

'No, it didn't work out.' A pause. 'Hadn't we better work out your programme for the evening ahead? I need to get home to feed and walk the dog. Do you like the blues? There's a blues club in town with a great band on this week. A girl in the shop was there last night and she says they are terrific. I love blues bands. Some of us are going to hear them on Friday evening.'

'Why wait?' asked Alistair with affected boyish eagerness. 'Why not let me take you this evening? We could meet here, and then you lead on to the club.'

She laughed out loud, in spite of herself. 'And how do you know I haven't other plans made for this evening? Maybe my diary's full.' Alastair allowed his face to fall like a disappointed schoolboy. 'Just teasing,' she relented. 'I'd love to see them this evening. Thank you for the invitation. Look, it's a small club so we'll need to get there early. I better get a move on. Thanks for the coffee. I'll see you right here at eight.'

Danielle was out the door, leaving Alastair planning other things for the evening.

She looked tremendous in her crisp white pintuck blouse, tight black jeans, and high heel platform court shoes. The few customers in The Bluebird looked up with interest when she entered.

'You look great,' said Alastair, as she joined him at the table they had shared earlier, but his face was somehow at odds with the words. Danielle spotted the expression right away. 'What's wrong? You look a bit glum.'

'Yes, I'm angry with myself. I always try to tell it like it is, but don't always succeed. I should have said earlier, but I didn't want to sound ungrateful or picky, or let you down, but the truth is, simply, that I'm not a blues fan, never have been, never will be. It's like this, I don't want the band spoiled for you because of a sorehead at your side. I should have told you this earlier. You'd be better hearing them on Friday with your friends. Sorry, Danielle.'

She looked confused. 'Do you want me to go home again?'

'Oh no, no, that's the last thing I want. I was thinking maybe we could have a few drinks and a chat, a quiet relaxed evening.' Silence. 'Not good, is it? Your head's full of crowds and music and dancing, and I'm suggesting the exact opposite.'

'No, it's all right, I don't mind, but I couldn't drink much. I'm driving. The car's parked outside.'

'You're driving?' He was genuinely surprised. 'Well, that's the end of that idea.'

'No, not necessarily. Look, let's go across the street. There's a nice wine bar and you can have a few drinks, and I'll risk a couple. I brought the car only because we were originally going to the Blues Club on the other side of town.'

Alastair had a large gin and tonic, and Danielle a glass of red wine. He told her all about himself, none of it true. She listened to the inventions, some of them embellishments or distortions of the truth, with interest. Alastair had to visit the Gents when his narration was over, and when he returned there was another large gin and tonic waiting for him.

'That's from the scary type in the shop,' said Danielle. She studied him in silence for a moment or two as he lowered the drink, and then suddenly said, 'I've a bottle of gin at home, and a bottle of fine Merlot. How does that sound?'

They were driving through the outskirts of the town. Alastair had been surprised by her sudden invitation back to her place, but his other feelings were mixed. First there was relief and satisfaction that things had turned out so well regarding a venue for what would follow, but there was also an anxiety that it would be all too easy, that it would be consensual. That would ruin the whole show. He needed to force her, overpower her, take her against her will. He always enjoyed their shock and fear when Mr. Nice Guy suddenly became Mr. Very Nasty Guy. That's where the pleasure would lie, in the coercion, the domination; that's how full gratification would be achieved. She had to resist, to struggle, just like the best of the others had done. The ones he had drugged had been poor sport.

It was about twenty minutes since they had left the pub and the excitement was rising in his mind, but at the same time, oddly enough, a sleepiness was descending on him. Usually, a couple of large gins would rouse him, enervate him, but Alastair now felt instead an increasing drowsiness. He reached to open the window and was aware in a far-off kind of way that his movement was slowed, heavy, and worse than that, the drowsiness had grown to a distinct dizziness.

'Howmuchfurther?' he tried to ask, but his words were slurred together, and he found that he couldn't focus clearly on his hand in front of him. Added to these sensations were slight tremors starting to run all through his body.

'It's the Rohypnol kicking in,' came Danielle's voice, in a coldly matter-of-fact tone. 'The date rape drug. You should know all about it, Alastair, just as I know all about you. That's what you spiked Naomi Sargent's drink with. Do you remember Naomi? Here she is.' Alastair was dimly aware of a photograph in front of him, but it was little more than a blur. 'Her dad gave me this picture when he hired me to kill you, Alastair. Can you still hear me OK? You know, of course, that Naomi took her own life after you were acquitted? In a few minutes I'm going to pull over, by which time you'll be totally unconscious, and then I'll administer your lethal injection for you. Sorry I can't promise a decent burial. At least Naomi got that much.'

Danielle's last words were like someone shouting from miles away, and then total darkness took over…

Danielle, or Kayleigh Coates as her passport read, sat back in her seat and waited for take-off. Her long blonde hair swirled over her shoulders, and the dark eyes were now greenish blue. She closed her eyes and reviewed the job.

It had been one of the straightforward ones. Youle had believed everything she had said, she had believed nothing he had said. Naomi's father had provided her with the necessary information regarding Alastair Youle and his itinerary. She had cased the town well in advance, waited for Youle's arrival, and when all was ready, had followed him from his hotel. How easily he had been deceived by her little bookshop manager role play and her subliminal French accent. What satisfied Kayleigh most in this assignment, however, was the ironic justice of the Rohypnol she had put in Youle's drink. As for the lethal injection, she was a traditionalist and had used the standard three-drug combination of pentobarbital, pancuronium, and potassium chloride. She had picked out his burial spot a few days earlier, and he now lay deep in a ditch where the likelihood of early, chance discovery was infinitesimal.

What was it Mr. Sargent had said? '*Just as a wealthy man has the right to buy private health if the State can't provide it, so should he be free to buy private justice*'. The thought pleased Kayleigh. Back home in the States, private medicine and private consultation didn't come cheaply. Neither did private elimination. She was one of the top people in her field, a real professional. Fifty thousand dollars? Worth every cent                    of                    it.

## The Cat Detective

Chester Maxwell, real name Bertie Davis, was a consummate con artist, a man who, throughout his fifty-five years, had lived by his wits, without recourse to the world of hard work; by craft rather than hard graft, as he liked to put it. It wasn't always an easy occupation, but for the most part, Chester had enjoyed a satisfying and rewarding career. The life of the con man is one of duplicity, secrecy and occasional imprisonment, and is, of necessity, a solitary business, but it had taught Chester the self-dependence and resilience that are valuable assets for any man in his mid-fifties who learns out of the blue that he has type 1 diabetes.

The symptoms were sudden, and the onset rapid. The tiredness, which Chester at first put down to his age, developed steadily into daily drowsiness and lethargy, in spite of the prolonged periods of rest he allowed himself. Chester wasn't a man who paid much attention to his own physical condition, or worried about his health, but when his clothes began to feel loose on him, even though his hunger had increased and he was eating more, Chester finally consulted the scales and found he was definitely losing weight. A further change in his bodily state was a thirst that was fast becoming a craving, accompanied by the frequent and irresistible need to urinate. The most unusual factor of all, was the sweetness in his mouth and breath that reminded him of his consumption of cheap wine in his youth.

Nobody who discovers that he is diabetic would claim that his way of life or attitude to life remains unaffected, but, ever positive, Chester tried not to be overwhelmed by the diagnosis. His initial dismay was understandable, but he took some comfort in the reassurance the doctor gave him that he himself had not caused or contributed to the disorder by his lifestyle or diet, although equally it could not be definitely attributed to hereditary factors. His doctor also encouraged him with the information that he was fortunate his vision had not been affected. As for the news that he was going to have to inject himself three times each day with an insulin pen and measure his blood glucose daily, Chester told himself these were routines he would get used to, just as he had been obliged from time to time to accustom himself to various routines in prison living.

The real adjustment was a 'professional' one. His diabetes, in all probability, was going to alter his approach to his work: Chester was convinced that he could not successfully live behind bars with the condition. No, he would have to be a good deal more circumspect in his job selection to avoid or reduce the risk of going inside; he had heard stories of vindictive warders withholding medication from prisoners as a punishment, or form of persuasion. They had the power to do it, he was in no doubt about that. He would never forget the unfortunate coincidence when one of the prison officers happened to be the nephew of a lady he had conned and fleeced.

The man had made his eleven months in jail seem like eleven years of misery.

The bigger the scam, the greater the danger of getting caught, and with his record, that would mean a lengthy spell inside. What he needed was some form of smaller swindle, where the income would be more modest, but the means safer.

Ironically, it was the medical complaint which had prompted the need for some different method that fortuitously helped him to find one. Chester was in the local pharmacy with his prescription for a batch of medication when he saw a notice that caught his interest and attention. It was pinned to a notice board for local advertisements and announcements:

**MISSING**
**'Bagley'**
**White Persian Longhair cat**
Lost on evening of Tuesday 5<sup>th</sup> August in Maltow district. Light-blue collar and name tag. Generous reward for return of Bagley or information leading to his recovery.

**Police Notified**

Below the picture of the missing cat were contact details for the owner.

Chester was thinking how some lucky local who happened upon the missing moggy would stand to make some easy money when the idea hit him. Why depend on luck, on a chance find, when you could fashion the whole lost-and-found process to suit yourself? All he would have to do would be to kidnap the cat, wait for the reward posters, and return the creature to its relieved and grateful owner. The idea took hold, and Chester's devious mentality immediately started to generate various techniques and refinements.

*

Rhoda Easton was in a distraught state of mind, and had been for a week since her darling boy, her lovely Pickles, had mysteriously disappeared. She just could not understand or accept that it had happened. She had let him out as usual the previous Tuesday at dusk, into the back garden for his 'comfort break', something he had been doing as a matter of routine for three years – but this time he hadn't come back in by himself through the utility room cat flap. Rhoda blamed herself, she should have noticed sooner, but she was absorbed in University Challenge, and realised only after the programme was over that Pickles wasn't back in his fluffy igloo.

When increasing frantic calling of his name and repeated searching of the house, garden, and laneway beyond the back garden wall all drew a blank, Mrs. Easton feared the worst. The days that followed were a nightmare series of phone calls to neighbours, desperate searches of sheds, garages, gardens and outhouses, poster displays showing a laminated Pickles on lampposts, trees, telegraph poles, and in newsagents and public buildings, and visits to the local police station, and finally to her doctor for sedatives to calm her distress. Rhoda hardly dared admit it to herself, but the sense of loss over Pickles was more acute than what she had felt when her husband Arthur had died a few years back. When a friend remarked that it was almost like losing a child, Rhoda's reply was that Pickles was her child, her only son.

After all her efforts had resulted in nothing and realising her beloved cat had seemingly vanished into thin air, Mrs. Easton gave herself over to a period of mourning. She was inconsolable.

*

Chester had already done four cat returns, each in a different leafy suburb of the city, but otherwise identical. He had bought a cat carrier at a car boot sale for a couple of quid and kept it in the back of his small van when he was making the snatch. The only other expenditure was on a bag of cat litter and some sachets of cheap cat food. Small investment, good profit, the key to success in any business. He carefully cased each job and knew in advance which cat he would lift, when, and where. Chester's worry was that they might be hard to catch, but they were all pampered creatures, used to being given titbits, and he had little bother enticing them over to the van. Once he had grabbed them and thrown them inside, he drove off a short distance and performed the trickier business of getting the cat into the carrier. It was a wise decision to bring his leather gloves with him; better they bore the scratch marks than his arms and hands. No cat scratch fever for Chester Maxwell.

This new case had the makings of a minor classic. It could be a case study for those wanting to analyse frauds and fraudsters. He had waited over a week after he had taken the cat before presenting himself at the door.

'Mrs. Easton? Good afternoon. I've seen your posters around the area and wondered if you've had any luck finding your cat.'

'No, I'm afraid not.' She had trouble speaking the words.

'Sorry. Look, forgive me, I should have introduced myself. My name is Chester Maxwell and I belong to a voluntary group who might be able to help you. We call ourselves The Cat Detectives. Could I take a few moments to explain what we do?'

She hesitated for only a second or two, and then invited him in. Chester knew the importance of appearance. What she would have seen on her doorstep was a tall, very well-dressed man who spoke his name in a cultured accent. Chester. What a good choice, suggestive of the public-school world he used to read about in the comics, Jones Minor and tuck shop and all that, a world in which even the bullies were well-bred. How many criminals would be called Chester? Mrs. Easton led him into the drawing room and invited him to sit down. He went straight into his routine, telling her about The Cat Detectives.

'We're a small group of people, mostly men, mostly retired, and all of us cat lovers. Some of us have been through what you're going through now, the pain of losing an adored pet. Our aim is to help, as far as is humanly possible, to bring about the return of the missing cats to their owners, and that's why I'm here talking to you now. Would you mind telling me all you can about your boy and how he disappeared.'

Mrs. Easton was more than ready to do so, and relayed in every detail the events during and since that terrible evening a week or so earlier. She spoke with a kind of relief, as if in recounting the facts she was at least doing something that might assist in finding her beloved Pickles. Anything was better than the sitting and waiting and simply hoping. Chester had taken out a little book and was making meaningless notes in it.

'Thank you,' he said when she had finished her narrative. 'Is there anyone else in the house who might add anything, or do you have any regular callers?'

She informed him that she lived alone, her husband having passed on some years earlier, and that apart from an elderly neighbour who cut her grass once a week, she had no regular visitors. As she was speaking Chester was thinking that just a few months ago he would have been sizing her up for a big hit, a major scam. A well-to-do widow in a fragile emotional state and with her own house in the fashionable Crofton area would have been a prime target, but now he was settling for something quicker and neater. In truth, even without the influence of his medical condition, he no longer felt like undertaking large deception campaigns. He was really enjoying his new 'working from home' ventures and was happy enough with the smaller income.

'Would you mind showing me where Pickles disappeared from?' She led him through the house into the large garden at the rear. He surveyed the area in professional manner, making some measurements and further notes, and opening the gate that led into the laneway. 'Was Pickles in the habit of jumping up and sitting on the wall? He wasn't? OK. Shall we go back in and I'll tell you what I'm thinking?'

Once they were seated again, he made his report. 'It seems to me there are a number of possible explanations. That wall at the bottom of your garden is five feet high, easily low enough for a cat to jump on to. Pickles may have done that and then jumped down on the other side and absconded, or...' he hesitated, 'or, someone might have lifted him down.'

'No, no, Pickles isn't active or athletic like that. He's a heavy boy and doesn't exercise himself much. I've never known him to jump up on the wall.'

'Good, good. There is another possibility that we have to consider. A tallish person could quite easily reach his arm down over the wall and slide open the bolt on the door. There's no lock on it.' This was exactly what Chester had done the previous Tuesday when he had stolen the cat. 'I don't want to alarm you, Mrs. Easton, but believe me, there are people out there who steal cats to order, and from his picture on the poster, I'd say Pickles would be a very desirable acquisition. It's something we need to take into account, but don't worry, it's much more likely that he has taken off on his own. Has he ever gone missing before?'

'No, never. He's perfectly content. He's very much a creature of habit.'

'Good, good. Just the same, cats are sometimes known to go off for no apparent reason and return under their own steam when the mood takes them, and that may well be the case here. They are unpredictable, you can't always know what's going on behind those lovely green eyes. Yet, in my experience, their behaviour is not as irrational as some people would like to believe. They may go off for reasons they might not even understand themselves. Do you mind if I ask if Pickles had any girlfriends?'

'No, definitely not. We had him seen to by the vet when we first got him.'

'Fine. Have you had him since a kitten, or do you know where he came from before he came to live here?'

'Yes. We got him four years ago when he was two. My husband Arthur's cousin got him for us from a friend on the north side, Criswell district I think it was.'

'OK. That might be helpful. We recovered a Siamese a few weeks ago that had gone missing. We found him over ten miles from his home wandering the streets of the district he had been born in six years ago. He hadn't been unhappy or neglected, it was just some instinct that amazingly drew him back to where he had started.

That's why we cast our net wide, Mrs. Easton. We start locally with what we call a deep seek, checking out all outbuildings in the area even though they may have already been searched. Cats can hide further in, behind boxes and mowers and the like, if a place is being searched. We carry this out discreetly and very thoroughly as a first step. Our team is experienced, dedicated. Needless to say, we are in continuous contact with the relevant agencies and authorities, the local vets, animal shelters, cat homes and catteries, and the like.'

'I've already notified the police,' Mrs. Easton said, anxious to show that she had done her bit. Chester had seen the **Police Notified** on the posters and had snorted at the very notion of it. As if the police would take the slightest interest in a missing moggy.

'Well done. Has Pickles any distinguishing marks or features, a missing tooth or claw, notches on the ears, lumps on the body, anything like that?'

'No, nothing. He's perfect. He's never been in a fight. I keep him away from the local cats.'

'OK. Just a few other things. First of all, we can't guarantee we'll find your boy, or if we do, that he'll be safe and well. I'm hopeful. We have an almost 90% success rate, but, as you probably know, there's been a recent spate of cat thefts across the city, and it would appear there are professionals behind it. You're better not knowing why these villains are taking them, and for what purpose. I've seen enough to understand why you're so concerned, but don't worry, there's only a very small chance of that happening to Pickles.'

He was good at this, playing with her emotions, raising her hopes, then her fears, implanting worries he was apparently discouraging. It was good psychology; he didn't want to make the undertaking sound too easy, and needed to raise her desperate dependence on him.

'Some things you need to understand before we proceed. First of all, we are not the police, even though some of our team are former police officers. We do not prosecute or bring charges if we discover that a crime has been committed. Our sole aim is to reunite owner and pet. Secondly, anonymity is key if we are to carry on our work successfully. If criminals learn that we are actively involved against them, not only are we putting ourselves at risk, but we are more than likely endangering the safety of some innocent cats, and that would be unbearable. If, or I'd prefer to say when, we find Pickles for you, we will not tell you exactly how or where we found him. What you don't know you can't tell, because telling can accidentally imperil our future operations.

Now, we're volunteers, but we don't work for nothing. There are necessary expenses involved, not to mention our time, so it's best, I'm sure you'll agree, if we sort out the cost first so that you can decide if you require our involvement. Let me say right away, that if we do not find your boy, then there is no charge at all. Your loss will be great enough without having to pay for no result. Our costs vary according to the difficulty of the job, the minimum charge being £500, and the maximum in very extreme instances being £1,000. It's very unusual for us to have to ask for the maximum, but it does happen, I have to advise you. Obviously, we won't know in advance how difficult it will be to find Pickles.'

'How long does it usually take?' she asked, and he could see at once that the money didn't matter to her. He informed her that if they hadn't found Pickles in ten days, the likelihood was that they were not going to find him at all. He asked for a copy of the Missing poster, and if she had another picture showing him in full. No bother, she had an album full of them.

'Would you like a cup of tea, Mr. Maxwell?' she suddenly asked.

'A coffee, no sugar, would be great, please.' Sure enough, just as he had guessed it would, the coffee arrived in a fine china cup on a fine china saucer. Chester smiled inwardly at the contrast between this delicate crockery and his coarse, cracked mugs at home. The request for no sugar allowed him to go into a recital about his type 1 diabetes. 'I was diagnosed as a teenager and I'm well used to it now after thirty-five years, if you ever can get used to jabbing insulin into yourself every day. I had to take early retirement, I was getting too tired to continue working, but came out with a good lump sum and pension.'

By the time Chester left he was calling her Rhoda and they were talking together like friends. In the back of his mind was the idea that if he did decide at some stage to go back to large scale cons, here was one with the groundwork already prepared. As for Rhoda, it would have been inconceivable to her that a man speaking so intimately of the illness that had made him vulnerable and dependent could in fact be practising an act of deception on an unsuspecting victim.

Ned Birkett's year-long contract as a highly paid mercenary fighting unofficially for the government forces against the pastoralists in the North Rift region of Kenya had ended, and he was spending his last day in the town of Eldoret, waiting for a charter flight from Eldoret International Airport to take him to Nairobi. From there he would fly home. With a few hours to spare, he strolled through the town and in one of the dusty squares away from the main business quarter, came upon a local market.

Birkett was sauntering up and down the aisles when he saw the cat in a crudely made cage on the counter of one of the stalls. His interest was caught immediately. He had been at one time, as a young man in his twenties, a cat fancier, breeder, dealer, and something of an authority on the more exotic and rare breeds. Unless he was mistaken, what he was looking at now through the roughly bound sticks of the cage was the native domestic cat called the Sokoke, a highly prized and admired species among cat lovers and collectors back home. The animal was lying, sleeping, possibly doped, on the floor of the cage, but he could see clearly the distinctive long legs, tabby markings and short coarse hair that were its hallmarks. He indicated to the stallholder that he was interested.

'Ah, khadzonzo, khadzonzo, lovely cat, lovely cat, only two hundred shillings, two hundred shillings.'

Birkett calculated that two-hundred Kenyan Shillings was about £1.75p, but he knew he was expected to haggle, and without too much bother he had the asking price cut in half. He paid the man and carried his purchase back to the small hotel. For a man like Ned Birkett, who lived by his own rules and broke most of the others, there was little difficulty in getting the cat out of the country and back home without regard for the quarantine regulations. He rang his friend, Colonel Kairu Abasi. The Colonel was the number one fixer in the region, the kind of man who could have arranged for snow to be supplied in the desert. Abasi had contacts in every government department, and with top and petty criminals, and local tribal leaders. His favourite saying was, 'If the money's right, anything is possible.' In a country where corruption was accepted as normal, and bribes were necessary before any business could be done, the Colonel was a very useful enabler. Birkett explained that he needed a cat flown back home 'without any bother' and gave the name of his hotel in Eldoret.

'I'll call you back inside an hour,' Abasi promised, and he was back in twenty minutes. 'It's done. Six thousand Kenyan Shillings, and that includes safe packaging and handling, a sedative for the animal, and delivery to you in person at the other end. Transfer the money into my account and email me your flight number from Nairobi. I'll send you the details, and somebody will arrive to pick up the goods.'

Six thousand Kenyan Shillings, just under a hundred quid. That's what Birkett loved about Kenya, the economy and efficiency of its corruption. He wasn't sure if he would keep the cat for himself, sell it on for a substantial profit, or present it as a gift to his favourite niece.

The box was handed to him by some minor airport official outside the Heathrow Terminal, exactly as arranged. He took a taxi to his flat, that reeked of a year's stale emptiness, and immediately opened the box to inspect his purchase. He was impressed by the packaging job, with the ventilation holes hidden under flaps but allowing ample access for air. It was a professional job. The occupant, his Sokoke cat, was in a caterpillar curl, its long back legs completing the circle. It was still unconscious from the drug.

Birkett was unpacking his large canvas rucksack and putting the contents into drawers when he heard a scuffling noise behind him. The cat had scrabbled out of the box and was standing on the wooden trunk near the door. It wobbled unsteadily over to the edge of the trunk and fixed a crooked stare on him. Birkett assumed its odd movement resulted from the after-effects of the drug. Next it scrambled down on to the floor and started circling the room in a manner that suggested lack of muscular coordination. It was at this point that he noticed its jaw was dropped, and a warning bell started to sound in his head. The animal's circumambulation of the room was getting faster by the minute. Its whole manner and appearance spoke of growing excitability, extreme excitability, and into Birkett's memory slid identical behaviour he had seen twenty years or more back in a film on feline rabies.

He reached at once into his rucksack, rummaged for a pair of gauntlet style leather gloves, and put them on with some haste. By this time the cat was stopped at his feet. It turned up on him an expression of overt aggression, the dilated pupils appearing deepest black as it prepared for attack. If its new owner was not yet fully convinced that these were the signs of what is known as 'furious rabies', the sight of frothy saliva dripping from the open mouth was the clincher. With the trained reactions of a professional soldier, he grabbed the carrier box and in one movement turned it upside down and slammed it down over the cat just as it was poised to spring on him. The frantic screeches and scrabbling coming from the box as he held it down tightly on the floor sounded like he had trapped a demon.

So that was why the market trader had sold so easily and cheaply. What Birkett didn't know was that the Sokoke had been bitten by a rabid bat-eared fox and the virus in its saliva had been transferred to the cat. In any case, the details of its infection didn't matter, all that mattered was that he would have to get rid of it. He couldn't take it to a vet without inviting all kinds of awkward questions. Ironically, this man who had killed any number of his fellow human beings, couldn't, as a committed cat lover, bring himself to kill the thing now shrieking and scratching beneath him. What he could do would be to turn it loose in some 'civilised' place and hope that a good citizen might find it and take care of it. Birkett chose to ignore the distinct possibility that the good citizen might very well need taken care of himself if he fell foul of the creature's saliva infected bite.

Chester called Rhoda Easton three days after their meeting to 'report in'. He told her the search, as a project of elimination, was going well and according to plan, and that they were following a definite lead. She thanked him effusively for being so assiduous and confessed that all her peace of mind now depended on the efforts of his team. Chester rang next day again with the bad news that their lead was a dead end. He could hear the disappointment in her voice even as she was thanking him for keeping her so well informed. He told her not to worry, that they were following up another line of enquiry, possibly an even stronger one. It was the old mix of sweet and sour, good news and bad news. Chester knew that something is valued and appreciated even more when it is thought to be irretrievably lost. He also knew the power of delay, and waited for two days before calling her again. His call was answered immediately; she had been sitting by the phone anxiously waiting for it.

'Rhoda, are you sitting down? I've some good news for you. We've found your boy, safe and well.'

He heard sobbing on the other end of the line. Chester couldn't believe it, couldn't understand it. He had seen tears when he had returned the other four cats he had stolen, and on each instance the owners were the only ones showing relief and joy. The feelings were clearly not reciprocated, at least not openly. All the cats had done was to amble over to the dishes looking for food. A dog would at least have wagged its tail, or barked, but the only love these felines seemed to have, if they had any at all, was of the cupboard variety.

The reunion of Rhoda Easton and her 'boy' Pickles was indeed an emotional one. Chester knew to stand back and wait until the rapturous reception of her lost child had subsided a little before speaking.

'We won't tell you how and where we got him, Rhoda, but we can assure you that the person who had him fed and looked after him well. He's back now where he belongs and, as they say nowadays, my work is done here.'

'Thank you, thank you, a thousand times thank you. You'll never know how grateful I am. Please tell me how much I owe you so that I can make at least some show of my gratitude.'

Chester had charged £600 for the first four returns but knew he could raise the tariff a bit here. 'I'm going to have to ask you for £825, Rhoda. There were, how shall I put it, some additional expenses in this particular operation. Cash would be best, if possible, because I have to pay my colleagues and grease a few palms.'

She left the room, came back a few minutes later, and handed him a large thick envelope. 'This is for you all. Please pass on to your friends my thanks and gratitude. If you are in this area again, Chester, please call and see Pickles and me. I promise he'll not go missing again.'

Chester parked a mile or so away and counted the contents of the envelope. A grand. She had added a bonus. He rubbed his hands together in satisfaction. This was the business, quick, clean, and in this case, open-ended.

He was still on a high when ten minutes later, driving down a tree-lined avenue in the Wynnfield stockbroker belt, he spotted a cat on the pavement outside two imposing pillars. Normally he would have driven on, but flushed with his success, and with cats miaowing in his head, this seemed like an invitation from the gods to continue the roll he was on. He pulled up just past the entrance.

Chester was certain that in this posh area the Missing posters would be up in no time, and he'd soon be repeating the kind of success he'd just achieved. His leather gloves and the cat carrier were still in the van. He lifted an open sachet of cat treats, checked that the avenue was empty of traffic and pedestrians, and, pulling on the gloves, approached the cat. It was lying in an odd shape, angled against the base of the pillar, apparently asleep.

Chester looked quickly round him, bent down, grabbed the cat, and fury was unleashed. A hissing, spitting fiend ripped itself from his grasp, leapt up at his face, and sank its foaming teeth in his cheek. Chester actually screamed out in pain and shock as the beast clung on, clawing for purchase at his neck, until he was able to pull it free and fling it to the ground. He instinctively put his hand to his face to check it and saw that he was bleeding freely.

The animal had righted itself on the pavement and was crouched in crooked, terrifying readiness for another attack. In panic Chester managed to kick it away long enough to scramble back into the van. He took off at speed. When he checked in the driver's mirror, he could see blood dripping down on to his shirt collar.

The nightmare was slow and stealthy, but steady in its progress. Chester was surprised that nearly a month after the incident with the devil cat there was still a tingling round the wound, but he didn't connect this minor sensation with the barrage of health problems that started to assail him. He had always been a healthy individual, and could nearly have counted the number of his visits to the doctor during his lifetime on one hand, so this onslaught of ailments was outside of his previous experience. Initially Chester accounted for the tiredness and lack of appetite as a by-product of his diabetes, and then the subsequent headache, fever, sore throat and cough the symptoms of one of those bugs that seemed to be continually in circulation. Even when the abdominal pain started, followed by nausea, vomiting and diarrhoea, Chester wasn't much worried. He recalled a bout of food poisoning that had produced the same effects.

It was the eventual mental or psychological disorders that finally convinced Chester that there was something seriously wrong with him. He began to experience a sense of deep worry, something that was entirely alien to his optimistic personality, and this anxiety was accompanied by an equally uncharacteristic irritability. For the first time in his life, Chester Maxwell then found himself suffering from depression, and experiencing bizarre hallucinations. It was at this point that he made an appointment with his GP.

The doctor examined him thoroughly and gave his diagnosis. He had concluded that as a result of Chester's diabetes his immune system had been compromised, and he was exhibiting the symptoms of a viral infection which might well be affecting his brain. He prescribed the strongest antibiotics he could to combat the possibility that the condition might be an autoimmune one where the immune system could actually work against the person, and ordered Chester to call in with the nurse to have a blood test.

Just as he was leaving the surgery, Chester asked, as a kind of afterthought, if there was an ointment he could use for a cat bite that wouldn't stop tingling and, just recently, was stiffening his facial muscles. The doctor himself stiffened when he heard this, and even more so when he then learned that it was over two months since the man had been bitten. Doctors do not usually test their patients to see if they have been infected with the rabies virus, and reliable test results are normally not obtained until the disease has progressed to an advanced stage, so how was he going to tell his patient that if his suspicions were correct, and he was now certain that they were, that there was no hope for him? That no successful treatment was available once the disease had progressed to this point? It was way too late for the two doses of rabies immune globulin vaccine that are needed in sequence, one immediately after the infection and the second inside three days. What the patient had presented with, the doctor now recognised, were the classic symptoms of paralytic rabies which starts at the site of the infection, the bite wound, and leads inexorably to asphyxia, convulsions, paralysis, coma, and ultimately, death.

## *Victim*

He was ready. Everything was ready. It had taken almost a year of careful planning and preparation, but he was ready. There was more to it than that, however, more than just planning and preparation. It seemed, right from the beginning, that everything – luck, fate, opportunity – had combined to bring him to this moment of readiness.

Checking once more that he had left nothing behind, had forgotten nothing, he eased the van out of the shed behind the house and down the bumpy, dusty track towards the county road.

From the beginning? And when was that? That vital instant when he had first glimpsed her through the trees, watched her in the early morning light jogging round the edge of the lake? Strictly speaking, no. He would have to go back a few years before that, back to the day both his parents, without a word to Gemma or to him, had bowed out of things for ever.

He had been the one to find them in the shed, the car's windows taped with all his father's efficiency, the engine running, a length of rubber hose leading from the exhaust into the front interior through a hole drilled to the exact circumference.

He couldn't say that either his sister or he had missed their father and mother very much. The big thing was that the house and property and all that money were now theirs. It was assumed that Gemma, six years older than himself, would be in charge of things.

Gemma. Things could have been all right, in fact, things could have been fine, had it not been for her. Her hardness ruined everything. She went out of her way to bring him misery, just because he had always been the favourite, and used her new position of authority to take her jealousy and resentment out on him. Sometimes she would lock him down in the basement room for days at a time, feeding him nothing but cornflakes and water. The only consolation during those long days of imprisonment was that he was free from her bullying and slave labour, and could spend uninterrupted hours doing what he liked best – painting watercolour pictures of scenes and animals. He had to hide his paintings from Gemma. She would have ripped them up.

He slowed the van at the road, at this time on a Saturday morning it was empty of traffic. Another unnecessary check over his shoulder into the back of the van. There they were, the wheelchair, the painting items, and the bag holding the bottle and cable ties and gaffer tape. He relaxed and returned to his reflections.

Three years of patient enslavement and then, just short of a year ago, on his thirty-second birthday, he had dealt with Gemma. It was carefully planned and much easier than he had feared. It was a tidy job. Afterwards he chose at random an isolated patch of forest from an Ordnance Survey map. It was on the far side of the town, about seven miles west of it, and reached by a side road. He drove out to inspect it. Perfect. Overgrown, deserted, with traces of a path around the dark lake, and enough remaining of old forestry tracks to allow vehicle access deep into the trees. The road itself stopped at an abandoned tin mine, and he wondered absently how such a poor thoroughfare could have coped with heavy traffic and industrial comings and goings. Next day, Saturday, very early, he had delivered Gemma and made sure she was well covered over.

It was what happened then, as he was returning to the car, that had dictated virtually all his thoughts and actions since, right up to and including the present moment. A movement on the far side of the lake had caught his eye. He involuntarily moved behind a pine tree and from its cover saw a figure at a point immediately opposite his position. It was a woman running round the edge of the black water. She was in a blue tracksuit. A blonde ponytail swung behind her, and her white trainers showed distinctly against the dark background of trees and undergrowth.

He watched her progress round the lake until she was directly in front of him, no more than twenty feet away. In the stillness he could hear her panting and see her breath in the cold morning air. She was about twenty, pretty, slim, and elegant, even in thick-soled sports shoes that pounded over the trail's coarse grass and encroaching brambles. His mouth was dry and his heart thumping as her figure started to recede towards an arch of trees bending into a small bay.

All this happened nearly a year ago, but he remembered it as clearly as if it had been the previous morning. Equally clear, if not recalled visually, were the impressions and thoughts that attended the experience. They were still present now as he motored south towards town, careful to observe the speed limits, even though the likelihood of a police presence just after dawn was negligible.

From the start he had known in his head that it meant something. The coincidence was too big not to mean something: in a place he had chosen at random, and at the moment immediately after he had deposited his sister, there had appeared, as from nowhere, exactly the kind of girl he had always wanted, always dreamed of, as a sister. Meaningful or what? In the silence of the forest, beside a dark lake still as glass, he sensed, was overwhelmed by, a feeling of destiny and by an instant powerful need to possess the girl he had been directed to by some force of fortune. One thing was certain, he had to find out more about her, everything about her.

And so, his mission had begun. Arriving every morning that week about an hour earlier than on the Saturday visit, he had parked the car well hidden from view, and watched and waited. Nobody, nothing. Then exactly a week later, on the Saturday morning, he saw her again. He was thrilled even now as he recalled that pulse of movement and colour in the misty morning stillness of the dark trees. This time she was wearing a light pink tracksuit but with the same swinging ponytail.

The pattern was clear; she jogged only on Saturdays. But why should she choose such a remote place, why so early, and how did she get there? These were just three of the delicious questions waiting to be explored. For that moment he was content to absorb her appearance as she completed five circuits of the lake, before vanishing again through the same archway of trees. He waited half an hour and then made his way along the weedy path and under the arch. At the head of the small bay, he found another entrance to the forest, and half a mile beyond that a tiny parking area at the side of the road. The tyre marks answered one of the three questions.

The road was just about car-width, and straggly grass grew in a line down the middle. He found out later that it forked on to the road he had used, about two miles from the town, but he hadn't noticed the junction before. She must be a local girl, he inferred, probably from the town, to know a shortcut road so minor that it didn't feature at all on the Ordnance Survey map.

He suspended his retrospective as the van neared the town boundary. A few vehicles were about, very few, mostly mail and newspaper delivery vans. Nobody would take any notice of his anonymous little van, and with the false number plates on, what if they did? A quick look at the watch, and yet another check into the back. Every time he scanned forward to the business ahead, he felt this compulsion to check the equipment. It was just a natural response now that he was so near the finishing line. He knew he had made no mistakes. That was why the whole plan had gone without a hitch.

He allowed his memory to swim back to the Saturday morning he had parked on the edge of town and waited for her to return from her run. She had finally passed by in her little yellow Clio, and he had followed her at a careful distance until she parked outside the block of flats he now knew so well. He also replayed in his mind that precious day when, disguised in a woollen cap, tweed suit and thick glasses, he had slipped on to the bus behind her and, sitting in the back seat, had learned her name from her conversation with several girls going to play hockey with her. Mandy. He liked the name a lot. Sporty but feminine, business-like but friendly. He enjoyed saying it in his plans: *'Today I'll follow Mandy on foot.'*, *'Thursday: Mandy's evening class tonight'*.

How much he now knew about her, from her workplace and daily routine right down to her taste in clothes and her favourite colours. Wearing his father's gaberdine coat, slouch hat and rimless glasses, he had followed her one day into a store and watched her buy a cream sweater and brown corduroy jeans. That was why he had chosen the brown and cream duvet cover for her bed in the basement. It was good not to take chances with colour schemes and details like that. These little things mattered to women.

A part of him regretted that the watching and following stage was over. He had enjoyed it, but he knew that it was only a means to the end, which was now only a few miles and an hour or so away.

The basement. What a great job he had done there. Its conversion into a fully contained bedsit, complete with modern bathroom facilities, had been his father's big project, but now, thanks to his own additions and extras, it was a showpiece. He had added a shower cubicle unit and carried out the additional plumbing work to perfection. A tidy job.

Privacy. Decency. These were key elements. He had read of men who held women captive as slaves to satisfy their filthy lusts. Disgusting. There would be nothing of that in this relationship.

A pity he had to anchor the length of chain and metal fetter into the centre of the room, but it would be necessary only for an initial period. He had padded the inside of the ring to protect the ankle. Little kindnesses like that would be important in the early months to help strangeness soften into dependence and dependence into need. From this would develop, in time, the respect and obedience owed to a big brother.

As for the exercise cycle, he would keep it upstairs until she had settled in. The holes were already drilled in the floor for the brackets he would use to bolt it down. The important thing was that she should stay fit; he would not like to see her grow fat and heavy. That would remind him of Gemma.

The cooking would be his preserve and would be done upstairs. He knew the dishes that would please best, and looked forward to conjuring up little surprise treats, to be followed by the perfect cappuccino she so enjoyed. At the start he would have to restrict her to plastic cutlery, perhaps only a spoon.

With a smile of satisfaction, he moved on to his masterpiece, the security door down to the basement and its concealment. Tricky, skilled, and painstaking work, but worth every minute of planning and construction. He would defy anyone to suspect that there was a door behind that tall bookcase in the big living room, a bookcase that would swing smoothly open or closed at the touch of a hidden switch. He kept it deliberately untidy, with loose sheets of paper and magazines disordered on the shelves. Anyone who might be looking for a special cupboard or bookcase would expect it to be tidy and trim, not in this scruffy state.

He was starting to leave the town. There were no real suburbs in this district, the scattered buildings just seemed to peter out to make way for rocky fields and moorland. He was so close. He swallowed hard.

The disposal of Gemma had taught him a couple of valuable lessons. Getting her bulk into the boot of the car and back out again, not to mention carrying her to the chosen spot in the forest, had been the hardest parts of the whole operation. It was this that had prompted him to buy the van to replace the car. He bought it at a shady car auction, cash down and no questions asked. The back doors were ideal.

Even better was his wheelchair brainwave. Apart from its practical usefulness to transport a person, conscious or unconscious, living or dead, it would provide him with the appearance of harmlessness, helplessness, someone to be pitied other than feared. The disabled sticker on the windscreen completed the effect.

After the mission had been accomplished, he knew he should get rid of both the van and wheelchair, but a little voice deep down in the back of his head was whispering that, if the Mandy friendship didn't work out, he would need them again. He'd definitely scrap the number plates.

Lucky again with the weather, dry, and promising to be a lovely day. He knew that it wouldn't have mattered about rain, Mandy would arrive anyway. She had done so every Saturday, all forty-one of them, except for the week it had snowed. Not much likelihood of illness either. He had been watching her the previous day and she had been fine.

It was two Saturdays ago that he had finally shown himself, made contact of a sort. It was a special moment indeed, staged through his painting profile. He had watched Mandy as usual until she was well into her third circuit of the lake. Then he had driven the van from its hiding place right down to the edge of the water and parked it in a small clearing a few feet from the path, where he had set up the easel, small table and paints. Finally, settled into the wheelchair, he had started on the painting of the lake scene before him. He was careful to have the front number plate concealed by the bushes, while the wheelchair hid the back one. He made sure he faced the direction she would appear from, with only the back of the easel in her view. Curiosity might play a part.

When he heard her feet on the path his hand shook and splodged dark paint over the sky on the canvas. He was sure her stride faltered for a second with surprise when she saw him. He kept his head down and then she was past him, for a second or two no further than a yard from him. Nothing was said. He wondered if he was the first person she had seen in all her early morning runs. Probably. In ten months he had never seen any other person. They were alone in their silent world. Adam and Eve. Babes in the wood.

On her final lap, by which time the painting was starting to take promising shape, he hoped she might offer a greeting, or perhaps even stop for a glance at his work, but she passed just as before, except there seemed no hesitation in her stride this time round.

Then the breakthrough the following Saturday. He repeated the artist set-up in identical fashion and waited. This time, it seemed to him, she slowed a little on her approach, but the real difference, the huge difference, was the 'Good morning' she threw, without turning her head, as she passed. It was as though they were acquaintances. He managed to return the greeting but couldn't be sure if she heard him.

It all came together next time round. Mandy slowed to a halt just yards from him, bent over with her hands on her knees, and called over through deep breaths, 'It doesn't get any easier.' He smiled back, not sure what to say. 'How's it going?' she asked, nodding towards the easel. 'Can I have a look?'

It was easier than he could have hoped. Perfect. She was genuinely impressed by his landscape and complimented him on his artwork. For his part, he was shy and polite, and modest about his talent.

'You're out very early, like myself,' she said. It was more a question than a statement.

'Yes. I like the early morning light. It's special for this kind of scene.' His explanation hit the right note.

'I love it,' she came back, with real feeling. 'It's the best time of the day. Sometimes I think it's the best part of the week.'

Face to face she was even prettier, with the fresh pink of wild hedgerow roses in her complexion, and perfect white teeth when she smiled. For a loose moment he was sorry he hadn't included her in the painting, but he controlled the notion immediately. That would have been too familiar and might have scared her off. Patience. Before long he would be painting portraits of Mandy all by herself.

'If the weather's good, I'll finish this one next Saturday,' he added. 'Maybe if you're here you'll see it completed,' and he watched her set off on her final lap.

That week was over and here he was now approaching his own final lap. There was only one little hurdle, but he had devised a solution. He knew he would have one attempt to seize her, one only, and if it failed, he would never be able to catch her. The timing was critical. He had to judge the moment perfectly. Once he had seized her, he was easily strong enough to force her into the back of the van where the cloth and chloroform were waiting. Her screams wouldn't be a problem, nobody would hear them.

He had rehearsed at home jumping up from the wheelchair to a standing position, and it was a total failure. Useless. She would be off like a shot, shock or no shock, if he tried that. No, he would have to grab her while he was still in the chair. He couldn't risk having the dosed cloth on his lap below the blanket in case she smelt the chloroform in the air. What he would do would be to drop, as if by accident, a piece of sketching paper just when she was a few yards away. He'd make an awkward attempt from the wheelchair to retrieve it, knowing for sure she would rescue it for him, and just when she was handing it over, that would be the moment.

He was about half a mile short of the little fork that Mandy took when without warning the van suddenly started to pull sharply to the right, so strongly to the right that he couldn't straighten the steering wheel. In fact, the wheel was pulling him down with it in a twist. At the same time something strange was happening, the light was dimming, and things were stiffening, slowing down, getting heavy. He seemed to be sluggish, losing control of the van, or himself, and unable to do anything about it. His thoughts were of a car jack and spare wheel as darkness closed over him…

Nurse Adams came on night duty at eleven and had a quick look at the admissions. 'What's the story on the new patient?' she asked the gossipy staff nurse, who could be relied on to give a more rounded account than the night sister's official version.

'Stroke. A bad one. They brought him into Casualty this morning. Overturned his car out in the wild somewhere. There's some bruising and abrasions and a few cuts, but it was the stroke that did all the damage. Paralysed down the right side and has lost his speech. They think there's probable brain damage.'

'Who is he?'

'That's what the police would like to know. They've been in and out of here all day. They're still not able to identify him. He's a mystery man. They got plenty of prints from the car, I believe, or was it a van, but they can't find a match. They think he's been up to no good. I heard he was using false number plates. They found a bottle of chloroform and other bits and pieces. There was a wheelchair too, but it must be somebody else's. The doctors couldn't find anything wrong there.

One of the paramedics was saying they had a real job getting him out of his vehicle and into the ambulance. Apparently there was a fair drop down into the field from the road, but not only that, he was a ton weight.

From what I hear, he's lucky to be alive. If he hadn't been found he could have been lying out in that field for days, weeks even. Nobody ever goes out there, they say, but by pure chance a girl was out running or training or something and she saw the vehicle overturned in the field when she was driving back to town. She called for help. Just shows you, even the bad guys have a guardian angel.'

## Game Plan

She'd never agree to murder. Irene hated Morrow just as much as he did, perhaps even more, but she'd never agree to killing him. James was certain of it. He had tested her once after one of her daily outbursts.

'He's ruined our lives, James, Morrow has ruined our lives, and here we sit doing nothing about it. There must be something we can do, there has to be something. Our lives are a nightmare.'

'Getting rid of the body's always the problem,' he joked experimentally.

She glared at him. 'Don't be stupid, James. I'm serious. We can't go on like this.'

Just like a woman – Irene would pile up a mountain of affronts and grievances, plead for an answer to them, and then dismiss the best and only solution.

She was right to an extent, though. In many ways he was stupid. It was stupid, for example, to go on blaming their former neighbour Ingram for starting all their troubles, but if only the mousy little accountant hadn't been fiddling figures and taking backhanders from his high-profile clients, or at least if he had not been caught. The case had made the front pages for a day or two; Ingram had been given a two-year suspended sentence, had had to put the house on the market to meet fines and legal costs, and Irene and he had suffered the punishment ever since.

Yes, they were the ones paying the penalty for the crime. It came in the form of their new neighbour, their tormentor, their scourge, Todd Morrow. James recalled his first sighting of the man who had totally wrecked their contented existence. The removal van was offloading its contents and as James watched from behind a curtain, he assumed that the man shouting instructions and threats to the other two was their boss. It was a real surprise later that evening when he answered the knock at the door, saw the 'removal man' with his hand extended, and heard him pronouncing the life sentence: 'Hello, I'm Todd Morrow. I'm your new neighbour.'

Next thing, the man was in the lounge, talking non-stop, mostly about himself, lifting Irene's best ornaments and checking their base, exploring the downstairs rooms. Irene and he found themselves trooping along behind, as their guide led them through their own house. He was like a tornado. The best they could do was watch for breakages, as they did every time Irene's sister arrived with her two dreadful children.

Their 'guest' was in full flow. 'Looking back I find it hard to believe myself how fast it all happened. Yes, started with just one car, done her up myself, sold her on and bought two more, and look at me now.'

They looked and hated, instantly and permanently. Morrow was in his thirties, well-built and with fairish hair gelled into tight curls. Irene was sure afterwards that his tan was real, in spite of her husband's hope that it had come bottled. One ear was studded, bolder jewellery encircled fingers and wrists. The open red shirt showed a medallion nestling in a hairy chest. His aftershave seemed to permeate the house like disinfectant. The business success story was building, 'Then came the famous day when the manager was off sick, and they put me in charge till he came back. Management – I got a taste of it, and I liked it. From that day on I knew I was going to be boss of my own business. Let me tell you this, I had to learn fast, and I expect my staff to learn fast too. Ask me once? No problem. Ask me a second time? Well, OK. Ask me a third time?… Oh brother!!'

As Morrow laughed at the fate awaiting a slow learner, James got an opening to offer him a drink.

'Thought you'd never ask. Used to be a pint man, but a man's tastes change as his fortunes change, as my old man used to say. Can still put away a pint with the best of them, mind, but nowadays it's the old G and T for yours truly.'

They were shell-shocked by the man's crassness and familiarity. 'This here's what put me where I am today,' tapping his head. 'The slogan did the business: *BUY THE CAR OFF T. MORROW* – get it? Nice one, eh, love? I was always good at gimmicks and stunts and the like.'

Later, 'So, just the two of you, no son and heir. No lead in the old pencil, Jimmy?'

Still later, 'Bit of luck for me, Ingram getting caught out. I got the house at the right price, cash up front. I knew the guy needed it right away. Cars, houses, it's all the same to me. Know your man, know your money, that's my motto. Must have been a surprise to the neighbours, him being involved in a scam like that. Different if it had been the likes of you or me, eh, Jimmy?' Laugh and wink.

Morrow kept on refilling his glass and splashing in tonic, while his hosts sat nervously sipping theirs. When he finally left, with darkness starting to settle, James found himself making a mental note to add gin to the weekly shopping list.

'Tell me it's not true, James, tell me I've been having a bad dream. Tell me that creature isn't real, that he's not really going to live in Grangeview Court, that he doesn't intend to settle next door to us.'

Irene was slumped on the couch, exhausted. James took her hand and in a thin voice told her all the things he hoped were true, but knew in his heart were not. 'It'll be all right, Irene, it'll be all right. He won't stay. It'll be too quiet for him here. Anyhow, he can't be that obnoxious all the time. We've just seen the worst of him, that's all.'

Grangeview Court was a long, curving avenue where, for once, the developers had shown sensitivity and good sense. It had formerly been the drive of an eighteenth-century mansion. The original ancient firs and pines that had bordered the drive had been carefully landscaped into the individual gardens of the development to complement the Georgian style dwellings. The sweep of the avenue was such that the two houses at the top, those of James and Irene, and Todd Morrow, were slightly removed from the others, and partitioned from them to some extent by the alignment of the trees. As a result, they were seen as the most private and exclusive. Another consequence of the geography was that the other residents were unaffected by the arrival of Morrow into their neighbourhood, and largely unaware of the activities that soon began to blight the lives of James and Irene.

The trouble started almost immediately. James was having breakfast a few mornings after Morrow's self-introduction when he heard a loud buzzing outside, followed by a shriek from the kitchen. Irene came rushing in, her face white.

'He's cutting down our hedge, James, he's cutting down our hedge.'

James rushed out, scattering toast crumbs from his napkin, and sure enough, there was Morrow busily barbering their precious beech hedge with a chainsaw.

'What do you think you're doing?' James spluttered. 'That's our hedge.'

Morrow heard him at the third splutter and allowed the saw to idle for a moment. 'What do I think I'm doing? I know what I'm doing, old son. This is a march hedge, and by law I can cut it down if it's causing a nuisance. Well, it's cutting the light out of my back patio, so I'm entitled to take it down a bit. I know the law, my son. You have to, in my line of business.'

Then he was addressing the hedge again with the chainsaw, and James found himself trailing back inside with his mouth hanging open.

That was the first of a series of brushes James had with Morrow, and in every one, whether it concerned sheds, fences, parking or boundary lines, he came out a very poor second. They all ended the same way, with a humiliated James sitting afterwards, thinking of the things he should have said or should have done. The business of the weedkiller was a case in point. Morrow had been spraying weeds at the side of the house and enough of it had blown over to wither a bed of Irene's roses, and leave several large freckles on the back lawn.

'One of those things,' Morrow shrugged, when James bowed to his wife's pressure and confronted him. 'Nobody's fault. It's what's called an Act of God. In law the wind would be an Act of God, so nobody would be held responsible. These things happen, old son. Nothing to do with me.'

What could the mild-mannered James do in the face of a bulldozer like Todd Morrow? Every day Irene and he came home from work dreading what lay at the top of the avenue. The front lawn of *Dunroamin*, as the house was now called, was populated by B&Q gnomes clustered near a PVC gazebo. Coloured light bulbs were strung round the house and garden, their illumination assisted by plastic Victorian gas lamps and a reproduction coach lamp at each side of the door.

All this, of course, was a mere sideshow. James and Irene could have lived fairly readily with Morrow's tastelessness, perhaps even derived some fun from it, but it was the man's antics, activities, lifestyle, whatever name best described the goings-on, that were destroying their peace and threatening their sanity. How naïve they were to regard the first party as a one-off, a housewarming do where excesses could be expected as part of the celebration. Irene was sufficiently relaxed to try a joke. 'Maybe they're celebrating Morrow living somewhere else, well away from them.'

The guests started arriving about seven. James was in the front garden expurgating dandelions with a kitchen fork, and could hear the music of clinking bottles that conducted them from their cars to the front door. Cigarette smoke and perfume drifted across in the mild autumn air, and giggles and high heel clickings reached him over his sweet escallonia hedge. Morrow, in a polo shirt and biting on a slim cigar, was feinting punches at the men and clutching the women. James caught himself watching the women. They had their hair piled high, deep cleavages, long legs, and wore very heavy make-up, short dresses and impossibly high heels, giving overall an appearance not unlike the saucy blonde barmaids and naughty nurses of the seaside postcard. James swallowed hard and went into the house.

'Thank goodness that's over. My nerves couldn't take much more.' Irene's head sank back into the pillow. The doors of the last car had slammed, its lights swung across their bedroom wall. Lying with eyes open and bodies tense, they had listened until almost four in the morning to the thumping music and drunken squeals, laughter and shouting that were to become the signature tune of the parties next door. The pattern was set.

When midnight arrived the next weekend with another riotous party in full swing, James took a deep breath and marched across to a house lit up like a Mississippi riverboat. He was met at the door by a pneumatic blonde who, assuring him that things were just starting to warm up, instructed him to leave his drink in the bar on the left.

James eventually located Morrow in the kitchen, overhearing him promising a couple of excited young women that he'd have the swimming pool ready before the end of the year. He spotted James. 'Come on in, old son. What's your poison?'

When he learned through the tobacco smoke that James was there to complain about the noise, his tone changed. 'A moment, friend. Nobody's causing any bother here, nobody but yourself. You'll need to learn to live and let live, my son. That's my motto, live and let live. You go ahead and have as many parties as you want, and it won't bother me. No, you'll get no complaints from me.' He drained his glass to affirm the promise.

James returned home wondering what version of the meeting would distress his wife least. He noticed, for the first time, how quiet their house was, like a library. Some little rebel part deep inside whispered that it preferred the perfumed noise and movement next door, but he squashed the insurgent thought in an instant.

As the noise and nuisance of Morrow's parties continued, they called the police, of course, but even as Irene was starting her lament to the policeman and WPC who called, James knew it was a lost cause. He saw the woman constable take in the domestic order of the room, the little dusted glass ornaments, the magazines in a rack, the gleaming furniture, and exchange a smile with her colleague. James too smiled, in spite of himself. He was remembering the Christmas his father had stayed over, and had thrown on the fire the group of small, varnished logs that Irene had arranged so artistically on the hearth.

The policeman was speaking to him. 'We'll have a word with Mr. Morrow, sir, and make sure he turns the volume down, so to speak. Maybe you can keep an eye on things.'

How could they do otherwise, when Morrow was keeping a dozen or more of his used cars at the front, and his visitors were repeatedly parking on their lawn, blocking their driveway, littering the area. James felt like a solitary fireman trying to fight a forest inferno. The men were all as obnoxious as their host, it seemed, and had the same disagreeable habits, such as addressing James as 'squire' or 'sport' when he protested about their behaviour. One morning, about two o'clock with a party at its height, James saw three of them urinating on his lawn. He prevented Irene from watching and, still fully dressed, marched downstairs and outside.

'Would you mind not doing that,' he called out in the sternest voice he could muster.

'Keep your hair on, chief. This'll make the grass grow quicker,' and they sniggered loudly. James felt his bald head glow in helpless rage.

As for the women, they were another matter. In a different way they caused James greater disquiet. Irene and he had agreed early in the Morrow tyranny that they would stand firm together, not allow themselves to take out their frustrations upon each other, and never move house. If anything good could be said to have come from the arrival of the neighbour from hell, it was that husband and wife presented a wholly united front, suffering bravely together under the same persecution. Then James found himself watching the 'sluts' in secret, with a dry mouth and hollow tummy, sneaking looks, strange desires stirring, whether half remembered or half forgotten, he wasn't sure. Afterwards, terrible feelings of guilt and shame would assail him – where Irene felt nothing but outrage and dismay, he was poaching little private satisfactions and sensations. There were nights when James lay sleepless as a traitor.

The strength of her resolve served to sharpen these stabs of guilt. One day when Morrow had lit a fire in his garden and the black smoke had blown straight into her washing, an extraordinary thing happened. Irene used the F word. James had never heard her swear before. He admired her defiance and resistance, but a little part of him was saddened – Morrow's coarseness was like a plague, affecting everything in its path, including the finest flowers.

James was starting to have other feelings too, feelings even more disturbing than those aroused by the females on the guest list next door. They started with fairly infantile fancies – smashing all Morrow's windows, slashing his tyres, spraying graffiti on his walls, the usual imaginings of a bully's victim. These revenge fancies, however, began to deepen into something darker, heavier. At first the violence was in the form of disturbed dreams, in which James saw himself, or felt himself, inflicting horrifying injuries on people he didn't recognise, often using sledgehammers or axes or iron bars. At no time in these dreams was Morrow the one on the receiving end of the terrible blows. James would awake instantly from the nightmares, breathless, his heart thumping, the nerves in his stomach churning. He said nothing to Irene about them, but the dreams were so unlike anything he had ever experienced before that they affected him greatly, making him anxious and nervy.

Then the thoughts started, appalling thoughts, thoughts of sadistic torture and killing, thoughts that the meek James would never have believed himself capable of conceiving. He thought of kidnapping Morrow, chaining him to a wall in some remote building and watching him die in agony from starvation; he'd sit gorging delicious meals as his captive begged for a scrap of food. Some of the thoughts and imaginings were so barbarous that he had to drag his mind to other things to avoid facing them. Yet, they kept coming back – Morrow hanging by his feet as James blinded him in each eye, Morrow tied up and helpless as James doused him in petrol and lit the match… What was happening to him? Was he going mad? He dared not share these frightful pictures with Irene, in spite of his best intentions, the bond between them was loosening.

The solution to everything was clearer by the day: he would have to get rid of the source of all their troubles, Todd Morrow, and he would have to do it by himself. It was just a matter of how…

The programme was one of those needless pre-match analysis pieces, the expert in the studio bland and infallible, but for James his words had the authority of an instruction manual: *'They're the weaker side and they'll be on the back foot throughout the 90 minutes. Their only hope is to play to whatever strengths they have, sit tight at the back, and hope the other team gets careless. In every match there's always a half chance, a gap that a quick break from defence might be able to exploit. Who knows, they might even sneak a result.'*

James waited until Irene had gone to bed, got a sheet of A4 paper, and ruled a line down its middle. He headed the left side 'MY STRENGTHS' and the right 'MORROW'S WEAKNESSES'.

The sides balanced better than he dared to hope. In his favour, apart from the motivating force of total hatred for the enemy and determination to destroy him, were two key elements. First, his job. As Distribution Manager of Pharmacom, the largest pharmaceutical company in the county, he had unhindered access to virtually every drug and chemical substance in the book. The second factor was equally advantageous – he had direct entry into Morrow's house. Morrow himself always drove into the garage through the electronically controlled door and entered the house by the inside door, but on a number of occasions, from behind his curtain, James had seen employees let themselves into the house through the back door, using a key they took from a shelf in the greenhouse. They always returned the key when their errand was over.

As James underlined, and then circled, these two vital strengths, a kind of excitement was building in him, the excitement of criminal secrecy. It was a feeling new to him, and he was surprised by its power. When he glanced across the page the excitement increased. Written there, and underlined, were the words *Routine* and *Habits*. Were these weaknesses, able to be exploited? In the early days, before the cold war had set in, Morrow would confide to James his success formula, confident that it would be found interesting. One of his practices was of particular interest now. He kept his used car showroom open late two nights a week, Tuesdays and Thursdays.

'Work hard, and play hard, but don't mix the two. That's my motto, old son, and I haven't done too bad by it. A couple of snifters from Mr. Gordon when I come in on the late nights, a little bit of the old TV, and I'm into the straw. Even the top stud needs an early night or two to recharge the batteries.'

Thursday. James added the word to the other two and drew a box round it. Thursday, the evening Irene went to her Italian class. He dropped her off each week at the college before half seven and was home again in ten minutes. A woman from the class left her at the bottom of the avenue, and she got back about ten. Morrow got home around half eight. Plenty of time. James felt a nervous satisfaction as the thing started to take shape. He gave a kind of laugh, and instantly looked over his shoulder. Was this really happening? Was he, all by himself, in his own armchair and surrounded by everyday familiar things, sitting, planning murder?

The mission was almost aborted before it got off the ground. Irene's gold bracelet somehow came apart just as they were leaving the house, and by the time he had found the small pliers and mended the fault, they were running late. His hands trembled as he did the repair.

'Never mind, James, it doesn't matter. I'll just miss the class this week. Don't get into a state over it.'

He dropped her off, but the anxiety stayed with him as he drove back. Should he go ahead as planned, or was the delay an omen?

Strangely, once he got into the plan itself, as he had rehearsed it again and again in his mind over the past few weeks, his nerves steadied and he was back in control. First, he phoned Morrow's house, prefacing the number by 141, to confirm there was nobody home. Then he slipped out the side door and slid through the gap in the hedge into Morrow's back garden.

For a moment he worried that the greenhouse door might perversely be locked, but it lay open as usual, and his surgical-gloved hand found the key immediately. Everything now depended on the back door of the house having no interior lock or bolt.

The key turned smoothly, the door pushed open, and he was in Morrow's house.

Every house has its smell. This one was a blend of pub, cinema, and Indian restaurant.

James stood breathless, motionless, listening to the hammering of his heart. He counted to ten, and then made his way softly into the room with the massive television screen in the corner, facing Morrow's wide leather armchair. James gave a sigh of relief. On the small table beside the chair was a bottle of Gordons, half full, attended by a plastic Family Size bottle of tonic. His heart raced, but his hands were remarkably steady as he took a phial from his inside pocket and poured its contents equally into both bottles. The Strychlometoxamen 22, according to its report, was lethal, instant, virtually undetectable, producing the symptoms of occlusion of coronary artery leading to myocardial infarction. In less than a minute the back door was relocked, and James was in his own garden, walking just a little too quickly.

The big fear was that Morrow might have other plans that evening or, worse still, would arrive home with a colleague or woman friend. James's plan was predicated on his belief in the man's vanity. Morrow felt that everything he did was right, perfect, and, in the interest of continuing success, routines were not to be altered. When his car rounded the curve just after half past eight, and he the sole occupant, James sagged with relief. He had unconsciously been holding his breath. He watched the car enter the garage and the automatic door close.

This was the worst part. What if Morrow decided not to have a drink, or chose something other than gin? But no, he'd said it himself, he was a G and T man. James paced up and down, up and down, afraid of the phone ringing, the doorbell ringing, afraid even to look out the window. How long should he wait? Might Irene arrive back early? Was the Strychlometoxamen as effective as its dossier claimed?

He kept putting back the deadline to make the call, but at a quarter to ten he knew he dared wait no longer. With dry mouth and pounding head, he pressed redial, finger poised to cut off the call should it be answered.

Nothing. No reply. James let the ringing continue for a minute. He had to be sure, before returning to get the bottles and whatever glass or glasses Morrow might have used. He'd kept the key and would replace it on the way back.

The house was totally silent inside. Why was the TV not on? Did Morrow somehow suspect something, was he hiding, waiting to spring out? Had he perhaps gone straight to the gin bottle? James tiptoed towards the room, his temples surely going to explode. He stopped outside the open door, needing to look, afraid to look, then took a deep breath and stepped inside the doorway.

James's knees went weak, his heart stopped. The armchair was empty, the room unoccupied. As his mind reeled and he sensed that Morrow was standing right behind him, he suddenly realised that the table was bare, the two bottles missing. In an instant all was clear. Morrow had gone to bed and taken his nightcap with him.

The thick carpet made no sound under his feet. The master bedroom was the second on the landing, its door half open. James listened outside for a moment, eyes closed in fear and concentration, but there was no sound of breathing. Suddenly he took two paces inside and opened his eyes.

Morrow lay naked on the bed, his mouth drooling, his eyes wide in death. Across him was slumped the naked body of a woman. James did not need to turn the face. The dead hand clutching at Morrow's chest had a bracelet on its wrist, with a mended link in its gold chain.

## *Patience is a Virtue*

Three senseless murders, three women dead, and still no leads, no clues, no witnesses, no suspects. DI Moore was feeling the strain as much as the rest of the team, but as Senior Investigating Officer, he could sense more keenly the general sense of frustration. He began to hear hopelessness in his colleagues' voices, see it in their faces.

Tuesday evening's incident was evidence of the mood that was taking over. At the end of another day's sterile enquiries, Moore had met up with four of the team for a drink at The Mill Pond. They were sitting in their usual corner, flatly talking over the dwindling lines of enquiry and the progress, or lack of it, in the investigation of a series of apparently random killings that seemed to have deadened the life of the city.

'OK, the papers are putting the boot in, but forget about them, forget about public opinion, forget everything but the facts, and what are we left looking at? Long hours of stumbling about in the dark and we don't even know if it's a he or a she we're looking for. If we were on 'payment by results' we'd all be in serious trouble with our mortgage repayments.' DS Craig lit another cigarette and gulped the smoke down like medicine with the remainder of his pint.

'C'mon, Sam, can you seriously see a woman doing this, killing three other women in cold blood? The shrink's right there at least, our killer is definitely a man.'

Their talk was low, earnest, unlike the racket coming from a group of men at the bar. One with a balding head and mousey pigtail must have recognised them. He began to direct his remarks in their direction.

'The police catch him! Don't make me laugh, I've a hack on my lip. The police couldn't catch VD in a brothel.'

His mates were sniggering at the witticism when, without warning, Andrews jumped up and strode round the table, shouting, 'I'll put a hack on your lip, you scumbag.' What happened next was straight from a Boys' Own Comic. Sam Craig's perfect rugby tackle brought his colleague down on the dirty tiles, right at the feet of the startled drinkers. The loudmouth was quiet as a statue, and got going again only as Moore was ushering his men out the door and into the street.

Andrews. That was what concerned Moore most. DC Andrews was the thoughtful one, the 'steady fellow', the last one likely to detonate. What tensions and pressures were being wound up by the killer out there, and where would he strike again?

Moore poured himself a Johnny Walker Black, dribbled in a little water from the tap, and sat down with the file. He took a mouthful of the whisky, swilled it round in his mouth, opened the file, and started again into the case of the first victim.

The body of Mrs. Lorraine Henley had been found by her husband just outside the front door of their Woolner Avenue home. Wilson Henley had come back about nine o'clock from his weekly squash game at Brandon Sports Centre. The lights of his car had picked out his wife's form lying a few feet from the front door. Her bunch of keys was hanging in the lock, her handbag lay a few feet away on the tarmac. At first he thought she had tripped, or taken unwell, but when he saw the blood on the collar of her coat and traced it back to the small hole in her left temple, the case had opened.

As they figured it, the killer had been waiting behind the porch and had stepped round and shot her cleanly in the head as she was reaching to open the door. That meant one of two possibilities. The first was that Mrs. Henley had been simply a target of opportunity – some marauding nutter had seen her parking her car in the garage and had decided on impulse to kill her. That seemed very unlikely. The more probable scenario was that the killer was someone who knew Lorraine Henley and her routine well enough to plan the shooting, or someone who had watched her over a period of time and timetabled her killing.

Mrs. Henley had owned a stationery business left to her by her father. It was a small but successful company with a profitable contract for local government work. Her husband and she had been running the business for twelve years and had no obvious financial worries. They had no children, no enemies, and, it seemed, no secrets that might account for such a brutal killing.

The crime scene provided no clues at all. Moore skimmed over the facts. The gun used had been a small .25-calibre automatic, a low velocity weapon, light and accessible. There was no exit wound. The powder burns on the skin showed that the shot had been fired at very close range, probably from only a few inches. There were no suspicious marks on the body other than the bullet hole. The post-mortem examination showed that Mrs. Henley had been dead no more than an hour before she was found.

Moore flipped over the technical stuff. It was the bizarre details of the murder that had intrigued him from the start. The killer had carefully arranged the body so that the victim was found lying *with her arms folded*. Equally unusual was what was found in the pocket of her coat. Among the other contents was a playing dice, a red dice on which only the 6 was visible, the yellow dots on the other sides having been painted out. Forensics showed that Cutex nail varnish had been used to erase the numbers. Smudges, and light lines, possibly made by tweezers, ruled out the hope of fingerprints.

As always in such cases, the husband was the first needing to be eliminated from the enquiries. The police investigation into Wilson Henley was sympathetic but thorough. DS Craig suspected him from the beginning.

'All right, so his alibi checks out and he's putting up a good show at the grieving husband bit, but you'll find I'm right. There's probably a bit of skirt in this. He's paid somebody to do the job for him. He can easily afford it. All that folded arms and dice nonsense is a smokescreen, decoy stuff.'

Moore went along with this as a matter of course, but only to get it off the list. The one thing he trusted, the thing that had propelled him up the ladder to become the youngest Detective Inspector in the Division, was his instinct about people. It was what the older detectives called 'the nose'. Moore could read suspects, could see through the lies of the cleverest of them, their smoothest performances. Equally, he sensed when to believe statements that seemed flawed by inconsistencies or contradictions. In this instance, his nose told him that the bewilderment of Mr. Henley, his grief, his confusion about certain times and dates and his inaccuracies in some other details, were honest.

Henley was adamant about one thing – Lorraine would not herself have had the dice in her possession. This certainty reinforced Craig's belief that it was a plant that Henley had organised. Moore allowed Craig to keep an eye on Henley from a distance, especially since there was little else to follow up. The door-to-door enquiries and appeals for witnesses had produced nothing; neighbours and friends were in a state of shocked incredulity and could throw no light at all on her murder. The overall view was that she had been 'a really lovely, quiet person'.

Yes, and what were he and his team of highly-trained professionals doing to catch her killer? Moore's mind slid away from the question and back to his childhood. He must have been about thirteen when his uncle was suddenly taken into hospital, and he was charged with helping to look after the small paint and wallpaper shop for a week or two. The stultifying boredom of it. Sitting there all day hoping a customer would come in; watching people walking past, mentally urging them to enter; depending entirely upon the public, helpless to influence them. Sometimes a whole day would pass without a single customer opening the shop door. For the first time in his young life, Simon Moore had thought about the terrible dreariness of some adults' lives. As early as a boy, just into his teens, he determined never to be trapped in a job like that. Perhaps that was a factor in his choosing a career in the police.

Yet what was he doing right now? Sitting and hoping for some passer-by on the street to come into his cop shop with a piece of information to restart an investigation that had come to a total halt, a dead end? Worse, an investigation that had never got off the ground. Moore forced himself back to the job in hand. At a time when his mind needed to be at its sharpest, he couldn't allow it to take trips down the side streets of his past.

'He's telling us he's thrown his six, he's got started,' he'd said at the first briefing of the team he had assembled, 'so the game's only just got under way. We have to assume there'll be more killings.'

'Are we sure it's a man, sir?' DC Cooper developed her question. 'I mean, there's the nail varnish, and then the gun. It's the kind some women might keep for self-protection, legally or not. Maybe it's another woman, a rival.'

As for the folded arms, Meadows, the forensic psychiatrist, had mixed ideas. 'The killer may be reaching back to a female authority figure, perhaps a mother or stepmother, a teacher or instructor of some kind. A dominatrix, if there had been sexual abuse, but I rather doubt this. It's a bit of a stereotype, the stern matron type with the folded arms. I'd think it improbable that someone would connect experiences of personal abuse to that popular representation.

On the other hand, the folded arms can represent, not the perpetrator of domination, but its victims, as in the child made to sit with arms folded as a mark of obedience. The murderer may have had sexual failures or humiliation, for example, and may want to deny or counteract these experiences by inflicting total submission and obedience upon women he sees as occupying power or position. The victim in this case would be just such a woman – wealthy, independent, and socially, and perhaps therefore sexually for him, superior.

The odd thing, though, is the suddenness of the death. These people usually want some kind of acknowledgement or recognition from the victim, some kind of relationship almost. Serial killers choose victims they can control or dominate. Simply shooting the victim in the head, as seems to have been the case here, would give the killer no satisfaction. The normal motivation for a crime like this is usually robbery, or revenge, neither of which seems to fit here.'

Moore had questioned Mrs. Henley's employees and former employees, but drew a blank. Craig's pursuit of her husband led nowhere. Visits to gun dealers and to various cosmetics outlets were merely routine. The trail grew thinner and thinner. Without saying so to each other, the police were simply marking time until the next killing. The expert's view was that psychotic killers acted in homicidal cycles, and there would probably be an interval of about two months.

The whiskey was burning in his belly. Why was he unable to enjoy something he really enjoyed? Moore reached for the Rennies and moved on to the murder of Linda Devoto.

The criminal psychologist had got his timing wrong. The body of Mrs. Devoto was found one month after the first murder, and, as it emerged, that interval was a calculated one. Moore read over the statements and reports, he now knew almost off by heart. The killing was identical to the first one except that it took place in broad daylight. Mrs. Devoto had been tending the grave of her father, something she did every Friday afternoon, at the old end of the Municipal Cemetery. It appeared that the killer had simply walked up to her as she knelt to place a bunch of flowers and shot her in the side of the head. He may have been in wait for her behind the large old yew tree that shadowed that corner of the graveyard.

Moore went through the statement of the council employee who had found her lying half across the grave with her arms folded, like one of the stone or marble figures that adorned some of the larger tombs.

The number left on the dice in her pocket was 4. It was DC Andrews who saw its significance – it was four weeks to the day since the death of Mrs. Henley. Was the killer throwing a dice to schedule the murders, and if that were so, how could he target his victims successfully?

Moore finished his whiskey and poured himself another, this time omitting the water. He'd pay for it shortly with bitter acid reflux and incineration of his stomach lining, but what the hell, pleasure and pain, pain and pleasure, weren't they always bedfellows in one way or another. In any case, he almost welcomed the burning. Why should he deserve enjoyment when he wasn't doing his job right?

Nobody had heard the shot, nobody had seen anything or anybody suspicious. As for Antonio Devoto, he was inconsolable, frantic in his grief. Even Craig felt bad questioning him about where he had been at the time of the killing, especially when it was established beyond any doubt at all that he had been working in the small prosthetics factory, that had come to him like a kind of dowry when he had married Linda.

'There's a connection there,' Moore had noted. 'Both women were the bosses, the president of the board so to speak. The killings aren't so random after all. Our man has maybe a whole shopping list of suitable targets, and plans to time their deaths according to the throw of the dice. I'll run it past Meadows and see what he thinks.'

'And I'll check what Henley was doing at the time of the murder,' growled Craig, who seemed unhappy to let go of his original suspect. 'Maybe this second one is to throw us off the scent.'

Meadows was uncomfortable with developments. 'Fine, the dice could be his way of taunting the police, showing them it's a game he's playing and everything is loaded in his favour. It's odd, just the same, for two reasons. Why is he indicating the day of the killing *after* it has been carried out? You might have expected the dice to be sent by mail or some other means *before* the killing, as a challenge to the police. These people take meticulous care to avoid detection, but at the same time many of them need the satisfaction that provoking the police gives them. That element of danger and defiance underlines their cleverness, their superiority.

The second thing that puzzles me here is why he should choose something as uncontrolled and unpredictable as the throw of a dice. The serial killer has to believe that he is in total control, not subject to the chance result of any gamble, whether he throws the dice or not.

As for the victims having had positions of power and control in their business and possibly marital relationships, I've met the full range of the downtrodden male, from the common henpecked husband right up to the entrenched misogynist, but none of them with sociopathic tendencies deep enough to make them serial killers. Even if such were the case, our man would need his victims to see and suffer their loss of control, and his domination. An instant bullet in the brain would do nothing to meet the needs of such a psychotic personality.'

Moore rubbed his eyes and stretched. He thought over what Meadows had said. It had occurred to him too, that a dice was an unusual means for a methodical killer to choose to programme his work. Methodical, even fastidious. The nail varnish had been chosen from a range of brands and shades to match exactly the red of the dice. Then the killings themselves. They were more like professional hits, assassinations carried out by a contract hitman, than the compulsive or obsessive actions of a deranged psychopathic killer.

A whiff of sweat reached him. Another shirt to add to the pile in the basket. Fortunately, tomorrow was Thursday and Mrs. Davey would be in. Suddenly tiredness set in. He wouldn't read the file on Wendy Barrett, he'd been through it often enough. He did, however, go through it once more in the busy brain that denied him the rest his body so craved. Five on the dice this time, the victim's bare arms folded peacefully in death on the sun lounger, the murder as motiveless and baffling as the others.

The killer had put a bullet in the head of Mrs. Barrett as she lay sunbathing in the back garden of her Green Park Court home. She had probably fallen asleep in the heat, allowing her killer to approach and fire at point-blank range, but how had he known she was there, and how long had he waited and watched for his opportunity?

As with the first two victims, Mrs. Barrett had been a woman of independent means, running a private employment agency. Her husband, who found her when he came home from work early in the afternoon after she had failed to answer his series of calls to her mobile, was, if anything, in even greater distress than

Henley or Devoto had been, and had to be sedated by the scene of crime medical officer.

For a time, they had seemed to have a lead. Neighbours had seen a dark blue or black car, possibly a Citroen, cruising up and down the broad leafy avenue, and a man who had been working in one of the laundered gardens had got a good look at the driver. There was a buzz among the team in the Incident Room, a feeling that finally they had something to follow up. Car dealers, garages, licensing authorities, and private motor clubs were contacted, and an appeal was made to the public. Hopes died as quickly as they had arisen when the driver turned up at his local police station and identified himself as a financial adviser on a home call looking for the house number of a new client. The client quickly verified his story.

Three meaningless killings. Three women from different parts of the city, all married, middle-aged, successful, apparently happy. None had children, in each case by choice. Meadows regarded this latter fact as of possible assistance in his attempts to build some kind of profile of a serial killer who, in his words, 'broke all the rules'.

Moore adjusted his pillow and focused his thoughts on forming an overview of the criminal and the crimes. This was no longer a random psychopathic killer but an extremely organised one, somebody capable of selecting and targeting a particular type of victim, somebody with the time, means, and mobility to carry out his work across the city without leaving one clue or making one mistake. Was he unemployed, perhaps unmarried, to have the opportunities to stalk and label his targets? Moore was certain that each murder was carefully set up, perhaps even rehearsed, which involved a long period of learning the victims' routines and daily programmes. The team had already checked delivery men, service men, repair men, anyone who might have had some connection with the three murder victims, but had drawn a blank.

When Moore woke at six the next morning, his mind went instantly back to work, trying in something close to desperation to get a toehold on the mountain of glass that the case had become.

'I knew there was something wrong when the oven buzzed and she wasn't back. She's always back before it buzzes. She's never been back too late for the oven buzzing.'

The man was clearly in shock. His mind had stuck at that point; the only thing out of order was his wife's uncharacteristic failure to get back in time, even though he had found her lying, arms folded and with a bullet hole in her head, a five minutes' walk away. He had wandered into the house next door and told the neighbours what had happened and that the timer on the oven was buzzing.

The murder scene was the rural equivalent of an alleyway, a lane that ran along the bottom of the back gardens of an avenue of well-appointed suburban houses bordered by the outer reaches of a golf course. The laneway was cordoned off and a small tent had been erected.

Moore knew that somewhere on the body, probably in the pocket of the cream cardigan, there would be a red dice reading only a two.

DC Cooper had got hold of the dead woman's little Scottie and was soothing its whimpering. Moore and she left the pathologist and forensic team to their business and walked back to the house to try to piece together, from Mr. Warburton and his neighbour, the circumstances of the killing.

There wasn't much that promised to be helpful. Apparently the deceased was a lady of strict habit. 'You could set your watch by Anna Warburton,' the neighbour said in sad admiration. Each evening when she returned from work, she would prepare the meal and place it in the oven with the timer precisely set. She would then take Chippy for his daily walk round part of the rim of the golf course, timing her return to beat the oven by a few minutes. Her husband's duty was to set the table and try to catch the sports section of the TV news.

'She's never back late. That's how I knew something wasn't right. It went on and on buzzing. I didn't know how to stop it, so I went looking for her. That's when I found her, when I went to get the buzzing stopped.' Mr. Warburton didn't want to go beyond that point, and it was the neighbour who finished the story. It was he who had phoned the police when 'John was at the door saying his wife was dead and the oven was buzzing.'

Predictably nobody had heard the shot, nobody had seen any suspicious characters or activity. It was the time of day when people in a district like Oakwood were inside having their evening meal and watching the news. Moore had the entire area, including the golf course, sealed off, but turned up nothing. The pathologist's on-site report simply confirmed what they already knew or presumed, and beyond corroborating the number on the dice, forensics could find nothing of worth. The body of Mrs. Anna Warburton was removed for a full post-mortem examination. Mr. Warburton's doctor, after giving him a strong sedative, ruled his patient not fit for further questioning that evening.

Other than the fact that the victim was in her late fifties, the Warburton killing was a perfect match for the others. She was a Polish woman who had met John Warburton literally by accident when he was a young man in her country alone on an angling vacation. She had been the only nurse in the small hospital who spoke any English when he arrived with the broken wrist that had cut short his fishing holiday. A year's correspondence and one visit each way later and they were man and wife. The marriage had produced no children.

Like the others, Anna Warburton had been a successful and enterprising woman. She had run a small chain of health food shops, and advised on healing methods and treatments such as reflexology, aromatherapy, and acupuncture. John helped behind the counter or made collections and deliveries.

Moore made a mental note to check if any of the first three victims had availed of these services, and arranged for home deliveries over the past year to be examined, but didn't expect to find any connection. His nose had already told him that his time spent with Warburton was only for the form book.

Craig was there if any sweet and sour was needed. Moore nodded him into the background. They were in the stiffly furnished front room, light filtering through the slatted blinds. Warburton seemed to have aged, his shoulders rounded as if the weight of the realisation of what had happened the previous evening was a physical one. He was a wispy man in his late forties. Moore noted absently that he had married an older woman. He wondered idly if the marriage certificate had been, for Anna, no more than a passport or work permit.

It was clear that the man was more concerned about himself than about the death of his wife or the identity of her killer. 'What am I going to do? I can't run the business on my own, I left all that to Anna. I'll have to sell it, I'll never be able to cope by myself. How could I manage it? I couldn't handle things on my own. You can't expect me to take all that on.'

The tone was self-pitying, almost petulant, with none of the grief the other bereaved husbands had shown. Craig caught Moore's eye and raised an eyebrow, but Moore shook his head. Nothing suspicious, the natural anxieties of a weak swimmer facing deep water. For some people the how and why questions about a murder were things that came later, only after they had settled in their minds its effects upon themselves. Moore had seen this many times before. True, Warburton fitted the profile of the male in a subordinate position to his wife, but then, to varying degrees, so did the husbands of the three other victims.

Moore avoided the inane questions that were almost written into the murder detective's script. He had never been given the name of someone who might have wanted to harm the victim, nor had witnesses ever been able to remember where they had been on the dates of previous incidents. The average person didn't know today's date or remember what he was doing two nights ago.

'No luck with the fishing, then? I don't see the pictures on the wall with you holding up the catch of the day. I thought every angler had at least one of those up on display?'

Warburton gave a sad, shy little smile. 'Gave it up years ago. Haven't the time.'

Moore nodded sympathetically and asked a few more questions about Anna's friends and employees. Suddenly he darted, 'And do you tie your own flies?'

Warburton looked up with surprise and interest. 'No, I didn't. Do you? Are you an angler?'

'What was that fishing thing about, sir? D'you like him?'

Craig was a good detective, but he watched too much NYPD. 'I love him,' said Moore savagely. 'Turn the car and go back, I forgot to give him a kiss.'

The needle daubed red varnish over the head of the fly. It was a Thunderflash he had tied. He waited for the varnish to dry. It took a little longer than nail varnish. He unclamped the fly from the vice and put in another size 8 double hook. That had been a 'dicey' moment when the big one in the dark suit had thrown the fly-tying question. He laughed at his little joke and chose a pinch of yellowcrest feather to tie in at the tail.

It was two weeks since the funeral. He'd 'throw' another four. It would look better, more convincing, if the same number came up twice. He didn't really want to kill a fifth one now that he'd got Anna over and done with, the job completed, but it might draw attention to him if the killings stopped with her. No, he'd do just one more.

The mylar body was neat; he'd wind a rib of oval gold tinsel and use some yellow beard hackle for the throat. Lovely.

Patience. It was all about patience. He was a born angler, a man of patience. What had he to do with herbs and treatments and appointments and deliveries and remedies? Why should he have to use up his life on Anna and her worried, wrinkled women? No doubt he could expect some further police attention, they'd go on looking for their serial killer, not knowing the real work was over. They'd never appreciate the years of patience needed, the care he had taken to make sure there were no children involved. Yes, it had taken a real angler's time and patience to find the ones with no children, but it was worth it. It would have spoiled everything if he'd felt guilty over a child having to suffer the way he had suffered.

A length of black squirrel for the overwing and a couple of strands of Flashabou next. Warburton rubbed his hands in satisfaction. All he'd ever really wanted was now his but, patience, he'd wait a year or so. They might be watching him, or wanting to keep him informed. Then he'd start with the salmon season in Russia. The Kola Peninsula trip, fishing the Kharlovka, the Eastern Litza, the Rynda. After that, probably Alaska, Prince William Sound.

Now just the build-up of the tidy head secured with whip finish and the joy of the red varnish. He finished the fly with patient pleasure, folded his arms, and allowed himself another little                                                    laugh.

## *Stealth*

One day he would kill. That was something Lee Hollister knew in his head. He knew it not in any calculating, pre-meditated way as part of a long-term life plan, but in the same way that he knew he had black hair and a susceptibility to sore throats. It was as much an unplanned certainty as getting older. Had he considered this part of his mental make-up intellectually, or studied it academically, Lee would no doubt have arrived very quickly at the word 'psychopathic', but thinking and studying were terms he associated with school, and school had been for him an environment he was glad to leave behind. His school reports had always centred on his personality and behavioural problems, the irritability and aggressiveness, the physical fights and altercations, including on one occasion, an assault on a teacher.

His teachers would no doubt have been surprised, and probably concerned, to learn that Hollister had found employment, even of an auxiliary nature, with the caring professions, and, of all places, in a hospital. The idea of somebody so uncaring, so callous, somebody so totally without a sense of empathy, acting as support staff in the healing and caring of others, would have provoked incredulity and indignation from those who would have remembered him clearly as a youth, missing any sense of ethics or the rights of other people, a young man with an inborn unconcern for everybody around him.

Lee worked as a hospital porter. Some might have seen it as a lowly job, but it was important in the overall workings of the place in the same way as paperboys are important in the giant newspaper industry. Patients had to be moved from ward to ward, from ward to theatre, from ambulance to ward, and so on. He liked his job; his high sense of self-worth told him he was much smarter and sharper than his co-workers. They in turn disliked him for his over-confidence and superior attitude. Working with him or alongside him allowed them opportunities to see aspects of his nature and character that were far from agreeable. He had a low tolerance to frustration and would become aggressive if his workmates opposed him or if something happened to hamper his plans.

On one occasion, Hollister needed an afternoon off and asked another porter, old Bobby, to swap shifts with him. Bobby refused, having himself been on the receiving end of Lee's selfishness over a similar matter.

'When I told him no, his eyes went black,' he told his workmates later, 'just the way my cat's eyes do when she's about to attack. I was sure he was gonna go for me.'

Some days later Bobby came back to his car in the staff parking area and found a series of deep scratches and scrapes running the length of his Fiat on both driver's and passenger's side. It was serious damage. A couple of other cars were scratched too, but only lightly in comparison to what Bobby's had suffered.

'This doesn't look to me like an act of casual, spur of the moment vandalism,' commented the policeman called out to investigate. 'Whoever did this took his time, like he really meant it. This vehicle here took the brunt of it, obviously. The other two look like decoy jobs. Pity the security camera doesn't cover this area.'

Bobby told the officer he hadn't any enemies he knew of, and he couldn't think of anybody who would want to do this to his car, but he wasn't alone in having a pretty good idea who was responsible. The porters talked about the incident in front of Hollister and watched him closely for a reaction, but he said nothing and showed no sign at all of guilt or remorse, even when he heard that neither the hospital's nor Bobby's insurance covered the damage. They weren't really surprised. They were familiar enough with Lee's shallow social emotions not to expect to see evidence of shame.

Then there was the business of the old lady on the trolley. Lee had been taking a female patient in her seventies to the geriatric ward and had left her on a trolley in one of the side corridors while he went to get a paper from the shop. Uncharacteristically, it must be said, he forgot about his charge and she lay alone for a full twenty minutes, until another porter found her helpless and distressed on the trolley. It was a wonderful chance to have Hollister disciplined, but the unwritten code of loyalty among the low-paid staff meant that the negligence went unreported. What most irritated the body of porters afterwards was the unwillingness, or inability, of the man to take the blame, to admit responsibility. He seemed to have no feeling of embarrassment at all about the slip he had made.

The nature of the job was such that from time to time the porters were obliged to witness very upsetting sights and situations, especially in emergencies, and even the most experienced of them occasionally admitted to feelings of revulsion and nausea in the face of cases like severe mutilation or foul-smelling gangrene. They could hardly fail to notice at instances like these how Lee Hollister had such a high threshold for disgust that he remained unaffected.

More than anything else, though, the other porters were wary of him. They recognised a danger in him, a menace behind the superficial charm. There was a coldness in his eyes, and a kind of contradictory mix of self-control and impulsiveness in his behaviour and reactions that made him unpredictable. Without perhaps identifying it or analysing it, the men sensed a lack of fear in Lee Hollister that scared them, made them keep their distance.

The nurses and female ancillary staff certainly didn't feel inclined to keep their distance. A man about thirty, not bad looking with his Mediterranean black hair, tanned skin and even, white teeth, one who didn't have a paunch and didn't reek of cigarettes, was always going to have a head start over the other runners in the popularity stakes. The women liked his darkest-brown eyes, they found them 'sexy' and 'interesting'. They saw nothing cold or dangerous behind their steady fix, no absence of empathy beneath the dark brows. They knew Lee's fellow workers didn't like him, but they put that down to jealousy. For his part, Lee took a pride in the smooth way he could charm them, the control he felt as he exchanged easy banter with them and saw them giggle or nudge one another as he passed through a ward. It was a good feeling.

Lee met Joanna quite by accident but, as he thought afterwards, the encounter was something he would have been pleased with if he had contrived it. He was browsing around the Saturday afternoon market, turned to pick up an item from a stall, and bumped directly into a girl carrying a brown paper bag. The bag was knocked out of her grasp and fell to the ground, spilling its cargo of oranges. As he helped her pick them up, he not only managed a good look at the girl, but noticed that she was doing the same with him. After her oranges had all been recovered, she seemed in no hurry to move on. Lee was instantly all charm. They chatted and Lee asked if she would like to go for a drink, indicating The Town Crier Inn on the corner of the cobbled market square.

'Thank you, but I don't drink. I wouldn't say no to a coffee though.' They both laughed and introduced themselves. Joanna was twenty-four and worked in the university library. She had her own apartment in town. She hinted at some disagreement with her parents who lived in a staunchly middle-class suburb. Strangely, she had never learned to drive, didn't own a car. Lee told her how he enjoyed his job as a laboratory assistant at the hospital. Over the coffees they chatted more, Lee allowing her to do most of it so that he could get the right slant on her. Her subtle use of make-up and the very slight politeness in her voice reinforced the impression he had initially formed of a girl of good breeding and conservative tastes, so he was able to casually drop in some views and opinions that he felt would chime well with her outlook and values. Lee subtly conveyed his contempt for antisocial behaviour, yobbishness, drunkenness, bad language and such, and expressed his dislike of smoking, adding that when it came to drinking, he liked a glass or two of wine.

They had been dating for about a month, Joanna smitten with this cool, engrossing man she had met by chance, Lee controlling her responses and emotions, and delighting in his own glibness and pathological lying. The mastery he had over her was an end in itself, not a means to some further end; no doubt Lee would have soon grown tired of it and perhaps resorted to the exercise of control by different methods, perhaps emotional cruelty, psychological torment or even physical abuse, had events not overtaken whatever devices his moral depravity would in all likelihood have arrived at.

Lee had sensed an alteration in Joanna's manner on their most recent date. She had seemed a little distant, guarded, not the free and open Joanna she had been on every other occasion. Lee, of course, assumed that there was no fault on his side and that the problem, if there was one, lay with her. This suspicion was reinforced next day when Joanna rang him on his mobile and, for the first time, declared herself unavailable for the visit to the cinema they had arranged for that evening. In short, she cancelled the date. She was evasive about the reason, but eventually conceded that it was 'part of being a woman', and that in a few days it would be over. Lee knew she wouldn't lie to him. Lying was his area of expertise.

When he came out of work next evening Lee's car wouldn't start. The battery was completely flat. Nobody had jump leads to help him out, or if they did, they were not admitting it. In a very black mood he caught a bus, and this mood wasn't improved when he found that its route took in a series of detours through a succession of anonymous estates and housing developments, and involved halts at virtually every stop sign.

Lee was sitting moodily looking out of the window at one stop when the door of a house directly across the pavement opened and the figure of a woman came out. He was so sunk in his own dark thoughts that it took him a second or two to realise that the figure was familiar, and another couple of seconds to recognise that he was looking through the bus window at Joanna. He instinctively put a hand over the lower part of his face and withdrew his head behind the frame of the bus window. Next, a man followed Joanna out of the house, and they talked briefly before exchanging an embrace. The bus was just moving off at this point, but he got a clear look at the man, a young man, tall and lean with fairish hair. Lee made a note of the house number, 62, and the name of the street, Caupin Drive, as the bus turned the corner on to a main thoroughfare.

He felt no real surprise at the little episode he had just witnessed, nor was there any feeling at all of romantic or sexual jealousy; what feeling was there initially, was anger, anger that his control of things had been compromised, that Joanna was sufficiently independent of it to be able to undertake a relationship on the sly. Things weren't under his command as he had supposed, and he felt thwarted, cheated, but as he brooded on her secret liaison and how he would react to it, other feelings started to grow, principally a kind of dark excitement, the stimulation of a challenge by an opponent and the dark energies it aroused in him. The situation was tailor-made to allow full play to the deviousness that was central to his make-up.

In the next couple of weeks Lee became very familiar with 62 Caupin Drive. He was free to move in its vicinity without fear of recognition because the man didn't know him, but he was careful not to become so familiar a figure that he might raise suspicions. He was puzzled that Joanna was seeing someone who lived in this fairly rundown area, especially when he learned that 62 Caupin Drive had a communal entrance, and that it housed four one-bedroom flats. The place offered a sharp contrast to Joanna's smart apartment in the up-market professional quarter of the city centre.

Lee had actually taken a day's leave so that he could stake the place out. By good fortune, directly opposite No. 62, a house had been demolished, and some of the rubble roughly spread and flattened to form a makeshift car parking area. It was from his car, that first day, that Lee found out the man didn't work. He watched him come and go several times, twice to the shop at the corner of the block for milk, newspaper and the like, and once on a longer mission from which he returned carrying a Tesco bag.

It was a great feeling being the hidden watcher, the unseen presence, but not up there with the kick he got from stalking Joanna. The stalking was special. There was nothing random or hit-and-miss about it.. Lee would pretend to be arranging dates in advance with her so that he could organise a diary of events; those evenings she ruled out, the evenings she wasn't available, were the stalking ones, the highlights, better by far than any date could ever be. Lee could have simply waited in his car for her to arrive at No. 62, but he chose to watch and wait near her house, see her come out of the apartment building and stand at the bus stop, and then follow her progress all the way to Caupin Drive. The stealth was so satisfying, the lurking in the shades, the silent shadowing, whenever they came out of the house and he followed them on foot. Oddly enough, they stayed very little in the flat, and he inferred that Joanna maybe found it pokey, stifling. On several occasions they walked the half mile to a public park and simply sat talking on one of the park benches. The man was like Lee himself, not very demonstrative; they didn't walk hand in hand, nor did he kiss her in public. Sometimes he would put his arm round her shoulder, but that was his only show of affection.

Most men watching couples in a park from the cover of the bushes would have been classed as Peeping Toms, but a voyeur's salacious motivation would have been mild, harmless, compared to the intentions behind the cold, dark eyes of Lee Hollister.

It was on that first Saturday morning that the idea was born. With nothing else planned for the day, and really enjoying the undertaking, Lee drove round early to his vantage point opposite 62 Caupin Drive and waited. He didn't have long to wait. Just after 9.30am he saw Joanna's other man come out and set off down the street. Lee watched him walk on past the shop on the corner, and at that point he decided, for novelty as much as anything, to tail him on foot. It was the first time he had followed him in broad daylight, and he enjoyed adjusting his pace to stay a steady distance behind him. The man went into the Tesco store on Bloom Street and Lee did the same. It was satisfying walking up and down the aisles a few paces behind his quarry, almost within touching distance but always out of sight.

Joanna had certainly gone for a change, for variety. Lee and he couldn't have been more different in appearance. No tan here, but a kind of chalky face beneath thin, dirty, fair hair which looked in need of a wash. His posture was loose and there was a kind of shifty quality in his bearing that invited questions about Joanna's judgement.

Lee lifted a few items and put them in his shopping basket. The man made some basic purchases, and then went into the alcoholic drinks section. Lee chose not to follow him into that designated area, which seemed to be empty of other customers. He watched him go directly to the wine shelves, select without hesitation two bottles of red wine, and put them in his basket. Even from the ten yards distance Lee recognised the red wine immediately, and it made him see red. It was the special offer he had availed of himself, two £8 bottles of Villa Agtuca for £12, the offer he had told Joanna about, the wine he had poured for himself when they had spent the evening in her apartment. So that was Joanna, sharing what she had learned from him with this creature.

Lee was enraged. The woman he thought he was controlling was using him, turning the tables on him. He would have loved to have smashed one of the creep's bottles and jabbed it into his face, but he controlled his rage by closing his eyes and biting the bulge on the back of his fist between thumb and forefinger. Amazingly, at that wholly unpropitious moment, the idea came to him. It was a moment of genius, a moment of justice. Lee abandoned his trailing of the victim, as he had now become, bought himself a cup of tea in the upstairs café, and planned the enterprise with icy clarity. It was beautiful; it was clever and sweet, better than all the crude stabbings and stranglings and suffocations, however good they might have felt at the time of their enactment. He bought a couple of the Villa Agtuca reds on the way out. The lady at the check-out assured him that the special offer was on for three more weeks, until the end of the month.

'If I was married to you, Carol, I'd be worried you'd put something nasty in my tea,' said Lee, looking around the packed shelves of bottles and containers and little boxes in the hospital pharmacy.

'It wouldn't be something nasty I'd like to put in your tea, whether you were married to me or not,' replied Carol with her throaty little laugh. 'In fact, it wouldn't be tea you'd be drinking.'

Lee had waited until Carol was on duty on her own while the other pharmacist was on his lunch break. She was a woman of about forty, one of those plump ones with the beautiful faces, the creamy complexions and shiny blonde hair. She wasn't exactly flighty, but enjoyed a bit of flirtatious banter. Lee had called in on the pretext of asking whether the herbal pills he was taking for his insomnia could be responsible for the light-headedness he was experiencing, explaining that he didn't like going to the doctor about something so minor.

'You're maybe suffering from a bit of night starvation,' Carol had suggested with a smutty laugh. 'I could offer you a private consultation.'

'How do you remember all these medicines and things?' Lee asked in mock wonder. 'Are you not afraid of prescribing the wrong thing and poisoning some poor soul?'

Carol was pleased by his interest and implied admiration, and flattered that he had appeared to enjoy her kidding. 'We can't afford to make mistakes,' she said, and then, in case she was sounding pompous, 'That's why we get the big money.'

'You're a foxy lady, Carol Watson. I happen to know that the dangerous ones have POISON marked on them, and a skull and crossbones.'

'What? What comics have you been reading? Yes, and robbers carry a bag with SWAG written on it, I suppose. You see this little cocktail here,' lifting down a small, anonymous bottle from the top shelf, 'we mixed this ourselves.' The pride was unmistakable. 'You remember old Bamford that was here? He used it to put down his Labrador. Too miserly to pay a vet. Man or beast, a sip of this and it's Good Night, Nurse. We keep it as a memento, or in case any of you porters step out of line.'

Lee left her still enjoying her own wit. How easy it was to deceive people, to manipulate them. A little teasing and a small sting and she had been wide open. He visited her again to thank her for the 'warm milk' and 'lying on the back' tips that had 'worked a treat' for his insomnia, then took his chance while she answered the phone, and the Bamford Formula was in his pocket, the work of seconds. He was away, with Carol's 'alternative' methods for getting asleep ringing in his ears.

The satisfaction Lee got in the piercing of the cork was matched only by the self-congratulation that followed it. Using the angler's dubbing needle that he had kept from his schoolboy fishing days, and with infinite care and patience, he pierced the foil seal and eased the tip of the needle down into the cork. With steady pressure, and resisting the urge to wriggle or twist it, he pressed the needle straight down into the length of the cork, the handle allowing him to exert good weight. Lee took his time. For someone so impulsive by nature, he could display exceptional patience. Many might have tried tapping the needle through with a small hammer, but he persevered with the steady downward force that was much less likely to shatter the needle. The moment when the tip pushed through the bottom of the cork was a triumph. He pushed the needle right through, and then slowly withdrew it.

The syringe he had 'borrowed' from the hospital was just about long enough to penetrate down through the pilot hole. Lee tilted the bottle and withdrew three full syringes of wine which he squirted down the toilet. He replaced the wine with the same three syringes volume of the poison. Perfect. No hitches, no complications. Once the top of the cork and the foil wrap had been pressed flat by his thumb nail, the infringement of the seal was undetectable. Lee turned the bottle of wine upside down. Absolutely no hint of leakage. The dark eyes gleamed with success.

He dated Joanna three times that week and turned the charm up to its maximum. He was Prince Charming. The more he played Mr. Nice Guy, the more he was in control. This was how he loved it, the master deceiver pulling the strings, playing her at her own game, miles ahead in his role as the good-hearted innocent. She couldn't know, at least not yet, that her duplicity and two-timing were affording him far greater pleasure and satisfaction than plain, honest dating and dealing could ever have done. Somewhere in his mind he hoped that all his relationships would be like this.

The plan depended on the behaviour of the creep, but Lee was fairly confident that he would conform to pattern, and his confidence was vindicated on Saturday morning when he again watched from his car on Caupin Drive and saw the target come out of No. 62 and head down the street. The whole thing was like an action replay. One vital difference was that when Lee followed him into the Tesco store, he was carrying with him inside his jacket the doctored bottle of Villa Agtuca. As before, he tailed the creep round the aisles, and put several items in his own basket. He waited until the prey was approaching the drink department and then made his move, getting there ahead of him and going straight to the wine section. He withdrew the bottle from below his coat and was standing reading the label when the creep approached and stood waiting patiently right behind Lee.

'This looks a good offer,' Lee said, half turning. 'Have you tried it?'

'I certainly have. In fact, I'm about to buy two more.'

'That's good enough for me. Thanks for the tip. Here.' He reached his bottle to the man, lifted another one and gave that to him too. 'Four quid saved is not too bad,' and he lifted two more for himself. 'Cheers.' The man smiled as Lee put the bottles in his basket and went past him.

Talking to his victim face to face, handing him his own death sentence, it couldn't get much better. A thrill passed through him. He felt replete. It didn't matter that Joanna didn't drink and wouldn't be affected. His father had told him once when they were on an angling outing, 'One at a time's good fishing.'

Joanna's mind was in turmoil. She had never felt this confused before. If only Alan hadn't been released on licence at this particular time. She felt guilty for feeling this, for wishing that her brother's parole had not been granted, because she loved him and felt sorry for him, but she was having to lie to Lee to cover it up. No, that wasn't true, she hadn't lied to him, but she was hiding things from him, and it hurt her deeply. Lee was so honest, so open, and would never have suspected that she had a brother just released after four years in prison for a serious sexual crime. She knew he would take a dim view of it. He was so upright about things, about antisocial behaviour of any kind, even littering, and she could picture in her mind the dismay in those deep, earnest, thoughtful dark eyes of his if she told him her brother had committed a terrible rape and would be on the Sex Offenders List for the rest of his life.

Her father and mother had disowned Alan. The shame of it had almost ruined them, but Joanna couldn't turn her back on him like that. She had visited him regularly in prison, and the rows those visits had caused at home had led to her moving out. Joanna had known that her brother was presenting a case to the Parole Board for early, supervised release, but these things normally took a lot of time, and it had been a real surprise when she learned that his appeal had been granted so quickly. NACRO had got him that awful flat in that horrible estate, and organised Jobseeker's Allowance for him. As a sexual offender, he had to conform to certain restrictions, and try to remain as anonymous as possible.

Joanna was torn between loyalty to her brother and her feelings for Lee. She didn't know if she loved him or not, she simply didn't have enough experience of men to be sure, but she certainly loved seeing him and being with him. At times she wished she knew what he was thinking, what was going on behind those lovely dark eyes, but she was sure it was something fine and proper. His behaviour this week had made her mind up about what she was going to do. He had been so kind, so attentive, so gentle, that she couldn't go on lying by omission. That evening she was going to tell him about Alan.

She had invited Lee round for a meal. He was in sparkling form the last time she had seen him, and told her this meal could be a celebration, but hadn't said of what. She had time to take the bus out to see Alan briefly. Her brother, no doubt, would be his usual doleful self. Joanna could hardly admit it to herself, but one of the reasons she visited him so loyally was the secret fear that he might do something dreadful to himself. She would do anything to prevent harm befalling him.

He invited her into the drab, cheerless living room. Joanna had brought a bunch of flowers to try to brighten the place up a little. Alan was drinking a glass of red wine, and she suddenly remembered she had forgotten to get a bottle for the meal. A glance at her watch said she hadn't time to get to the Tesco store. She looked over his shoulder into the tiny kitchen and there on the bench, by good fortune, was a bottle of the Tesco stuff that Lee was so fond of.

'Alan, I need a favour. I've a friend coming over this evening and I've forgotten about the wine. Could I possibly borrow a bottle? I'll replace it in the morning.'

'No bother. I got two this morning, so this one will do me all right in the meantime.'

They talked, or at least Joanna talked, and Alan listened dutifully. She arranged the flowers in a pint tumbler, gave him a hug, and promised to see him in the morning.

Lee was in such high spirits that Joanna just couldn't ruin the evening at the start by telling him about Alan. She decided to wait until he had enough wine to fortify his tolerance. She inferred that he had been given a promotion in work, because he kept going on about having had a week when everything went well for him, worked out for him. There was a certain mischief in his manner and tone that she liked very much. How attractive and personable he was in the candlelit setting. She knew he liked these little touches, the candles, the red wine nestling in its white napkin, the soft music.

It was when they had finished their main course and Lee had lowered half the bottle that Joanna judged it time to unburden herself of the weight that had been oppressing her during a period in her life when she should have been happy. She took a deep breath and opened with that line that has spelt ruin for so many relationships down the ages. 'There's something I have to tell you.'

Joanna had been expecting Lee to react badly to the news of her criminal brother. He sat immobile, expressionless, during her narration, the only change being that the light seemed to have dulled in the dark eyes. When she finished, he sat looking straight ahead, saying nothing. She could almost hear him thinking. Next thing he was slowly getting up from the table and she heard him saying, 'I have to go. I'm not feeling well.' His voice was tight, strained.

A kind of panic seized her. 'Lee, I'm sorry. Will you not stay for dessert? It's your favourite, strawberry pavlova.'

He said nothing. She knew from his face that he was controlling his feelings, holding them in check, and she knew he was doing it for her, to avoid hurting her. Then he was moving towards the door.

'Lee, please.' Then in desperation, 'At least take the rest of the wine with you. You know I'll not drink it. Please take it and think of me.' She punched the cork into the neck of the bottle with the heel of her fist and offered it to him. He hesitated and then took it and was out of the door. Joanna sat there alone a full fifteen minutes, at first very upset and regretful, but gradually rallying and calling up a little bit of defiance to help her. If that was the kind of man Lee was, unyielding and judgemental, then he was no better than her father and mother. She was better off without him. She would go and see Alan next day and take him out for a pizza.

What was the little bitch at? That story about her brother. She was playing with his mind. The pair of them somehow knew they had been rumbled. How well she had told it, and all that soft lights and sweet music stuff. She was good, very good. It was the first time he had been outmanoeuvred, the first time he had had to get away to get things sorted out in his mind.

Lee hadn't, in all honesty, invented the not feeling well bit. He was indeed feeling a bit bilious. Probably the little slut's cooking. He was glad to make it home and get into a chair. He poured himself a glass of her wine. '*Think about me*'! He would do that, all right, and she would get the benefit of it, and so would that wimp of a boyfriend. He drained the glass and tried to get things straight in his mind, but it wasn't working right, and the sick feeling in his stomach was fast becoming a pain. He reached for the bottle as a medicine to ease the burning and something caught his eye; a drop of blood was oozing stigmata-like from the cork lying on the table, and a terrible truth hit him, the last coherent thought he would ever have – they had double-crossed him, they had used his own device against him. Then the thought was slowly rubberised and stiffness was his body and heaviness was happening to him. A thickening muffled his head and his eyes were bursting and closing down and a raw bonfire was burning in his belly and his tongue and throat were welded in pain, and his skin crinkling so that the darkness could    blacken    him    in    its    flames.

## *The Collector*

Michael went along to the hotel, more in hope than in expectation. As a true collector, he did not dare miss even one of the Collectors' Fairs, just in case. Like all the other hopefuls who would be there, Michael had heard the stories, (probably apocryphal, but you never know), of innocents bringing in precious, rare posters, found in an attic or spare room, and sold for a song. Likewise, he had heard too the 'tragedies' of whole collections lying in a dusty room in an old cinema, amassed over decades, and dumped or burned by philistines before they could be rescued and treasured. Every serious film poster collector dreamed of such a discovery. To arrive at a scene of sacrilege just too late, as Michael had done on one terrible occasion, was the stuff of nightmares.

This Fair was just as he had guessed it would be, with the same familiar dealers circulating the same familiar film memorabilia, old postcards, newspapers, comics and such, and the same familiar punters trawling and anxiously hoping that a rival collector wouldn't make a chance, worthwhile discovery. Nobody seriously believed that some great find would be made at these dos, but all hoped for at least a modest deal or trade to justify their presence on a precious Saturday.

Michael hated going home empty handed, so he bought the poster for John Wayne's final film, *The Shootist*. He might be able to use it somewhere down the line in a trading transaction. He stayed longer than was sensible, in case somebody arrived late with a rare gem. Fat chance. Then he made one last quick check of the stalls to be absolutely certain that he had missed nothing, and left the Snowdon Room.

He made his way to the tabled square in the corner of the Reception Area and ordered a cup of tea and shortbread. Michael was feeling a little down. These Fairs were a waste of time, but how else could he find something to add to his collection. The whole scene had changed, shrunk. People had become too 'educated' about the value of old cinema memorabilia and the like. It was those antique shows on TV that were doing the damage, ruining for genuine collectors the hope of finding something of worth at a sensible price. Thank goodness he had started collecting when he did, almost forty years ago when he was in his early twenties. He had got in just in time and had built up his collection fairly easily in the relatively short space of about a dozen years. Since then, the pond had slowly started drying up, and every single acquisition now had to be chased after, or waited for, or fought over.

Yes, and the number of items still possibly in existence wasn't inexhaustible. There could only be so many left out there waiting to be discovered, waiting to send reverberations through the collecting world. Michael took comfort in thinking about his collection at home, a collection recognised by all, even his jealous rivals who would never concede it, as probably the finest in Europe. He was enjoying a little smile of satisfaction at this thought when a voice said, 'Is this chair taken? Do you mind if I sit here?' It came from a young woman in her twenties. She had long shiny, black hair with a full fringe.

'No, go ahead,' said Michael, making ineffectual shuffling movements. The girl set down her bag and was just easing herself down into the chair when her knee caught the leg of the table which lurched to one side enough to overturn Michael's half cup of tea. The liquid spread in an instant flow across the table. A small run dripped over the rim on to Michael's lap.

The young woman's mortification was total. 'Sorry, so sorry, I'm really sorry. Please give me a minute. Really sorry.' She was back in seconds with a handful of paper serviettes. She gave one to Michael, who was wiping his pullover and trousers with his handkerchief, and set about mopping and soaking up the small pool of tea that had formed against the table's chrome surround, all the while reciting a 'sorry' to accompany each dab of the napkin. A waiter appeared with a tray and collected the wet napkins. The girl said something to him as he left.

The incident was really very minor, with no injury to person and virtually no harm to clothing, but it was clear she was deeply embarrassed by it. Michael reassured her that all was fine and invited her to sit down.

'Thanks,' she said. 'Honestly, I'm so cack-handed.' Michael smiled, never having heard a woman use that term before, especially about herself. 'I'm Penny, by the way,' she added, as though that somehow accounted for her clumsiness. 'I'm waiting for my sister, Annette. She'll be late. She's always late. That's why I wanted this seat, facing the entrance, so I could see her. She'll be late for her own wedding,' and she smothered a giggle with her hand.

*A bit scatty*, thought Michael. Just at that moment the waiter arrived as if by magic, and offloaded cups and saucers, a big pot of tea and a plate of finely cut sandwiches on to the table.

'These are on me,' said Penny, organising the cups and saucers and the rest the way only a woman can do. Michael thanked her and bit into a sandwich. Very good. 'Are you here for the Fair?' he asked, as she sampled her tea.

'Yes. Annette's getting married in October. I'm her bridesmaid. I'll probably drop the bouquet, or something,' and she aborted another giggle.

*Daft answer*, he thought, *she's more than just a bit scatty*.

'Are you here for the Fair too? You are? Let me guess, groom or father of the bride?' and yet another giggle was stifled.

The cross purposes and confusion were quickly resolved: there were two Fairs going on in the hotel, the Collectors' one in the Snowdon Room, and a Wedding Fair in the McKinley Room. Michael explained how, as far as he was concerned, his was over.

'Was it no good?' she asked. 'Did you not get anything? I hope this wedding thing isn't a flop.'

Michael didn't want to sound like a moan. 'It was all right, I got this,' and he held up and half opened the John Wayne poster. She went off on some tangent about bridal veils and table favours, but Michael was only half listening. He was getting tired of her, and was retreating into himself, when suddenly everything changed. At the end of her seemingly interminable ramble there came across the table a sentence that sprang him into instant alertness. 'My grandad's got a load of those things.'

'What? What things?'

'Those poster things. He's got two or three piles of them up in the loft. They've been there for donkey's years.'

Michael couldn't stop the instant jump of his heart or the dryness in his mouth, but he was too seasoned to get excited too quickly. He had learned from hard experience that people often exaggerate, that piles can translate into half a dozen, that donkey's years, especially to young people, can be a few months. 'What are they like, these posters?' he asked as casually as he could. 'Are they like this one, with a picture on them?' Many times the old posters he had been promised had turned out to be hand-painted jobs, crude lettering of the film's title, often wrongly spelt.

'No, they're not as good as your one. They'd be of no interest to you, I would think. They're too old. He's had them since before he got married, and he's coming eighty now.'

Michael felt his face go red and his temples start to pound as thoughts he hardly dared entertain surged up in his racing mind. He wanted to cross examine her on every detail, but at the same time he had to remain composed and sound disinterested. He liked her valuation of the posters as worthless. Normally the poorer a poster was, the more highly an owner would value it. For young people, however, what was new was best, and anything old was fit only for jumble sales or the dump.

'Where did your granddad get them?' he managed to ask in as indifferent a tone as he could master.

'He used to work in the old Meteor Picture House. He was the... the man who showed the films.'

'The projectionist,' Michael offered helpfully.

'Yes. Couldn't think of the word.' Half giggle. 'It's ancient, his stuff, out of Noah's Ark.' Full giggle.

'Are you sure he's still got them?' Michael asked. 'I mean, when was the last time you saw them?'

'Oh, he's still got them OK. I was up in the loft a couple of weeks ago and I had to go around them to get out mum's old cat basket for Nina. She's our new kitten, and she's ripped the new one to shreds. You should see her, she's lovely but a real rascal.'

Shreds. A new fear arose in Michael's trembling mind: he pictured a pile of precious, priceless posters reduced to crumbling ruin by damp and decay, or eaten away by mice. Unable to tame the fear, or affect an interest in Nina, he blurted out, 'What's the loft like?'

Penny looked at him in surprise. 'It's at the top of the house, in below the roof, above the two bedrooms. It's bigger than you'd think.'

'Sorry, no, I don't mean that.' Michael braked hard on the urgency of his enquiries. 'No, what I meant was, is your granddad's loft nice and dry and insulated. I mean, there's no damp in it?'

She didn't seem surprised by his concern for the condition of a loft he had never seen, and a few minutes earlier didn't know existed. 'Oh no, there's none of that. Grandma got him to floor it all properly and keep it in good shape. You see, she kept her out-of-season clothes in it. Grandma loved clothes. The wardrobes wouldn't hold them all. I remember one Christmas, I was only a little girl, mum and she brought them down and tried them all on. It was great fun. And one time, you won't believe this, grandma dug out her wedding dress, centuries old, and mum and I tried it on. I was about fifteen then.'

She was off and running, Michael all the while burning to get her back on track but not wanting to press her too much on the posters, and maybe accidentally antagonise her. He just couldn't let this opportunity slip. It could be the greatest one of his life.

'Gosh, I'd better go and look for Annette,' Penny suddenly said, and Michael felt a rush of panic. He had to get something firmed up.

'I haven't even introduced myself,' he tried. 'Michael,' and they shook hands. 'Would you like some more tea?'

'No, thank you just the same. I'm off to find and kill that sister of mine.'

'About those old posters. I'd love a look at them some time, if your grandad didn't mind.'

She hesitated. 'I don't know. He's got a bit odd recently, in fact he's been odd since grandma died. He doesn't like people about the house, not even the carers who come in about half nine to make him his breakfast, and they're only in for about fifteen minutes. Mum calls with him nearly every day and keeps an eye on him. I don't know how he would react if a stranger arrived wanting to see his stupid old posters.'

Michael was at a loss. He couldn't push too hard, maybe raise her suspicions, but he couldn't just let her walk away, taking with her the possible find of a lifetime, a dream come true. 'Tell you what, Penny,' he said. It was the first time he'd used her name. 'If you could bring me a few of them, even a couple, I'd be very grateful. Just to have a look, that's all. As you say, they might be rubbish. We could meet here next Saturday for lunch, on me. Provided you don't spill tea over me.' The joke worked, and she liberated a full-blown giggle.

Penny was due to visit her grandad that week, so she promised to bring a number of the posters away with her for his inspection. They arranged to meet in the hotel restaurant at one o'clock the following Saturday. Before they parted, they exchanged mobile numbers in case the arrangement had to be changed.

Michael had never known such a week of roller-coaster emotions. Nothing in all his years of collecting even came close. They started almost immediately after his parting from Penny. She must surely have infected him, because as he was driving home, he suddenly and involuntarily emitted little truncated giggles. He repeatedly checked in his driving mirror without quite knowing why, and sneaked quick glances into the back seat of the car, as instant, nameless fears overtook him.

The mood swings continued all weekend and into the new week, troubling his sleep and affecting his nerves. At one moment he would be actually laughing aloud at his good fortune, the next he had sunk into gloom as he imagined all the things that could go wrong. Again and again he was tempted to phone Penny, but his good sense forbade him. He had to play it cool, even though he was churning like a washing machine inside.

When Penny rang him on Wednesday to say that her grandad had taken unwell and she would not be able to see him until the following week at the earliest, it was like a death blow to Michael's hopes. She postponed their meeting on Saturday and promised to rearrange it as soon as she could. He managed to contain his disappointment on the phone, and wished her grandad well, but when he came off the line he indulged himself in overblown despair, actually dramatising some of his misery aloud. 'I knew, I just knew, it wouldn't be straightforward. When have I ever had anything easy, so why should I expect things to work out now? I know what this means; it means I'm not going to get them. It's an omen.'

This was the tenor of Michael's thoughts and feelings all next day and most of Friday, so he was totally unprepared when Penny rang him at tea-time with the news that her grandad was feeling a little better and she was going to see him that evening. The death sentence on his hopes was lifted, the meeting for lunch next day was reinstated. Michael's joy and relief made him quite silly. 'I knew it, I just knew it would work out. I'm due a break, and this is it,' he told himself. 'I've a good feeling about this.'

The good feeling suffered a little setback when they met at the restaurant next day and he saw immediately that she was carrying only a shoulder bag that clearly wasn't holding film posters. Michael refrained from asking about this serious omission and contained his impatience until they had ordered from the menu.

'Well, how's your grandad? Did you get to see him?'

'He's OK. He's moved down into a bed downstairs. Says the stairs are too much for him. I'll tell you about him in a minute, but let me tell you about the posters first. They're still there just the same, and I opened a few of them out. The top one on the pile was covered with dust, but the rest are clean enough. They're very big and hard to manage. It's like wrestling with a newspaper. Anyhow, I didn't like to take them with me. It seemed a bit off, him lying in bed in the front room downstairs, and me sneaking them out of the house.'

'What were the ones you looked at like?' asked Michael, hiding his disappointment.

'I don't know. I didn't recognise any of them, but I wrote some of the names down. These are the ones I wrote down. I didn't take down the names of the actors,' and she handed him a small sheet of lined paper torn from a notebook. Michael's brain reeled when he read down the short list: *Niagara, The Big Heat, From Here to*

*Eternity, Roman Holiday, Gentlemen Prefer Blondes*. He couldn't speak, his hands were shaking. He hid them under the table.

'You see, I told you, they're old ones nobody has heard of. Sorry. I don't know about you, Michael, but I'm going to order a bottle of wine. I'm not driving, so why not. If you're driving, I might have to drink the whole bottle myself.' She'd kept her best giggle for this moment, it seemed, but the real laughing was going on inside the sober-faced Michael. At random Penny had skimmed off five of the rarest, most valuable, classic posters. Their value on the American market would be through the roof. He knew immediately that all five were from the same year, 1953. He must have them in chronological order. What other vintage gems lay further down in that pile, or in another pile? A shiver of excitement travelled right through him like an electric current.

His leg started shaking under the table, but his voice was back, and remarkably steady. 'They're not bad. I've seen worse. Let's forget about them just now and enjoy the meal. I'm here on my bus pass, so I think I'll join you in that bottle of wine. Waiter!'

For Michael, the lunch was intended to be merely a means to an end, but it turned out to be something of an end in itself. Penny had hit on the right formula in talking about her grandad's posters first because the list she had shown him put Michael in such high spirits that he would have enjoyed a meal of bread and water. As it was, the food was excellent and thoroughly enjoyed by both. Michael was not normally much of a drinker, although he was partial now and again to a good white wine, and the bottle of house wine he ordered was just the business.

Their conversation after the meal got off to a fairly unpromising start. 'You asked about grandad. Thank you. To tell you the truth, I'm a bit worried about him. He was always a bad sufferer – mum says all men are bad sufferers – but he's thinking now that he's really poorly. All you can get out of him is, 'I'm on the road out'. I did my best to cheer him up but no, 'I'm on the road out'. It was a bit depressing. You can see why I need this glass of wine.'

'Not a good time to be bothering him about film posters,' said Michael mournfully.

'I don't know. You could be wrong there. This might be a good time, for all you know. It might be good for him, help take his mind off himself, give him an interest, something else to think about. He was going on about all the stuff he'd be leaving behind, what would become of it, and saying it would all end up on a dump or on a bonfire. He was talking himself into a real black mood about it.'

Michael caught her drift. 'I can promise him this, Penny, and you can tell him so, that if I had his posters they couldn't go to a better home. They might not be worth much, but they're important to him, and they'd be important to me. I'll give him whatever he thinks they're worth, but more important than the money is that they'd be well looked after.'

Penny laughed. 'You sound like you're about to adopt a child. Honestly, I don't know what you see in these old posters. In fact, you wouldn't be able to see them at all, the way they're all folded up in piles. Who's going to go to the bother of opening them all up? It would be a day's work. There must be hundreds of them.'

How could she possibly know the thrill her words sent through him at the delicious prospect of what she had described. It was exactly what he had imagined over and over again in his fondest dreams.

'They wouldn't be folded the way I would have them,' he said. 'I'd have them all unfolded and lying flat.' The excitement and wine were loosening him up.

'Oh, I see. You live in a castle with huge empty rooms. You'd need to. They're yards wide, those things.' She was teasing him, humouring him, and he enjoyed it.

'Forty inches by thirty inches, actually, landscape format,' he returned, with the smugness of the expert. 'I should know. I've a collection of them, over five hundred, looked after like royalty.'

Penny laughed again. 'Very good, Your Majesty. So it's a palace you keep them in, not a castle.'

Michael brought the banter down to earth, in case she might start to think of him as some kind of fantasist. 'As good as. Have you ever seen a plan chest? It's perfect. It's a special cabinet for AO size plans. Before I retired I worked in a drawing office, and that's where I got the idea from. My posters are dry and clean and, above all, opened out flat. That's the way I'd keep your grandad's ones too. Tell him that.'

Michael was the last person in the world to boast, but a little flushed with wine and in a flutter inside about his big opportunity, he was uncharacteristically open about his arrangements. He would never have been this free to another collector, but it was a rare enjoyment to talk with pride and satisfaction to a total novice.

They didn't leave the restaurant until nearly three o'clock. Penny was to see her grandad again on Tuesday evening. She had promised to bring up the subject of the posters, and champion Michael's interest in them.

For the second weekend in a row Michael was in a fever of anxious excitement and expectation, tingling with the belief that he had stumbled upon a goldmine, but fearful that he would be forbidden to enter. Just the same, he couldn't help imagining the sheer pleasure of bringing the posters home, sorting them, repairing them, cataloguing them, and, above all, informing his rivals of his amazingly lucky strike. He had already a poster-type catchline to accompany the story: *He read the tea leaves and found a fortune.*

The agony of waiting ended when Penny called at nine o'clock on Tuesday evening. Michael picked up his mobile with a shaking hand, but controlled himself enough to ask about her grandad's health.

'He's not too bad, much the same. There's better news for you. I mentioned the posters and told him about you. You're to come up and see him on Saturday morning, if that suits you, and talk about the squads, as he calls them. Not too early, mind, about eleven.'

Michael almost sobbed with relief. He couldn't be too extravagant, however, in his gratitude for access to posters which he had valued so moderately.

'I think he means quads. They're called quad posters,' he said.

Penny released one of her distinctive abbreviated giggles down the phone. 'I thought he said squads, but he hadn't his teeth in, so it was probably quads.'

'Does your grandad take a drink at all?'

'Well, he's not a big drinker, but he enjoys a whisky when the mood takes him. Might be the first thing to lift him out of the mood he's in at the minute.'

Michael assured her that he'd be free on Saturday morning, and they arranged that Penny would be there to make the introductions. She gave him the address, 258 Mancuso Gardens, and directions. He lived in the suburbs in the south of the city, about an hour's drive, Michael reckoned.

Three whole days to wait before the Saturday that Michael hoped would be the greatest red-letter day of his life. He had to be doing something, so on Friday he set off to find the house. A recce. Penny's directions were perfect. He had transferred them from the notepad he'd used on the phone and printed them in a large hand on a piece of white card which he clipped to the dash. It wasn't really necessary, but it had helped him put in Thursday.

258 Mancuso Gardens was pretty much what he had envisaged, a large detached redbrick two storey house set back from the road. A gravel path sloped up one side of the patchy lawn that

had surrendered to a sprawling conifer of some kind. To think that this anonymous, undistinguished dwelling could contain treasures he had only dreamed of. People were living in the same street and driving every day past a storehouse of riches. Amazing. He drove back home with exaggerated care. Imagine accident and injury now, just when he was on the brink of a massive break...

He rang Penny that evening to ask about her grandad who, he learned, was in better form. Everything was still OK for the next day. 'See you in the morning,' she finished, and a shudder of excitement coursed through him. He decided not to wrap the bottle of Glenfiddich single malt whisky he had bought, or put it in a bag. It was more man-to-man style to hand it over as it was.

His exploratory journey to Mancuso Gardens had taken him an hour and ten minutes, but the traffic was much lighter on Saturday morning, and he arrived almost a quarter of an hour early. Michael parked a few houses farther up the street and waited in the car. His heart was hammering. In half an hour or so he should be back in the car with the single greatest scoop made by any collector he had ever known or heard of. It was frightening and exhilarating but he subdued the riot of thoughts and feelings and got ready to make history. That irritating *There's many a slip twixt cup and lip* jingle had insinuated itself into his head and was going round and round like a nursery rhyme. He finally eased the car down to 258, took a deep breath, marched up the gravel path holding the bottle of whisky like a battering ram, and with a shaking hand gave two raps with the rusty knocker on the blistered blue door.

The woman who answered his knock was small and in her fifties. Penny's mother, no doubt. 'Hello. Is Penny in?'

'Who?' She was looking at the bottle of whisky.

'Penny. I'm Michael. Penny's arranged for me to see her grandad at eleven.'

'You've got the wrong house. Sorry,' and she started to close the door.

'No, wait. This is 258, Mancuso Gardens, isn't it?'

'All right, you've got the right house, but there's no Penny and no grandad here. Sorry,' and the door was firmly closed in his face. Michael felt himself break out in a sweat at the same time as a coldness in his stomach was stealing his breath away. There was only one explanation, he had the wrong house number. Either Penny had given it wrongly, and that would not be unlikely, or he had somehow taken it down wrongly over the phone. He called her mobile. Nothing. It was dead. Three more attempts failed too. He thought about asking at another house, perhaps the one next door, but realised he didn't know Penny's grandad's name, or even Penny's surname. It was hopeless.

Michael felt sick. The strength seemed to go out of his legs as his hopes fell apart. What was happening? What had gone wrong, and what could he do about it? He got back in the car and sat with his eyes closed as his head whirled. There was nothing to do but drive back home. He could never, afterwards, remember one feature of the return journey. He must have gone into auto driving mode so that his disappointment, frustration, and confusion could be uninterrupted, concentrated.

The minute he entered the house he sensed something was wrong. Everything was in place, but by instinct he was aware of something different, unfamiliar. Then he identified it, the faintest hint of perfume and cigarettes in the air, such as would come off the clothes of a female smoker. His heart seemed to stop. Somebody had been in his house. With an indeterminate choking sound in his throat, Michael rushed through the sitting room and into his study, and his life was never the same. Where the plan chest with its forty-year collection of posters should have been waiting to greet him, there was nothing but an empty space.

Nothing in his 62 years had prepared Michael for this; he had never been the victim of a crime, never suffered shock. Now an onrush of bewildering thoughts and feelings threatened to overwhelm him. Foremost among these was sheer disbelief, failure to accept what his eyes were telling him. He kept staring at the empty space, waiting for it to go away, and for reality to return in the shape of his familiar plan chest, with its rows of drawers he had opened so often and so lovingly. He left his study and then returned, as though he had entered wrongly the first time and now everything would be all right and the cabinet would be back in its normal place. His unwillingness, or inability, to accept that it was gone led him to foolish searching in unlikely, preposterous places – behind doors, under the table, even below cushions.

Then came mystification, incomprehension. How had this happened? He sensed that it was connected to Penny and to his wild goose chase to Mancuso Gardens, but how? The pounding headache, thumping heart and churning in his stomach did nothing to assist him in his efforts to understand what was going on. A kind of melancholy started to settle on him, a weakness that made him want to curl up on the floor in pity for himself, close his eyes, and let everything drift into blackness. It was grief Michael was feeling, the emptiness and hopelessness of inconsolable loss. His posters were his family, the companions he loved and cherished most in the world. He knew all five hundred and twenty-two posters in his collection, where, when, and how he had acquired every last one of them. To think of all those years of wheeling and dealing, the last gasp deals, the overnight trips, the convoluted swapping, all for nothing, all gone in one go. Would he ever see them again, or were they gone for ever? The thought was unbearable. In just over an hour, he had plummeted from eager anticipation and hopefulness into black despair.

Mixed in with the emotional loss Michael was suffering was the nagging knowledge of the financial one. His house contents insurance cover didn't extend to his hobby; he had explored this on one occasion with the insurance company, but the increase in premium was prohibitive. Michael had never actually sat down and calculated the probable value of his collection, but, incredible as it might seem to the uninitiated, he knew beyond any doubt that they were worth, at the very least, a million pounds, and that was a big undervaluation.

Something in his heart didn't want to call the police. By bringing them in he would be acknowledging, confirming, even consolidating, the reality of the theft, and erasing his vague hope that it would all turn out all right, that all this couldn't really have happened, not for real.

'We've been after this team for some time, Mr. Faulkner,' the detective said. 'We're closing in on them. We'll catch up with them sooner or later.'

'But it's not a team, it's only Penny, the woman I was telling you about.'

'Believe me, sir, she was the only one you saw, but there's a team behind her. They're real pro's, these people. You were targeted. They've done their homework on you. They'll have been down here before today, getting the lie of the land, preparing the operation well in advance. They were probably watching you when you left the house this morning. No offence, sir, but you were a soft target for this crew.'

'But what about her grandad, and the posters in the loft?'

The detective smiled. 'There was no grandad. There were no posters. Did you actually see them? The only posters they ever had in their possession are the ones they stole from you. The whole thing was a set-up to find out exactly how and where you kept your stuff, and to get you out of the house for a couple of hours. That's why the address they gave you was well on the other side of town. Don't beat yourself up for falling for it. These people are good at what they do. They're well informed. They'll have been well read-up on your collection from magazines or the internet or some other specialist source. They know the market and the value of this kind of material.

I have to tell you this, Mr. Faulkner: we'll get them one day, I'm sure of that, hopefully sooner than later, but we can't be sure of recovering your property. In our experience they wouldn't set up this kind of scam unless they were sure of a buyer. It's possible that your goods are already on their way out of the country.'

Michael winced. 'Is there anything can be done to stop them? What about her phone number?'

'The phone would be first to go under the hammer, literally. So far we've found tracks on the waste ground at the back. They used a hand truck to wheel out your cabinet. Must have been a fair weight. You can see the faint little traces there on your flooring, those little indentation lines. A neighbour says she saw a small blue van parked on the waste ground this morning. We'll check the CCTV cameras in the area. We could get a break there.'

He set down an Identikit image of a woman with close-cropped fair hair. 'Is this anything like the woman who called herself Penny?'

'No, nothing like her. I'm sure.'

'What about this one?' The face in this one was set into shoulder length black hair and a distinctive fringe.

'Yes, that's her. That's Penny. Definitely.'

The detective smiled again. 'That's the same picture, except the hair has been changed, and the eyebrows darkened. A good wig does the same on a woman. Penny's last victim helped us compile the first picture, we just added the hair. Penny was Susie then, and it wasn't film posters she conned the lady out of, it was bonds and Travellers' Cheques.'

The news of Michael's theft sent shockwaves through the film memorabilia collectors' world, and resulted in widespread reviews of security and insurance cover arrangements. Michael tried to keep in touch with the detective handling his case, but every time he rang the man was 'at a meeting' or 'out on a case' or 'on leave', and Michael never did learn of any developments in the investigation.

The loss of his beloved poster collection had a profound effect on his personality. His fellow collectors, including those he would have regarded as his competitors, tried to rally round and show their support, but their visits were awkward and apparently unwelcome. The truth was that Michael didn't trust them, for all he knew, one of them might be a smiling assassin who had been an accomplice of Penny, or had hired her to steal his collection. Maybe the man shaking hands with him and sympathising with him was the treacherous new owner of his posters.

Michael grew moody and reclusive. He reached and recognised rock bottom one evening when a fellow collector, formerly his closest ally, rang to tell him of an upcoming Collectors' Fair, reputed to feature a number of new exhibitors with very interesting items for sale. Michael thanked the man for the information and invitation and told him he would think about it. As he made himself a cup of tea, he found himself formulating, and then saying aloud, the epitaph for Michael Faulkner, Poster Collector: **Nothing Seems To Matter Anymore**.

## *Play Off*

How had she always imagined panic to be something quick and dramatic – *panic-stricken, sudden panic, panic attack*? The feeling that had invaded her was stealthy and steady, but it was panic just the same. It had probably been working away in secret for some time, but she could pinpoint the exact moment the actual occupation began.

Brenda and she had met in town for lunch and were having the usual natter afterwards over a gin and tonic.

'That's the difference between you and me, Pat. You're too trusting. If Ross were my husband, I wouldn't let him away on all these golf outings and weekend things. He could be seeing somebody else, for all you know.'

Pat returned the serve neatly, 'I read somewhere that the best way to lose a man is to chain him up.' It was at that very moment, as she delivered the little epigram, that the panic which was now her daily companion made its move. Into her mind slid the realisation that she couldn't have cared less whether her husband was having an affair or not. In fact, it would have been almost a kind of relief to learn that he was being unfaithful. The beachhead was established, and panic's infiltration began from that quiet recognition – she didn't love Ross, probably never had loved him, and, worst of all, was almost repelled by him.

That first flare of insight lit up the poor wreckage of Pat Walker's thirty-four years of life. She had achieved none of the dreams that had vaguely coloured her early ambitions, no special talents or accomplishments, no qualifications or career in Art and Design, no circle of good friends, no children. Her one apparent success, marriage to a young, handsome husband, was a lie. Ross had done well from the marriage, acquiring social status and business opportunity, but from Pat's point of view the relationship had deteriorated so rapidly that she could hardly believe she was married at all.

Pat's sense of panic burned deeper each time she looked ahead, but instead of consuming itself in a fierce blaze, it smouldered and took even firmer hold. The only picture that appeared on the screen of her future was a fuzzy one of empty middle-age.

Pat poured herself a very generous gin, splashed in a suggestion of tonic, and returned to the couch. She could hear Ross rattling his clubs together in the hallway. The sound irritated her. Everything about him irritated her, right down to those little vulgar habits she had once overlooked or tried to find amusing: dipping biscuits in his tea was well up the list, but personal things too, like the way he put his tongue out like a budgie's when he coughed, were now unbearable.

'That's me away. I should be back about six or seven on Sunday.' He didn't come into the room.

'Cheerio.' Pat didn't have to try to sound dry; she would have found it impossible to put any warmth in her voice.

'If any calls come for me...'

'I'll make a note of them – name, time, number, message, if any. I know my duties by now.'

He fired up instantly, and came in from the hall, two little tell-tale flushes of red high on his cheeks. 'Don't start all that again. You're becoming tiresome. Sometimes I really think you're jealous of me – you don't like to see me enjoying myself. I wouldn't object if you were going away for a few days to enjoy yourself.'

'No, you'd welcome it. It's not so long since you were swearing you could enjoy nothing without me. To think I believed all that stuff. How did I not see through it?'

Ross was about to enter into the fray, but he thought better of it and went out with the clubs, slamming the outside door as he left. She heard the Volvo roaring off in a rage.

Pat felt no satisfaction from the skirmish, just a sad little pleasure in seeing again that his hair was definitely starting to grey at the sides. How had things been reduced to this. What was that phrase she had heard at school that had somehow stuck in her mind—something about people leading lives of quiet desperation. The words had meant little to her then, but they were bang on target now.

She emptied her glass, hardly tasting the drink. Pat's affair with alcohol was a volatile one; it could sink her into melancholy or spark her into friskiness, all in an instant. The school thought suddenly reminded her of Brenda and their arrangement, and in a moment, she was dialling her, excited and girlish.

'Brenda. He's away. Bring your own nightie this time.'

Brenda. Now there was a real person. When everyone and everything else let her down, there was Brenda. How would she have coped without her one true friend. She felt momentarily ashamed of all those times she had been aware of her natural and social superiority; yes, Pat was prettier and from a better background, but never once had her pal shown even a hint of jealousy or resentment. She blushed that, even now, in the midst of her remorse and gratitude, the feeling still persisted that however bad things might be for her, they were worse for Brenda. Could that be what friends were for? Pat fixed herself another drink to ward off the bad thought.

Brenda came in brandishing a bottle of wine in each hand. 'Daa Daa. The best that Tesco can supply at £4.99 a bottle.'

Pat laughed. 'I want to drink the stuff, not cook with it.'

Brenda unhooked her shoulder bag and made straight for the drinks cupboard. 'Give me a Gordons, quick. That stuff I've been buying tastes like ivy juice.'

'It's great to see you, Brenda. Thanks for coming over.'

'Sure, but what are your neighbours saying? Every time Ross goes off with his clubs, hey presto, I'm on your doorstep in a flash. It looks like classic *Golf Widow and her Lesbo Lover* stuff.'

Pat was already on a high, just having Brenda with her. 'Frankly, my dear, I don't give a damn,' she drawled. 'No suh, instead ahm gonna have me a gin and It.'

'Tell you what, you have the gin and give me the It. I've been looking for It all week.'

Pat giggled, Brenda laughed at Pat giggling, and the evening was off and running…

'…no, it's true, Brenda, and I'm speaking from expense, sorry, experience, or maybe I was right the first time, but anyway, believe me, any man who marries up always resents it, and any woman who marries down is never sure, never completely sure, if she's been married for herself or for her money… all right, so I'm a little tiddly, or my voice is a little tiddly, but my mind's as clear as a nun's diary—Ross knows what he stands to lose, so he'd better ship up, or shape out, or something like that.'

'Promise me this, Pat, and I want it in writing. If he goes on the market, I get first refusal. You can have my flexible friend as commission.'

'…what I'd like, and who wouldn't, is a secure relationship and a bit on the side. At the moment, I've neither.'

'Don't be greedy. I'd settle for either.'

'You know what I like most about you, Brenda—you never change.' Pat knew that part of her was fairly drunk, but she was surprised how clearly she was thinking and articulating her thoughts. 'Maybe it's all our own fault. We make men too important in our lives. Remember at school we always had to have a boyfriend, whether we liked him or not. It was social death not to have a boyfriend. I want you to do something for me, Brenda, just for a minute. Think back on those days, go on, think back on them, and tell me the truth—where did all the good times, the good laughs, the really good laughs, come from? From us, from ourselves, that's where from, without boys or men or whatever you want to call them, only we didn't know it at the time. Wait a minute, maybe you did, and that's why you stayed single.'

Brenda laughed. 'I hadn't much choice in the matter, and I can't say I've been laughing ever since. No, you're right, I have to agree, we did have some good laughs in those days. Remember we all bought those stupid T-shirts with our names on the front, and you had 'PAT' in big letters right across your breasts?'

'Yes, and nobody took up the offer. And they were good breasts too! Still are. Breasts. Doesn't that sound old-fashioned? Nowadays girls just talk about their tits. I'm not sure if I like that or not.'

Pat emptied her glass and set it on the glass-topped table. Her tone modulated, 'I'm serious when I tell you this, Brenda, I'm laughing but I'm serious—a good friend, a really good friend, is worth half a dozen husbands, and you're the best friend anybody could have, so how many husbands must you be worth?'

She picked up her empty glass and drank from it. Brenda seemed moved by the compliment but hid it in a joke. 'This sounds to me like a coming out. Maybe the neighbours have something to gossip about after all. Either that, or else you're like one of those stupid men who go all slobbery when they get a few drinks in.'

Pat didn't reply and Brenda, perhaps feeling she might have hurt her, abruptly changed the subject. 'Oh, nearly forgot, guess who I saw in Stanton on Wednesday.'

Pat snorted. 'Guess who I saw in Stanton on Wednesday—the daft things people say. There's just about ten thousand million people out there, and I'm expected to guess who you saw in Stanton on Wednesday. Hold on a minute, I'll just nip out and win the lottery. OK, game on, but you'll have to give me a clue. Male or female?'

'Male.'

'Male—I love him already. Married or single?'

'Don't know. I'm not playing this game. It was Tony Taylor.'

Pat looked up from twirling her empty glass. Her face was heavy and the mouth a little slack, but her eyes were bright and focused.

'Tony Taylor? *The* Tony Taylor from school?'

'Yessir, the very same, the Tony Taylor from school. He's the only one I know.'

'Are you sure it was him? I mean, it must be over twenty years since we saw him.'

'It was him all right. I was stopped at traffic lights and he walked right across in front of the car. Definite, sure.'

'Tony Taylor—I can't believe it. He was good-looking in a dark Christopher Lee kind of way. Saturnine.'

Brenda gave a little laugh. 'Saturnine. That's a good word. I'm sure Tony Taylor would be pleased to know that at this very minute somebody is describing him as saturnine. He'd probably be delighted to know he's being talked about at all.'

'Did I ever tell you I went out with him once?' and a strange little thrill of satisfaction ran through Pat when she saw Brenda's look of surprise.

'What? Now the secrets are coming out. You told me in about fourth form that you fancied him, but you never said anything about actually going out with him.'

Pat got up and opened another bottle of wine. She was tempted for a moment to dress the story up but, prompted by laziness, she opted for the facts.

'There's nothing to tell. The whole thing was a damp squib, or soaking wet squib might be better. He took me to the pictures, the old Tivoli. We didn't hold hands, we didn't even talk. Funny, I can remember what the film was, *Halloween*, I nearly peed myself with fear. Then he walked me home and the rain came on. That was the beginning and end of the big romance. Never even kissed me. I remember wondering afterwards why he'd asked me out at all.'

Brenda digested the account and pronounced judgement. 'Taylor was always a bit weird. I'm surprised he didn't bite you in the neck.'

'What, weird because he didn't kiss me?' Pat laughed.

'That too. I meant taking you on a first date to a film like that. He's more scary than the movie.'

They sat in silence for a few minutes, rethinking the past. Finally, Pat said, 'All right, maybe so, but he was interesting, if you know what I mean, and I bet he doesn't play golf and try to impress other people. I wonder what he does, where he lives, if he's got any little Christopher Lee lookalikes.'

'Maybe he's just normal and has a gay live-in lover,' said Brenda, breaking the spell.

Pat took a thoughtful sip of wine. 'Isn't it funny how all the people you used to see every day disappear and you never find out what's become of them? I'd love to know how some of the people in our year turned out.'

Brenda had been studying a table lamp through her red wine when she suddenly set the glass down and turned to her friend with the old familiar note of schoolgirl excitement in her voice.

'Why don't we find out? What's the term they use—run a check. We could run a check on your friend Mr. Taylor. Find out where he lives, stalk him. Yes, that's it, that's all the rage, stalk him. We could have a laugh like the old times, instead of shopping our brains out.'

For a moment Pat was back behind the Art Hut for an illegal smoke, planning to mitch hockey or some other stunt, but she touched the brakes of her feelings and remarked, 'You're loopy, you know that? Genuinely loopy. I'm the

217

one who's drunk most of the wine, and I'm making more sense than you are.'

'But why not? We'd be great stalkers. We need a bit of excitement, both of us. Think of the headlines: *Stanton Man in Stalking Terror.*'

'Or *Sex Starved Women Sought in Stanton Stalking Storm.*' The voice was Pat's, her face flushed with wine and excitement. 'But where would we start?'

'Some are born to lead, and some are born to be led. Aren't you lucky I'm one of the leaders? Where's the phone book? There can't be too many Tony Taylors living in Stanton. I'll just look up all the T. Taylors and check them out. I'll know his voice right away.'

Pat shook her head in resigned amusement. 'The great leader's an illiterate. It'll be A. Taylor, not T, Anthony, you ignoramus. Wait a minute, we used to call him Rat, do you remember? R.A.T. – Richard Anthony Taylor.'

Brenda was already leafing through the directory, keeping Pat at bay. 'Hold on, hold on, you're forgetting I wasn't in your class. You stay over there, or you'll make me laugh and give the game away. Taylor R., Taylor R., Taylor Robin, Taylor R.A... There it is, there's only one R.A. It must be him. Taylor R.A., 28 Treadle Avenue, Stanton.'

'Treadle Avenue? Doesn't sound too impressive, does it?' Pat felt vaguely disappointed that he had been located so easily, preferring him as a fantasy in her imagination to a street name, a house number. 'Arise, Sir Anthony, Lord of Treadle. Let me see.'

'No, get off, go away, you're going to spoil this before it gets started.'

Brenda dialled carefully from the book. 'Hold on, hold on, it's ringing...

...Hello, I'd like to book a table for four for this evening, please... What? Oh, sorry, sorry, beg your pardon...' putting the phone down, Brenda exclaimed, 'It's him, it's him, it's definitely him, I'd know that creepy voice anywhere.'

'It's not creepy, it's silky, you philistine. So, what now?'

Brenda closed the phone book in triumph and reached for the wine. 'First, we'll finish this, then we'll get a good night's sleep, bypass the shops in the morning, and it's straight on for Stanton, the ancestral seat of Sir Anthony. We can take a picnic and do a stake-out like the cops in the movies. I've always wondered what they do when they need a pee.'

'You're impossible. I know what's going to happen in the morning. We'll end up in Sainsburys buying Brie and broccoli.'

\*

'Treadle Avenue... Treadle Avenue... Let me see.' The man screwed up his face to assist the process. 'OK, you'll have to turn back and... Treadle Avenue? No, wait a minute, you're all right... You see them traffic lights where that red lorry's turnin' in. Go you on through and take the second, no, the third, yes, the third, the third street on your left. You'll come to a big roundabout. Go straight through and take the first on the left, no, it'll be right goin' this way, yes, the first on your right. You'll see a big church on the corner. You'll come then to another set of lights. Go left and about three or four hundred yards down on the right you'll see Treadle Road. Treadle Avenue would be the third, or maybe the next one down, on the left, off Treadle Road. You couldn't miss it.'

'Did you get all that?' Brenda asked, keeping her expression earnest.

'Great. The whole town to ask and we picked the local idiot.' Pat eased back into the thin flow of traffic.

'I'm nearly sure those are the lights where I saw Tony the Terrible. I wasn't expecting to be down here again so soon.' Brenda laughed to herself at the silliness of it.

They had slept late, very late, and had shuffled about while Pat made 'brunch for the living dead'. The drive down to Stanton had been uninterrupted except when Pat had to stop at a McDonalds for a 'McPee'. Both were surprised their hangovers weren't worse, but they were quiet on the journey and the excitement they were expecting had yet to kick in.

*

At about the same time as they pulled away from the kerb, Ross Walker, to the ribbing of his companions, missed an easy putt at the sixteenth.

*

They found Treadle Avenue independent of the man's directions. The area seemed in decline, the houses just a degree or so away from shabbiness.

'Well, this is it, the Taylor demesne. Any nerves?'

'Nerves?' asked Pat, and her voice sounded too loud to her. 'Why should I be nervous? You're the one who's going to do the business. I'm strictly an observer. Bit grubby, isn't it?'

'Slow down a bit... 18, 20, 22, 24, 26—that's it, 28, with the blue door and the FOR SALE sign. Look at those awful net curtains. Don't stop, don't stop, drive on down and we'll turn and park down a bit on his side where he can't see us.'

Pat did as instructed. They could see the front edge of the house, the patch of lawn and the agent's sign, but the angle was too oblique to see the windows or door.

Pat broke the little silence that had descended when she had switched off the engine. 'Just look at the two of us sitting here like a pair of fourth formers.'

'And why not? Why should fourth formers have all the fun?'

Pat was beginning to feel the delayed effects of the previous evening's drinking; an unpleasant heat settled on her, and she felt a little sweat on her brow. 'Knowing my luck, he's not in,' she said, not sure what her feelings were.

'Knowing your luck, he's sitting in there by himself hoping for somebody to take to see *Halloween 11* or *12* or whatever.'

Pat managed a smile, but the place was depressing. 'Sir Anthony doesn't seem to have done too well for himself. I think I'm glad our big romance didn't blossom.'

'You're probably right, but you never can tell. Some of these old houses can be – what's the jargon? – 'very desirable residences'.'

'Either that, or he's got a big place in the country, and this is just his secret love nest for a bit of cheap on the sly. Wonder why it's up for sale?'

Brenda was studying what she could see of the house. 'Don't see any swing or toys or evidence of young heirs to the estate. I'm going to have a look. He won't recognise me. I'll ask for directions or a kiss or something. I just want a look.' She broke into song as she unhooked her seatbelt, *'just one look, that's all it took, yeah, just one look.'*

'You're a nutcase, d'you know that?' Pat's voice had none of the lightness she intended.

Brenda was out of the car. She leaned in to Pat. 'D'you think he'll ask me in? If I'm not back in ten minutes, send in the cavalry or a SWAT team or something... You're supposed to say 'come back you brave fool' at this point.'

Suddenly Pat's mouth was dry and nervousness flooded through her, leaving a tingling that made her almost numb. 'Brenda, let's just go home. I've got a bad feeling about this. Please don't go into the house. I really hope he isn't in.'

But Brenda wasn't listening. *'It is a far, far better thing that I do than I have ever done...'*

The car was door closed and she was striding towards the house, her shoulder bag swaying with each step.

\*

Ross swung the bag of clubs on to his shoulder at the eighteenth, the first round completed, himself in the lead, and the prospect of a drink at the clubhouse lengthening the stride of all four golfers.

\*

Pat watched what was happening like a spectator with no control over the game. Brenda walked up to the house, looked back, knocked, and waited. Then she was in conversation with someone, but whoever it was stayed inside, and Pat couldn't see him. Next thing Brenda gave a comical little circular wave in Pat's direction and disappeared into the house. Pat discovered she had been holding her breath.

'She's in, the nutter. I knew she would, I knew it,' she said aloud to break the tension, a mixture of uneasiness and curiosity swirling in her head. Would Brenda run riot now and reveal who she was, and tell Tony that she was waiting outside in the car? Part of her cringed, another part hoped…

It seemed to Pat that twenty minutes had gone, she couldn't be sure, and there was no sign at all of Brenda. She found herself repeating over and over, 'Where is she?' and 'What's keeping her?', the irritation in her voice quickly giving way to anxiety and then to real fear as Brenda's words echoed round in her mind, *'Taylor was always a bit weird. He's more scary than the film. I'm surprised he didn't bite you in the neck'*. Pat found her hands were actually shaking and there was a coldness in her stomach that had nothing to do with a hangover. If only she knew what was happening, if Brenda was safe. Suddenly she thought of the mobile in Brenda's bag. Her mind raced so hard it couldn't get hold of Brenda's number, but she forced herself to calm down, and remembered it was one of the stored numbers on her own mobile's address book.

'Please answer, please answer,' she begged aloud as the number rang; *'I'm sorry, the person you have called is not available. Please leave your message after the tone'*. Not available. Why? Where was she? What had happened to her? There was no time to look for help, no other way, she had to go to Taylor's door and find out by herself.

\*

They had decided after a couple of drinks to have a leisurely lunch in the clubhouse restaurant and give themselves time for an easy-going second round in the afternoon. Ross studied the menu; he always ate fairly lightly when he was playing golf.

\*

The open door unnerved her. It had swung open when she raised the rusty knocker on the faded blue top panel. Her first tentative 'Hello?' told her instantly that the house was empty; the sound echoed down the dark hall and in the bare rooms, scaring her by its aloneness. She wanted to turn and run back outside, but concern for her good, true friend was stronger than even the terror that made her heart hammer and her legs weak. She moved deeper in, towards the centre of the house.

Pat was calling for her friend, calling her name, 'Brenda... Brenda?' when a gun came out of the semi-darkness and shot her at point-blank range through the temple. The flash lit up the gun for a second, wrapped in a nightdress as it smoked in Brenda's hands, and its muffled boom thumped in the heart of the desolate house.

The noise reverberated in Brenda's head long after the house was again silent. She still held the gun with both hands, arms out straight in front as Ross had shown her. '*Walk away when it's done,*' he had told her, '*don't look at her*', but she couldn't stop herself looking down. Pat's body lay against her feet, the face white in the gloom, a stream of blood moving slowly away from the head.

Brenda shivered and dragged her eyes away. She shuddered as she stepped over the body and sat on the bottom wooden stair. Her mind desperately tried to recall Ross's last words. They were in her bed, their bodies warm and exhausted: '*Once it's done you must stay calm. It won't be easy, but think of me, of us, and you can do it. When this is all over, we'll be free. Take some of the brandy and you'll be OK until I come for you. You'll have to wait until after dark, but you can do it, you can do it. I love you, Brenda, darling, you know I love you.'*

\*

Ross finished his drink, lit a cigarette, and motioned to the barman to repeat the round. The hotel bar was full with its Saturday evening regulars; Ross's group had finished their meal early to secure their favourite spot at the end of the long gleaming bar counter.

\*

The street lighting was poor, but there was just enough light in the hallway to pick out the two pale faces on the floor, both surprised in death; a mess of blood had leaked from one of them, while near the other something had spilled from a hip flask on the floor and had trickled into the darkness.

## Out of the Maze

Everything that she had admired in him, had married him for, Lillian now despised. The confident manner that had swept her off her feet she now knew to be empty swagger. The forthrightness and strength of mind that had made her look up to him so much were nothing more than loud-mouthed self-importance. The sociability which she had envied was embarrassing familiarity. How, why, Lillian asked herself a hundred times a day, had she allowed herself to ignore her little niggling warnings and doubts, and agree to marry a lazy, bullying know-all like Gordon McNally? Why had she not seen through him sooner?

Lillian was too self-honest to blame anyone but herself. The mistake, the blindness and bad judgement, had been hers alone. She had concentrated her mind on the trappings and fripperies of the wedding, and ignored the things that really mattered. The result was deadly – the wedding was a success, the marriage a disaster. Only eleven months into it, and she felt her life was a ruin. She was like someone who had entered a maze, instantly taken a wrong turn, and become hopelessly lost.

At times when she was feeling sorry for herself Lillian wished she had had somebody to advise her. If only her mother had been with her. As an only child, she had been so close to her mother that they were more friends than parent and child. The loss of her mum to cancer four years earlier had left Lillian almost inconsolable. As for her dad, his only interest seemed to be how much the wedding was going to cost. His worries stopped there. The nearest thing she had to a friend was Doreen, now Mrs. Doreen Courtney, whose thoughts and energies were totally taken up with looking after her year-old twin boys. Lillian had voiced a few mild misgivings to Doreen a month or so before the wedding, and the response had cut her deeply.

'Come on, Lillian, it's not a buyer's market out there. You're pushing thirty, the clock's ticking. You're hardly in a position to be demanding some Mr. Perfect. Be like me, be grateful for what you've got.'

And what had she got? A bad-tempered, bragging bore. Virtually every time she was with him, that little phrase she had picked up from her old Primary School teacher rang in her head: *'Empty barrels make most sound'*. At first Lillian had made excuses and allowances for Gordy, hoping maybe he was having teething troubles in adjusting to civilian life after nearly ten years in the Army. After a time, however, a very short time, she was weary listening to his claims that he was too good for the Army, that they were stupid donkeys, and that he wasn't considered officer material by his snobby superiors solely because he hadn't gone to 'the right school'.

'They don't like this in the Army,' he said, tapping his head. 'Intelligence. That's why I packed it in. If you're smart like I am, you'll get nowhere in the Army.'

Lillian found herself wondering just how smart he could be if it had taken him ten years to make that discovery, but, as always, she said nothing.

Then there was that day they were on the escalator in the shopping centre when a voice called across from the escalator going up in the opposite direction. 'Hey, Gordy. How's it goin? How're you copin' with being Private McNally DD?' The owner of the voice was a young man with a number one haircut and a distinct sneer.

'Who was that, Gordy? What did he mean?'

Her husband's face was tight with anger. He could hardly speak. 'Just a loser I used to serve with,' he finally managed. 'Like all the rest, jealous of me. Couldn't stand it when I got my DD, my Distinguished Decoration.' Lillian had tried looking up the Distinguished Decoration award on Google at work, but the only term she could find to match DD was Dishonourable Discharge.

The notion of his being 'too good' for certain positions extended beyond military circles. Prompted by Lillian, Gordy half-heartedly applied for a number of jobs advertised locally, but in every case came home from the interviews convinced that he was too good for anything they had to offer. Receiving no military benefits or pension, his only source of income was the paltry Jobseeker's Allowance which, oddly enough, he didn't find himself 'too good' to accept. Had it not been for Lillian's job in the library, they would have had difficulty most weeks in meeting the rent.

Financial problems, as real and serious as they were, were not, however, the cause of Lillian's deepest anxiety. That arose from her rapid recognition that her husband's personality, temperament, nature, call it what she would, was unbearable. She had been brought up in a gentle home where a voice raised in anger was unknown. She, herself, was softly spoken, mild in demeanour; she was simply not able to stand up to the shouting and swearing of her husband whenever she dared to question his conduct or even suggest a criticism of him. Gordy never actually threatened her, but his loud aggressiveness, at full volume when he was shown to be wrong, intimidated her into submission. Lillian felt on many occasions that the short temper and bullying manner were mere expedients to get his own way, and to prevent the weaknesses in his own arguments or opinion from being exposed. Whatever the case, she preferred to give ground rather than find herself cowering away from Gordy's red-faced rage.

Surely there had to be an underlying inadequacy or sense of inferiority to account for much of his behaviour. She had never known the likes of it. Those stories of his, with their schoolboy joke construction, and the inevitable triumphant ending favourable to himself; how juvenile, how phoney, '*they couldn't get that nut off, so they asked me to have a go. First go, wouldn't budge; second time tried a touch of the old WD-40 on her, she maybe gave a little, couldn't be sure; third time, put the heat on her and bingo, off she came, easy as pie.*'

In the first few weeks Lillian had asked around a few colleagues from work for supper with their partners, to see the flat and meet Gordy. Never again. He had dominated every conversation, dogmatic about things he knew nothing about, advising and instructing people of real ability and experience on matters they were fully proficient in.

'In your position, I would go for the short, sharp shock treatment, and then negotiate after I'd softened them up a bit.' Cringe, cringe. Her guests had tried to include Lillian in the chat, but Gordy had cut across her attempted involvement and answered for her, inferring from her quiet words that she wasn't up to a social situation that required his assertive contributions.

'I showed a couple of those smart boys a thing or two,' said Gordy after the guests had gone. 'They were probably expecting some thick squaddie, but I think they got better value than that. Lily, you'll have to learn to speak out a bit, like me. That's what impresses people, meeting somebody with strong ideas and good personality.'

The total absence of any subsequent mention of Gordy by Lillian's colleagues indicated just how impressed they had been by his character and intellect. They were free, however, from having to witness daily displays of his vanity and insensitivity. The school governor phase would no doubt have further 'impressed' them. A member of the Parents and Teachers Association of the local Primary School had called. There were rumours circulating that the Education Department was going to merge two schools, an idea that was strongly rejected by the local parents, and this man was collecting signatures opposed to the proposed merger. Gordy had answered the knock at the door, and in no time at all he was launched into a tirade against the current education system, a subject he had never before given a single thought to. Hidden in her armchair, Lillian was suffering more than the poor innocent buttonholed on the doorstep.

'You're right, you know,' said the unfortunate, ready to agree to anything to get the signature and make good his escape. 'It's somebody like you we need on that useless Board of Governors, you'd soon waken them up.'

Gordy was glowing the rest of the evening. He informed Lillian that he wanted the Gordy dropped, that he would be Gordon from that point on. He also demanded that she look out and press his flannels, and check his green blazer. A new image was being born, modelled on those he regularly denounced as toffee-nosed gits. Fortunately for Lillian she didn't have to see Gordon's efforts to ingratiate himself into the good opinion of the 'snooty, stuck-up bastards', as he was shortly to call them. She shuddered as she imagined his familiarity and forwardness. Piecing together what she could infer from his accounts, and reading between the lines, it was clear that Gordon had made a repeated nuisance of himself in the school, offering, and then demanding, to give talks to the children on his military exploits, and to demonstrate Army-fighting techniques. The headmaster had finally been obliged to tell him to leave, threatening to call the police if he refused to go, or chose to return. Gordon's only return was to Gordy and to jeans and a pullover.

Yes, the maze had closed round Lillian, and no mistake. She tried one day to think of something worthwhile in her husband, something positive. Surely it couldn't be all negative. What a struggle to unearth something beneficial, affirmative, but she managed two advantages, neither of them particularly constructive. Being married to Gordy McNally helped her enjoy her work more, to appreciate its value in getting her out of the house and among other people. Being married to Gordy McNally gave her a little time to enjoy her own company, because he had taken to going down to the pub some evenings as soon as he had finished his meal. The downside of this second virtue was that he was wasting money they could ill afford, but it was worth it to be free of him for a few hours. His snoring was a different matter altogether.

Gordy was on his way home from The Three Oaks. He was in a black mood. The Darts Team names were up on the board, and his wasn't one of them. You had to be fifty or over to get on the team, it appeared. He was out of money, hadn't been able to get himself a third pint. He had thought of asking the barman for one on credit, but the little sign behind the bar told him he would be offended by the refusal he would get. Gordy had put himself about, chatting to a number of the drinkers about his Army experiences, but not one of them had offered to buy him a drink. They had seemed anxious to get away from him, to avoid putting their hand in their pocket. Well, at least tomorrow was Friday and Lillian's payday.

This was Gordy's frame of mind when he noticed the figure moving towards him a hundred yards or so along the alley. The alleyway was poorly lit, but the person's movement was the slow, stiff-legged gait of the elderly. Suddenly the figure staggered sideways a step or two, swayed for a second, and then crumpled to the ground.

'He's had a few more than I did,' Gordy said to himself. He reached the man, who was sprawled on the ground on his back, his legs half bent to one side. 'Better get yourself up, mate, before the bin lorry comes round,' offered Gordy.

The man looked well up in years, probably in his eighties. He was clean and well dressed, not a down-and-out. No response to Gordy's words, no stirring. Gordy crouched down beside him to give him a hand up, and shook him roughly by the shoulder. His head lolled to one side a little, but no other movement. Gordy would have left him to sleep it off at this point, but then he noticed the badge on the breast pocket of the man's jacket and his attitude changed immediately. What he saw was the Crusader's shield and Gold Cross of the British Eighth Army, the legendary Desert Rats of General Montgomery's African campaign. The cloth badge was sewn to its original square of black backing material. Gordy knew about military badges and insignia, he had collected them as a boy, and he recognised the shield, chosen in recognition of the Eighth Army's first operation, Operation Crusader, and the cross in gold to prevent confusion with the Red Cross symbol.

Gordy shook him more gently and asked, 'Are you all right, sir? Have you a load on? Let me give you a hand up.' For the first time it occurred to him that something was wrong, that the man was unconscious, or worse. He put his ear to the mouth. No breathing. Gordy had been given basic First Aid training, and he now tried for a pulse, but couldn't be sure if he felt one or not. He slid his hand inside the buttoned jacket to feel for a heartbeat. Nothing. The man was dead.

Gordy was slowly withdrawing his hand in defeat when he felt a flat bulge against his hand. He squeezed the outside of the jacket. There was something in the inside pocket. He looked up and down the alley. It was empty. Gordy took a deep breath, eased his hand inside the dead man's inner pocket, and felt the unmistakable shape and texture of a wallet. He checked the alley again, and then started to slide out the object. Pressed tightly against the body, it offered a little resistance, but a slight tug released it. Gordy was holding an old leather wallet bearing the distinctive Eighth Army emblem of the shield and cross. The insignia this time was of metal, with the shield outlined by a broad black margin and the cross more yellow than gold.

In less than five minutes Gordy had put himself nearly half a mile away. He slipped into Ormond Park and behind the holly hedge bordering the Monument. Nobody was about. The wallet was empty except for five ten-pound notes, and a small card with the words: '*If found, please return to Clifford Newsome, 32 Chadwick Gardens, Chandley'*. Gordy transferred the fifty quid into his jeans and was about to throw the wallet into the bushes, but something stopped him. Perhaps there was a little bit of the collector left in him, or he thought the wallet might be worth a few pounds, or maybe there was just enough admiration in him for an old soldier not to disrespect the treasured keepsake of a brave Desert Rat. He licked a little dot of blood from a finger. Must have pricked himself on the holly.

Lillian hadn't seen him in such chirpy form for some time. He actually gave her a half hug as he combed his hair in front of the mantelpiece mirror.

'Well, it's not all downhill. What goes round comes round, as they say, and that's why I'm fifty quid to the good. Met an old buddy in the bar tonight, haven't seen him in years, and what's the first thing he does? Comes up, shakes me by the hand, and gives me the fifty quid I'd loaned him nearly ten years ago. I'd forgotten all about it, to tell you the truth. I was always helping people out who were a bit short of the readies.'

'That's good, Gordy,' said Lillian, thinking, 'A pity he doesn't show a bit of his great generosity where it's really needed.'

'We're going to celebrate, go out on the town, eat out, break open a nice bottle of wine. How does that sound to you, Lili Marlene?'

Absolutely dreadful, were the words in her head as her tongue somehow formed and delivered a toneless 'Wonderful'. The only thing she ever remembered afterwards about the meal was her urge to throw the jug of iced water over him. He had ordered a carafe of the wine the waiter had recommended, and then gone off on a pointless discussion with the poor fellow on its percentage proof and the accuracy of the 100 degrees proof spirit scale. The waiter, bored, busy and agitated, politely waited while the discussion inexorably made its way towards the inescapable conclusion. 'If it's strength you're talking about, have a go at my home-made barley wine – first glass, no bother; second glass, still OK; third glass, out comes the sledgehammer.'

The waiter looked like he would have had a ready use for a sledgehammer if one had been available.

The following Thursday evening Lillian was ironing. She was stinging inside. She had mentioned to him over tea that an opening had arisen for a Chief Librarian on the other side of town, and that she was considering applying for the post. Gordy had virtually ridiculed the idea.

'Don't take this personally, Lil, but you wouldn't have a look-in. They'll want somebody with drive and authority, somebody who can give orders and have the respect of their staff. Take it from me, don't bother. They'll be looking for somebody like me, a leader. You'd be too weak, Lil, too quiet. You're not cut out to be a boss.'

*A Helping Hand* was on TV when Gordy came in from the pub. The programme was produced as a service to the local community. The public was asked to help find lost cats and dogs, for example, and the police had a short spot where they asked for assistance to solve petty crimes in the area. The presenter was doing the lost and found section of the programme. Gordy was brooding over his continuing omission from the Darts Team and was only half listening, until the lady announced that an elderly citizen had lost his wallet and the family was offering a reward for its recovery. The presenter made it clear that the family didn't care about the contents of the wallet, that the wallet itself was their concern on account of its sentimental value; it had been presented to the owner by General Montgomery after the battle of El Alamein. A description of the wallet was read out, and a picture of the Crusader's shield and cross emblem was shown on screen. As always, at the end of the broadcast a list of telephone numbers was given, each one relating to a particular item on the programme, and Gordy surreptitiously noted down the number for the lost wallet. He could hardly wait until next day when Lillian would be at work and he could follow up on the offer of the award for the missing wallet.

The woman who answered his call next morning listened closely while Gordy told her how he had found an empty wallet the previous week that matched the description given on *A Helping Hand*. He had found it on a patch of waste ground near Criswell Road. Gordy had chosen an area between the pub and his flat, but well away from the alley. He explained that he didn't think an empty wallet would be worth handing in, and had kept it only because as a former soldier he was interested in the insignia.

'I'm so glad you did,' said the woman. 'Most people would have thrown it in the bin. Thank you so much. You see, my father has died suddenly. He was in the early stages of dementia, so we weren't surprised when we discovered he hadn't got the wallet with him. He had probably dropped it somewhere. He was always losing things.' She offered to collect the wallet, and 'square him up', but Gordy said he was happy to drop it round. She gave him an address a mile or so away and he arranged to call that afternoon.

It was a man in his forties who opened the door to him shortly after two. He introduced himself as Bob, shook hands with Gordy, and ushered him into the front room where a woman was standing by the window. She came forward and Bob introduced her as Valerie. She invited Gordy to sit down. He assumed she was the woman he had spoken to earlier, although her voice had sounded a little softer on the phone.

'Thanks ever so much for calling over,' she said. 'Maybe we'd better have a look at the wallet and make sure it's the right one.' No sooner had Gordy produced it than they both confirmed it was. They looked relieved, and both thanked him again.

'No bother. As a former soldier myself I'm only too happy to help. I'd have brought it to you, reward or no reward. That's me, always ready to be of service.'

Gordy was enjoying their gratitude and his role as the good citizen, with the forthcoming reward the icing on the cake.

'Can you tell us when you found the wallet,' asked Bob. 'We're trying to trace his last movements, not that it'll do any good, I suppose. The sad thing is, he was due to go into a Nursing Home at the end of the month, but he never made it. Heart attack, they think. He was found in an alleyway near Lessor Street.'

'Yeah, no problem. It was last Friday evening, about ten.' Gordy had instinctively switched from the actual Thursday to keep himself out of the time frame. 'I found it on that waste ground near Criswell Road when I was walking home from The Three Oaks. If I'd known it was of sentimental value, I'd have handed it in right away.'

Valerie gave a dry laugh. 'Well, it has no value of any kind to him now, but it's important to the family. We're wondering if he had the heart attack where he was found, or if it happened somewhere else and he was able to make it as far as the alleyway. It's upsetting to think he might have staggered there on his own, and maybe lay alive and unconscious with nobody to help him. Maybe he could have been saved, kept alive. Did you notice if he was breathing at all?'

Gordy stiffened. Something was wrong here. 'Did I notice what? All I noticed was an empty wallet lying on waste ground. You're getting a bit confused here.'

He hadn't taken the bait. 'Sorry, Mr. McNally,' the man came in. 'I'd better explain. I'm DS Bob Wood and this is DC Valerie Kelton. We're investigating the circumstances surrounding the death of Clifford Newsome. The wallet you found might be of use to us in our enquiries. I'm afraid we're going to have to hold on to it in the meantime as possible evidence in the case.'

Gordy sprang up from the couch. 'What? What's goin' on here? What kinda' trick is this? I come over here to do a good turn, no matter about reward, and the police are lyin' in wait for me! That's it. Keep the wallet if you want it, but I'm outta' here.' He made for the door, but the man was too quick for him and blocked it off.

'We can understand how you feel, but we have to do our job. This is a nasty business. We're waiting for the result of a second autopsy. Mr. Newsome did have a heart attack, but he also had suffered a blow to the head. The pathologist isn't sure if he was struck, or injured his head when he fell, or if he had the heart attack as a result of being struck. We have reason to believe that this wallet was stolen from him, either before or after his death. In either case it's a very serious crime, so you see why we're following up every line of enquiry.'

'What's this got to do with me? All I did was find the wallet. Somebody else must have done it, and dumped the wallet. I know nothin' about any of this.'

'Fine, and we appreciate your assistance, but there are certain procedures we have to follow in a possible murder case. With your permission, we need to take a DNA sample from you. It's routine, just a matter of minutes, and done to eliminate you if other forensic evidence is found. DC Kelton will take a saliva swab. It's in your interests. I should add that if you refuse permission here, you will have to accompany us to the station where a blood sample may be taken...'

Lillian noticed him uncharacteristically subdued for two or three days. Something seemed to be on his mind, but he said nothing to her about it. She hoped whatever it was would continue, but started to think her hopes were in vain when an outbreak of the old familiar blustering and browbeating occurred one evening. Ironically it was the very same evening that the police came. Gordy answered the knock on the door about seven o'clock, and next thing two plain clothes officers and a uniformed constable were in the flat. The PC stood with his back to the door.

'Hello again, Mr. McNally,' said the older plain clothes one. It was DS Wood.

'Sorry to burst in on you like this, but there are one or two little things we need to clear up with you. Shouldn't take a minute. You said last time we talked that it was on Friday 8th that you found the wallet, on the way home from The Three Oaks public house. Are you certain about the date?'

'Yes, definitely. No doubt about it.'

'I see. The odd thing is, we checked with some of the regulars in the pub and they were all fairly sure you weren't there that evening. Seems there was a darts match on, and you had made a point of not supporting it.'

'Well, they're wrong. I said I wasn't going, but I changed my mind and went. That's where they got it wrong.'

'OK, very good. And can you remember where you were on the previous evening,

Thursday 7<sup>th</sup>? Some of The Three Oaks people thought you were in the pub that night.'

'Wrong again. I was in here all evening. Never went out the door. Ask her, she'll tell you.' All attention turned to Lillian, who put up a good show of being puzzled.

'Why Gordy, how could you forget? That was the Thursday evening you met your old Army pal in the pub, and he gave you the fifty pounds he owed you. Don't you remember that next day, the Friday, you got me to phone up and book a table for Saturday evening in The Camomile Garden?' She felt a strange thrill of satisfaction pass right through her as she saw, for the first time in their relationship, that something she had said had rendered him speechless. Let him bluster his way out of this.

'Fifty pounds,' said the detective. 'That's a good round sum. I'll be very interested in talking to this old Army pal of yours. We'll get his details from you in due course. Thank you, Mrs. McNally, you've been a great help.' He smiled across to Lillian.

'She's got it wrong, as usual. The stupid bitch has got it wrong,' snarled Gordy. 'She's all mixed up.'

'Easily checked. What we're sure about is that we haven't got anything wrong. You see, when the body of Mr. Newsome was examined, a spot of blood was found on his white shirt. Stood out like a beacon. Small, but an ideal DNA source. We know whose it was and how it got there. The gentleman was getting a bit forgetful, you see, was losing things, so his daughter pinned his wallet pocket closed with a safety pin. A nuisance of a thing, a safety pin, always seems to manage to jab people. Whoever pulled the wallet out of the old man's pocket pricked his finger on the pin, and left that blood trace evidence behind on his shirt. A perfect match for the one you gave us, Mr. McNally. Maybe all those people down in the pub are wrong, maybe this lady here is wrong too, but the chance of our DNA match being wrong is about one in a hundred million.'

At this point the uniformed man moved away from his post at the door. He was carrying handcuffs. 'Gordon McNally,' continued the Detective Sergeant, 'I'm arresting you for the wilful theft of a wallet and fifty pounds from the body of Clifford Newsome on the 7th March. I have to caution you that further charges may be preferred against you. You do not have to say anything, but it may harm your defence if you do not mention when questioned something which you later rely on in court. Anything you do say may be given in evidence.'

Lillian read the letter through several times, just for the satisfaction of it. What a lovely phrase, *shortlisted for the position of Chief Librarian.* She stretched and sipped her tea. Gordy in custody awaiting trial for manslaughter, divorce proceedings in the hands of her solicitor, and now this good news through the mail. She smiled to herself; it was like one of Gordy's three-part, happy-ending stories. No doubt about it, every turn in the maze was now the right one, the paths were wide and free, the space ahead was opening up, and Lillian was well and truly on her way to freedom.

# *Confessional*

Jerry's instinct had been right – the party was a flop. As soon as he had entered the room, maybe even before he had entered the room, he had smelt failure. Funny things, parties. For no definable reason, one could be a big hit and another a total fiasco, even though both might have exactly the same ingredients. The only recipe known to practically guarantee success, he thought, was lashings of free drink, but that could be an expensive and possibly explosive formula.

This do never got off the ground. Thank goodness Jerry had brought his hip flask to help him through it. He half-regretted going to all the bother of the priest get-up, but had to admit he'd done a fine job there. For him, the clerical outfit and persona were the only good part of the evening.

Ronnie had sworn it was going to be 'a full fancy dress thing' when he was persuading him along, but only a handful had bothered, the obligatory Dracula was there, and a couple of cut-price Pink Ladies, a bedraggled Elvis, and someone of undetermined gender who was either Rasputin or a bearded Cleopatra. At least they had made an effort, which Jerry preferred to the antics of a number of giggly girls, in the early stages of drunkenness, cavorting to dance-proof music.

Jerry devoured about a dozen small but surprisingly good sandwiches, washed them down with potent Jack Daniels and Coke, took a look around, and decided he'd had enough of this particular shindig. He located Ronnie chatting up a Pink Lady.

'I'm going home. Can't take any more excitement. Doesn't matter about the lift, I'll take a bus.'

'Party pooper. Quitter. I'll tell you everything you've missed on Monday.'

'Good. That'll cheer me up.'

The bus was practically empty. Jerry sat upstairs near the back and wiped a peephole on the steamy window. His Jack Daniels finally started to work its magic. He closed his eyes from the blurred streetlights and cursed whoever had banned smoking on public transport.

It was at moments like this that Jerry regretted most the loss of his driving licence, although he wouldn't have driven now in any case. He'd become punctilious about the rules of drinking and driving. He was assessing how much worse the party would have been if he had been driving instead of drinking when he felt eyes upon him. A burly type of man in the seat across the aisle was looking over at him intently. Jerry supposed it was his priest garb that drew attention, closed his eyes again, and resumed his post-mortem on the party.

Next thing he knew, someone was sitting down roughly beside him and a voice was saying close to his ear, 'Father, I need to talk to you.' Jerry was so surprised that he couldn't reply, and the voice continued, 'I want to make confession.' It was the man who had been looking at him from the seat opposite. He carried with him the unmistakable reek of whisky.

That was the key moment, the moment when Jerry should have explained to the man his mistake, and confessed himself, that he was not a priest. His own mistake, and a more reprehensible one, was to say nothing. Looking back at that crucial moment he was able to analyse why he had stayed silent. Apart from the surprise element that had left him momentarily speechless, there were other factors at work, perhaps unconsciously. Jerry was pleased with the man's ratification of his guise, and a little mischievous side of him was excited by his role of confessor, and curious about what this penitent might tell him. There was another component, a certain bullishness in the man's appearance and manner raised the troubling question of how he might react if he discovered Jerry was a fraud.

'Have you seen your own priest about this?' Jerry asked. He was surprised at the steadiness of his delivery, and gave credit for it to the Jack Daniels.

'I haven't been inside a church for thirty years. Maybe you've been sent to me instead.' Something in the earnestness of the voice made Jerry uneasy, but he was beyond the point of recanting. What came next dispelled any idea of entertainment from hearing the confession. 'Father, hear my confession. I've killed a man. It wasn't an accident. I planned it. I don't regret it. I just need to tell somebody. Isn't that what you're there for? I don't want forgiveness, just to tell somebody, that's all.'

Jerry sat stunned. He didn't doubt for a moment that the man was telling the truth. Like Jerry, he had definitely consumed, liquor but was not under its influence. His tone was low and level, and chillingly controlled.

'Who did you kill? Why did you kill him?' Jerry managed.

'He was sleeping with my wife. Isn't that the polite term they use for it? He's sleeping a different way now, Father.'

'Does your wife know what you've done?'

'No. Now I'm saying no more. I don't want any of your Hail Mary's or penances, or your absolutions or whatever you call them. You just remember the Seal of the Confessional. I know about these things.'

With that the man was out of the seat and on his way down the aisle. Jerry heard the bell ringing, the swish of the door opening and closing downstairs, and then he was alone in the seat and shaking. The entire encounter had lasted no more than a few minutes, but its impact was permanent. Jerry could remember every word, both the man's and his own, as though they had been imprinted in his brain. Afterwards he couldn't recall where the man had got off the bus, and indeed he almost missed his own stop, so deeply was he sunk in retracing the meeting in his mind. It had really rattled him.

A kind of anxiety settled on Jerry when he got back to the flat. He thought of calling Ronnie but knew his friend would be in no mood, condition or situation to listen to him properly. He'd call him next morning. In the meantime, he tried to argue himself out of his uneasiness. After all, what had really happened? Very little, and nothing to worry him. He didn't know the man, the man didn't know him, and even if they met again it was unlikely he would be recognised in his regular workaday appearance. Maybe the whole story was the gibberish of a drunk man.

But it wasn't. Jerry was sure of it. The confession had been clear-minded, clinical. That meant a man was dead, murdered, and, apart from the murderer, he was probably the only one who knew about it. But wait a moment, maybe not, maybe the police already knew about it. Maybe they had found the body and had started an investigation that would lead them to the guilty man.

Jerry tried to comfort himself with that hope, but to no avail. It wouldn't wash. The truth was that since the business with the accident, he and the police were bad grammar. It wasn't that the police had a problem with him, he had a problem with the police.

It had clearly been that stupid woman's fault when she came out of a side street and drove into Jerry's passenger door. She had admitted as much to Jerry before the police arrived, but as soon as they smelt alcohol on his breath the focus was all on him. Jerry failed his breathalyser test, just failed it, and the outcome was a £200 fine and a six-month suspension of his licence. OK, he had had two pints and was just over the limit, Jerry accepted that, but what he couldn't accept was her going on her way unchallenged, while 'justice' took its course.

And yet, for all his sense of grievance, Jerry knew that this was police business. Where else could he go if he wanted to pursue the matter? After a restless night he called Ronnie early next morning. The call clearly wasn't welcome, and it took all his powers of persuasion to get his friend out of bed and into a taxi, which Jerry promised to pay for. He declined Ronnie's suggestion of sorting out whatever it was on the phone.

Ronnie looked 'a bit rough'. Jerry made him a strong coffee, took one himself, and recounted in full the events of the previous evening. He waited for his friend's response.

'And you've got me up, and over here, on my precious Saturday, to tell me this? Are you for real? Some smart ass was winding you up, taking the piss out of an idiot dressed up as a priest. He knew you weren't a real priest. A real priest, off duty, on a bus, wouldn't have been wearing all that gear. Either that or he was too drunk to know the difference. In either case he was taking the piss. Get serious, Jerry? I'm going home and getting back into the pit. You should have stayed on and enjoyed the party and got a lift home with Keith the way I had arranged it.'

The debate raged in his head. *Ronnie's right. I'm exaggerating the whole thing. Even if I'm right, why should I get involved? Leave it to the police. Why should I do them any favours. They certainly did none for me. But I can't let him get away with it. He might do his wife next. But the police will never believe me. They'll laugh at me, or worse still, I'll get myself in some kind of trouble...*

The Desk Sergeant directed him to a seat in a corridor and spoke into a phone. Jerry waited and watched until a plain clothes officer arrived at the desk, had a word with the sergeant and looked over in his direction. He motioned Jerry with his head to follow him, and strutted off down a different corridor where he opened a door, ushered Jerry in, and closed it behind them.

'I'm DC Fowler. What's this about?' His manner was of someone who wanted the matter over and done with quickly.

Jerry disliked the man instantly. He was tall and scrawny, with a long thin face and nose to match. The narrow forehead sloped back until it reached a crest of dirty fair hair perched like a crown. This feature, together with the receding chin, made Jerry think of a rooster, and it struck him there and then, remarkably, that the Fowl part of his name was bang on target. He took a dislike too, to the brown suit and matching suede shoes.

'I want to report a murder.'

Fowler looked up sharply and gave Jerry his full attention. After a pause he said, 'We'll better have a seat, then, hadn't we, and get a few details.' He faced Jerry across the worn wooden table, produced a notebook, and took down Jerry's name, address, and date of birth. 'Excuse me a moment, Mr. Moore,' and he eased out of his chair and out the door. He returned after a few minutes with a slim folder, withdrew a single sheet of paper from it, scanned it, and returned it to the folder.

'Now then, tell me about this murder of yours.'

Jerry settled himself and reported the events of the previous evening, from his preparations for the party right through to his return to his flat. Fowler listened intently without interruption, his eyes fixed on the table. He made a few notes in his book.

'Had you ever seen this man before? Did you know him or recognise him from anywhere?' he asked when Jerry had finished.

'No. I'm sure about that.'

'And you say you don't know where he got on the bus, or where he got off the bus?'

'That's right.'

'Would you recognise him if you saw him again?'

'Yes, I'm certain I'd know him again.'

'Were you drinking at this party last night, Mr. Moore?' Fowler suddenly threw in.

Jerry hesitated, and framed his answer carefully. 'Yes, I had a few drinks at the party, but only a few, and I certainly wasn't drunk.'

'I see. Only a few.' Pause. 'Why, then, if you certainly weren't drunk, did you hear confession from the man? If you knew what you were doing, why didn't you tell him you weren't a priest?'

It was an awkward moment. Fowler was good at this. 'I don't know. He took me by surprise. He was started before I could stop him. He was determined.'

'OK. So what have we got here? A stranger sees you on a bus, thinks you're a priest, and confesses a murder to you. You don't know who he is, where he is, or who he has killed. Not much to go on, is it?'

'Look, I'm trying to help here, to do the right thing. What about all these appeals on TV to give the police even the tiniest bit of information, no matter how small. The easy thing for me would be to do nothing, but I'm here. Do you think I've nothing better to do on a Saturday? Why would I be here if I thought it wasn't important?'

Fowler sniffed a little laugh. 'There's a lot of strange people come in here, Mr. Moore, believe me, a lot of strange people with a lot of strange stories, and even stranger motives. Some have a grudge against the police and like to waste police time. That's a criminal offence, by the way.'

'OK, OK, but from where I'm sitting it looks like you're wasting my time. Maybe I was hoping you'd found the body, or you were looking for a missing person or something, I'm not sure what I was expecting, but I'm here, whether you want to believe it or not, because I thought it was what a good citizen should do, schmaltzy as that may sound to a hard case like you.'

Just at that moment there came a quiet knock on the door and a policeman came in with a mug of tea. Jerry looked up and froze in shock. The breath left him, like he had been kicked in the stomach. He was looking at the face of the confessant on the bus, the man who twelve hours earlier had told him about murdering his wife's lover. Now here he was again a few feet from him, in a police station, and wearing a police uniform. There was no mistaking those heavy features, the reddened, slightly pitted skin and slack mouth.

A chill of fear ran through Jerry. A blizzard of thoughts swirled through his mind. He felt trapped. The whole thing had been some kind of set-up. But how? Why? What was happening? Just as panic was starting to shake his right leg uncontrollably below the table the constable set down the tea, said something to Fowler, and left the room. He hadn't given Jerry another look.

He hadn't recognised him! Of course – Jerry the priest had had his hair gelled flat and combed straight back with a tidy side parting, was clean shaven, wore wire-framed glasses, and the dark suit, collar and regalia of the cleric. This Jerry's hair was its usual tangled mess, the glasses were gone, he displayed early morning stubble, and wore a denim jacket and jeans. His heart was thumping and his head pounding but he managed to steady his shakes while his interrogator was sampling his tea.

'Maybe you're right. Maybe I should thank you for coming in,' resumed Fowler. 'Were you able to get parked OK?'

What a sly one he was, with the softened tone for the loaded question. In spite of dry mouth and residual shaking, Jerry swallowed hard and fielded it. 'I walked here. It's hardly a marathon. Anyhow, as you know from my sheet, I'm not allowed to drive at present.'

'But are you allowed to impersonate a priest, I wonder? To tell you the truth, I'm not sure on that one myself. Must look it up. There's probably something in civil law against it. You could run the risk of a civil suit against you for hearing confession.'

They sat in silence. Fowler finished his tea. 'Should have got you some tea, I suppose. Maybe black coffee would have been better,' and he smirked. 'Here's what I'm going to do on this one. We'll wait a few days and see if your dead body turns up, or if the killer comes in to us and makes another confession. I'll have to open a file on this, just in case, but in the meantime you go on home, and tell us if you remember anything more useful, or if you see the man again. We have your details. We'll get in touch if we need you.'

Jerry walked home with a terrible weight of dread slowing his footsteps, and at the same time a nervousness prompting him to walk quickly. The whole thing was unreal. The man who had committed murder was a police officer. It was like some phoney melodrama, except it was all too real and he was in the middle of it.

What if the killer were to find out from Fowler about Jerry's evidence? A man like that would think nothing of eliminating a witness, and he would have the means and experience both to do it and get away with it. He had done it already. A shudder of fear ran through Jerry, and a quiver of self-pity as he thought of his own vulnerability. His only hope was that Fowler would be too busy, or too sceptical, to mention Jerry's claims, or else be unlikely to mention them to a lowly constable.

There was absolutely no possibility of going back to the police. He tried to imagine telling Fowler, 'That man on the bus. I saw him again. He was serving you tea in the police station.' They would think he was some kind of nutter with a spite against the police. Even if they did give him a hearing, they would close ranks to defend one of their own; if they got so far as to investigate Jerry's charges, the man would have covered his tracks, left no evidence. His wife was hardly going to attest that her lover had disappeared.

Jerry knew that every day he would be looking over his shoulder, fearing every phone call and knock at the door. His peace of mind was shattered. If only he had never gone to that stupid party.

The priest knew almost immediately that the man on the other side of the screen was not a Catholic. He was clearly unfamiliar with the ritual of the sacrament, he ignored the kneeler, didn't ask for forgiveness or confess to have sinned, and made no reference to the period since his previous confession.

'Would you prefer to speak to me face to face instead of through the screen?' the priest asked. 'Some people don't like the Confession Box.'

'No, this is all right. I just need to talk to you.'

'Fine. I'm happy to listen and offer whatever help I can. I'm trained to offer advice and guidance, but I won't be able to do the absolution prayer.'

'That's OK. That's not what I want, I just want to confess. You see, Father, I'm ashamed of myself, my own fear and weakness. For over a month now I've known about somebody committing a murder. I know I should do something about it, but I'm afraid of him. I haven't got the strength to face up to him and all his friends. I despise myself for it, but I'm afraid. I don't want penances, or Hail Mary's, or absolutions or whatever you call them. I just need to tell somebody. I just need to tell somebody...'

## *John Nobody*

Detective Chief Inspector Martin Hennessy retired at the age of sixty. He could have gone at fifty-five, but the man was at the peak of his powers and the height of his career, a career that had made him one of the most successful and highly respected criminal investigation officers in the country. Unlike so many of his peers, whose aim had always been to get promoted behind a desk from where they could accept invitations to conferences and dinners, Hennessy was first and foremost a frontline policeman. He had declined a number of opportunities to advance to the power and prestige that Detective Superintendent or Chief Superintendent would have given him.

I was a civilian employee at Police Headquarters. My job as Press Officer was to prepare statements for the media and to be responsible for all internal releases, bulletins, PR, and policy documents. The work brought me into regular contact with Senior Investigating Officers on almost a daily basis, and I can say with all sincerity there was none that I admired more than DCI Hennessy.

A few months after his retirement, he rang me one afternoon at work and asked if we could meet at the Tanyard Tavern for a chat. His choice of bar was not the usual one, so I guessed the matter must be of a private nature. We met as arranged and he told me over a pint what our meeting was about – several family members, friends and former colleagues had prevailed upon him to consider writing his memoirs, and he wanted to discuss various aspects of the idea with me before making a decision. I was more than ready to offer whatever help I could, and told him I would be honoured to be of assistance.

'Here's my address,' he said, giving me his card. 'Could you come round to the house some evening and we could take a look at the dos and don'ts in privacy and comfort. I'm not a great one for these public places.'

The Hennessy home was a generous redbrick bungalow on the south side. Diagonal lattice windows and a graciously curved eyebrow window set in red fired-clay tiles looked along the curved length of the drive. Hennessy admitted me and showed me to an armchair in front of an open coal fire in the large front room.

'Thank you, sir.'

'Forget the sir bit. I'm retired now, I'm in civvy street. If anything, you're the SIO here,' and he laughed at the whimsy of it. 'What's your poison?' I asked for a scotch and ginger ale. 'I'm a vodka man, myself. Always have been. You'd be amazed the number of people who expect me to drink brandy. The name, you see. I should have got it changed to Martin Smirnoff.' He enjoyed his own little joke again. 'Irrational connections, irrational connections. OK, let it be known for the record that for the purposes of this interview I'll be known as Martin Smirnoff, and you'll be DC David Dundas.

Will you indulge me in a little matter, David? One thing I enjoy, have always enjoyed, is sitting in a room with just the light of the fire for illumination. I like the relaxation of it, the flames throwing shadows on the walls and furniture. Can you believe that many of the case-solving moments I had in thirty-five years in the CID came from this armchair here in this very room? By the way, we'll just be talking this evening, no writing, so there's no problem there.'

He was right, it was relaxing, and I wondered if this was some technique he might have used with a witness or suspect. Martin made it clear at once that he wouldn't expect me to talk about the legal side of the proposed book, the confidentiality and Public Interest issues, because he had more than enough legal advice to tap in to. I confined myself to literary and publication matters.

We were getting along very well, Martin asking penetrating questions and allowing me ample time to deal with them, when, without reason or intention, I said something really stupid. Maybe the third generous scotch played a part, or perhaps the flickering firelight dulled my brain, but all at once I heard myself putting to the revered ex-DCI Hennessy, the crass question of a rookie reporter, 'Is there a favourite case you remember best?' It was like asking an undertaker which funeral he had enjoyed most. My face was instantly ablaze, and not from the coal fire or the whiskey, but amazingly my gaffe didn't get the response it deserved. Instead I seemed, accidentally and amateurishly, to have pushed the right button, because Martin piled a few lumps of coal on the fire, refilled our glasses, settled himself deep into his seat, and was ready for take-off.

'I'm glad you asked that question, David. It gives me a chance to go way back in time, right back to the beginning. Not that we homicide detectives should allow ourselves to have favourite cases. We can't forget that in every case a life has been lost, can we? At best we're only reactive people, we always get there after the crime has been committed. There has to be a body, a victim, before we go to work on a job, so there's not much to take satisfaction from, even when we catch and convict the killer. The victims don't feel any sense of justice, that's for sure; the best we can do is help the friends and families to feel that justice has been done.

I suppose the closest we get to being proactive is if we can prevent a murder, a further murder, in a serial killer case, for example. That's what I'm going to go back to now, a serial killer case. Can you believe it was my very first murder case? We called it the John Nobody case at the time.

Let me say right away, David, this has nothing to do with what we've been talking about up to now. This case will not be in my memoirs, if they ever do get published. It started, as they all do in one way or another, with the finding of a body. I wasn't long out of uniform, in fact I'd been in plain clothes for only about a year or so, over in Walton. It was a large enough station, with about a dozen uniform men, three DC's, a DS, and a DI in charge. You've met him, Bob

Matthews, a good Inspector and a good man. Died a couple of years ago.

Well, the case began innocently enough when a widow in her mid-fifties, Miriam Torrens, was found dead, apparently from natural causes, in her back garden in the Corton district of the town. Her doctor estimated she had been dead 72 hours, or thereabouts. She had not been attending her GP and had been given a clean bill of health at her recent yearly check-up, so she was taken by ambulance to the University Hospital for post-mortem examination to ascertain cause of death. When the samples came back to the medical examiner, the toxicological analysis showed unmistakable evidence of poisoning. The victim had ingested a massive dose of Succinylcholine, one of the most lethal biological toxins known, and one most difficult to detect. Colourless, odourless and tasteless, it produces rapid muscular paralysis and resultant collapse of the respiratory system. Death occurs inside a few minutes.

At this point we were called in and a murder enquiry was opened. I'll not bore you with the details, David, the usual door-to-door enquiries, the appeals for information and witnesses, the checking of the deceased's bank accounts, relations, friends, habits. All to no purpose, I should add.

The back garden, now a crime scene, provided one result. Miriam Torrens had been well-liked and friendly, but had lived a lonely life since the passing of her husband some years earlier. She sought solace in her gin bottle, and was known to be a secret tippler, sometimes drinking herself to sleep on warm evenings in her cushioned garden swing seat. Well, the gin bottle at the crime scene had fallen from a small table on to the grass, but the SOCO examination detected enough residual liquid to establish that the poison had been introduced into the bottle. The inference was clear, Miriam Torrens had not been a random victim. Whoever had killed her had known her behaviour patterns sufficiently well to make use of them in her killing. The crime scene examination turned up nothing else, however, no trace evidence, not one hair or print or fibre that did not belong to the victim herself.

The press and local TV news broadcasts announced that the death of a local woman was, first of all, 'suspicious' and, a day or so later, 'being treated as murder', and appealed for assistance from the public, but to no avail. We tried to follow up with suppliers of the deadly Succinylcholine, but it was a lost cause. Without leads, witnesses, motive, suspects, forensic evidence, information, the investigation was at a standstill, or it might be fairer to say it had never got properly started. Somebody at the station remarked one day that the perpetrator was so anonymous, so unknown, that we should tag him John Doebody. Doebody was quickly refined to Nobody, and from that point on we referred to the murder of Miriam Torrens as The John Nobody Case.'

Martin got up out of his chair and stretched. 'For the record, Martin Hennessy is leaving the room at 20.50 hours. He's going for a pee.' He laughed in that same distinctive manner. Hennessy was clearly a man who enjoyed his own sense of humour. While he was gone, I looked around the room and was struck by the absence of photographs, free standing or on the walls. I knew he had been honoured twice at the Palace by the Queen, and had had a Doctorate conferred upon him by the local university, but there were no pictures of smiling handshakes or ceremonial occasions. I noticed a similar absence of photos down the wide central hallway when I accepted his invitation to use the bathroom. I mentioned this to him when I returned. 'I see you're not a man for displaying photos of yourself.'

'Photos? I've boxes of them, but I don't put them up. You wouldn't expect a top welder or plumber to be exhibiting pictures of himself round the house, so why would a successful police officer?'

I was back in my chair, and Martin resumed the John Nobody story. 'At that time, I was going out with a Walton girl. Joanne worked in the office of a leading Coal Importers Company. One evening I was recounting the progress, or lack of it, in the John Nobody case. 'It's like looking for the invisible man. We know nothing about him, assuming of course the culprit is male. He's a complete nobody.'

'If it's a complete nobody you want, I can supply you with one,' said Joanne. 'He works in our office. You'll never find a better match, if you're looking for somebody who is the total Nobody. He just has to be the World Champion Nobody, the uncrowned King of Nobodies.'

I was at a smart-ass age, and ridiculed Joanne in mock newspaper fashion: *Acting on information from the girlfriend of a grateful detective constable, police have arrested and are questioning a local man fitting the description of the suspect in the so-called John Nobody murder investigation.*

The actual investigation, such as it was, got a kick in the backside the very next day when an envelope addressed to CID, Walton Police Headquarters, arrived in the morning mail. It had a local postmark and had been mailed the previous afternoon. DI Matthews opened the envelope and took out the following message, carefully hand-printed on an A4 sheet of plain white paper:

*SO YOU ACTUALLY FIGURED THIS ONE OUT. SHE'S MY SECOND ONE. YOU MISSED THE FIRST ONE. THAT'S BECAUSE I LEFT YOU NO CLUES. THIS TIME I LEFT YOU THE BOTTLE. YOU LOT NEED ALL THE HELP YOU CAN GET. I'LL BE IN TOUCH SOON, VERY SOON.*

Well, Matthews hastily scrambled a team meeting for ten o'clock, and a worried meeting it was. There was little doubt that the letter was genuine, the reference to the bottle confirmed that. Equally, there was little hope that forensic examination of the envelope and its contents would throw up anything. We concentrated on three areas, the claim that he had killed already, the thinly veiled threat that he would do so again, and the reason he had sent the message in the first place. There was general agreement that the first killing must have been a trial run, to prove to himself that he could kill with impunity, or perhaps it hadn't been a safe kill and highlighting it to the police as a murder might have carried risks. Clearly the killer needed recognition of his work, needed his mastery to be identified and acknowledged, and had left the gin bottle clue in case the post-mortem wouldn't take place, or would be so perfunctory that natural causes would be assumed. The view that the killer had been found out and had been forced by the news reports into claiming the death was never seriously entertained. This was a serial killer, who would need to raise the stakes each time to satisfy his psychopathic urges and exercise his psychotic belief in his own superiority.

All of which was very fine to talk about around a table, but NOTHING was known about the age, identity, whereabouts, appearance, or history of the killer. All we knew was that he was probably a local man who had probably known the second victim. DI Matthews asked a couple of his men to check what work had been done to the Miriam Torrens house over the past year, and what deliveries might have been made, but everyone knew these were dead ends. The best hope of progress would come with the next killing.

I think you know me well enough, David, at least by reputation, as somebody who sets little or no store by such things as coincidences or hunches. I've always worked my way into cases through facts, solid checking and questioning and evidence, so why did I find myself a day or so later asking Joanne to tell me a bit more about her Nobody man? Let me tell you why. It was simply to be doing something, anything. I didn't think for one minute that the oddball in Joanne's office had any connection of any sort with the murder, or murders, we were investigating. Had there been even a sniff of another line of enquiry, the faintest whiff of a suspect, I would never have mentioned him to her again. The truth was that I felt so much at a loss, so guilty to be doing nothing, that it was a case of – what's that French phrase? '*Faute de mieux*'.

Anyhow, perhaps feeling a little ashamed and wanting to make amends for my mocking manner a few evenings earlier, I asked her for some details about her World Champion Nobody. Her answer surprised me a little.

'All I can tell you about him is his name, Cyril Roscoe. That's all I know about him, that's all anybody knows about him. I know nothing more about him now than I did six years ago when I first met him, the day I started work in Diamond Coal Importers. He's been there nine years, and some of the staff who have been there all that time don't even know where he lives. He watches people all the time in a sly kind of way, but he never speaks to anybody. And he's got horrible short flat white fingers, with the nails all bitten away,' she added as a clincher.

I wasn't supposing for a moment that this weirdo had anything to do with the killing of Miriam Torrens, but I promised Joanne I would make a few enquiries next day. As it turned out, there was indeed little information about him. I learned that he was 29 years old, lived at 15 Clipper Street, had no criminal record, no hospital history, no driving licence, no television licence. All I could get was his National Insurance Number, and that he had attended Walton Green High School. I called round to Clipper Street, which was the second in a series of parallel streets off Freeman Road, all terraced houses built in the 1920's. No. 15 was indistinguishable from the others, drab and nondescript. I decided I might as well take a look at its anonymous occupant, so I rang Joanne at her work and arranged to meet her outside the Coal Importers ten minutes before the end of the working day. I was really just trying to please her and show that I was taking my promise seriously.

At ten to five I parked on the other side of the street and Joanne arrived as arranged. We watched the trickle of workers straggling towards their cars and buses.

'That's him,' said Joanne, and I got my first look at Cyril Roscoe. I don't know what I had been expecting, or hoping for, but whatever it was I was going to be disappointed. Roscoe was a stringy, round-shouldered figure with thin, mousy hair, a pale flat face, and a distinct weakness of chin. He was wearing a light grey anorak. This much I noted as he slithered along the pavement towards the bus stop. The only noticeable thing about Roscoe was that while his fellow workers emerged in pairs or small groups, he was distinctly alone, and making no conversation with the others. We waited until the bus he boarded had moved off, and Joanne then got out of my car while I set off for Clipper Street, passing Roscoe's bus at the very next stop. I picked up Detective Constable Lucy Harbinson on the corner of Denning Road as I had arranged earlier, and we continued on to Clipper Street, parking a hundred yards or so down from No. 15 on the opposite side. The street lighting was good, and we had a clear view of the house fronts. DC Harbinson was an able and attractive officer, and had readily agreed to help me out on the quiet.

Approximately fifteen minutes later, Roscoe walked into the street from the Freeman Road end, went straight to his house, let himself in, and closed the door behind him. The street was empty and quiet. We allowed ten minutes, and then Lucy walked over to No. 15 and rapped the door. No reply. After half a minute she knocked again. All the time I was watching the windows for a tell-tale twitch of the net curtains, but not a movement. Lucy knocked a third time.

He was in there, I was sure of that. I was equally sure that he was watching her through the gauze curtaining, I was certain of it, and I felt for the first time a real stirring of interest in this Cyril Roscoe. Why would a man not answer his door to an attractive, well-dressed girl? What was he hiding, or what was he afraid of? As instructed, Lucy tried one more knock, and then walked away from the door and turned the corner into Freeman Road. I waited five minutes before driving off in the opposite direction. I turned onto Bauer Road at the bottom and then into one of the parallel streets, drove back up, and picked up DC Harbinson on Freeman Road.

'Well, that was a bit of a waste of time,' she remarked.

'Not at all, not at all, in fact I think I've just realised that's what I wanted to happen. We're looking for a Nobody, and the more he behaves like a Nobody, and is a Nobody, the more I like him. I'm starting to think I'd have been disappointed if he had answered the door. It's better like this.'

'Thanks very much, Martin. I'm glad I've been such a help. Remind me to be washing my hair next time.''

Hennessy laughed at the little memory and dribbled a gulp of Coke into his empty vodka glass. I had been sitting silent, impressed by his ability to recall the names of people and places, and impressions, and even conversations, from a distance of over thirty years. 'Did you share your suspicions with anybody,' I asked, 'or take them to the DCI?'

'No, not at that stage. I knew Matthews too well. I could just hear his response, '*What! Some weirdo who works with your girl won't answer his door at night, and that makes him a murder suspect? Get out and do some proper detective work.*' I suppose I should have told one or two of the DC's, we were always having the importance of being a team player drummed into us, but I wasn't sure myself where I was going. It was all too thin. Just irrational connections, like we were speaking about earlier.

Anyhow, next day I called Walton Green High School and spoke to the Headmaster. He was a youngish man, and very helpful. He undertook to speak to his staff, rang me back later, and invited me to the Staff Room after school, 'but only for ten minutes or so, they've all got other things to do.' There were seven teachers who had taught or known Cyril Roscoe. Without exception they were agreed that there was nothing to remember. The word 'loner' was the term of choice. One woman described him as 'creepy', somebody who watched, never joined in, never smiled. I struck it lucky with the geography teacher, a former pupil who had returned as a member of staff. He had been the Form Prefect for Roscoe's year and one of his roles was of a pastoral nature, to help integrate outsiders and make them feel part of the group.

'I tried everything and then I just gave up. He didn't WANT friends, he wanted to be by himself, inside himself. There was no point in trying to help somebody who didn't want or need help. I was made Head Boy in my Sixth Form Year and I asked Cyril if I could attend his mother's funeral to represent the school. His gracious reply was NO. Typical.'

'What happened to his mother? Was she elderly?'

'No, I don't think so. She fell down the stairs. I remember there was something in the Gazette about it.'

I heard a 'ping' in my head, thanked the teachers for their time, and rushed over to the Gazette Offices. The geography teacher had given me the month and year, and in a matter of minutes the archive girl had the microfilm item in front of me. *Tragic Accident Claims Life of Walton Woman*. The report was simply a factual statement of how 48 year-old Walton Woman Mrs, Dereva Roscoe had died from her injuries following a fall downstairs in her Clipper Street home. It added that there were no suspicious circumstances.

Sometimes our line of work, David, is like a traffic jam. For a while you have to sit still, even when you're itching to be on the move; nothing budges, and then one car moves, and another, and suddenly the block melts and every traffic light is in your favour. As soon as I left the Gazette I called into the station and saw that the Desk Sergeant on duty was Freddie Dawson, a man putting in his time to retirement, but useful for his local knowledge and sound memory.

'Hi, Freddie. Can I ask you something? Do you by any chance remember a woman falling down the stairs and breaking her neck in Clipper Street? It was about twelve years ago. Her name was Roscoe.'

'Remember it? I was there in person, in attendance'. He liked the phrase. 'Yes, I happened to be up there on the beat in those days, and a woman came running out of the street on to Freeman Road, and told me she'd found her neighbour lying dead at the bottom of the stairs, in her nightdress, like maybe she'd been up to go to the loo or something, the woman said. I proceeded to the scene and found the situation as described.'

Martin couldn't resist another little laugh. 'Freddie always went a bit formal when he was discussing business with the 'tecs. I've heard his language sometimes with the lower orders – choice. I got from him that this was about eleven in the morning. Nobody else was in the house, the woman had called over to borrow milk for her elevenses. Sergeant Dawson had rung for an ambulance, 'but she was stone dead'. On the neighbour's insistence, he had also called Dr.

Bruce, the family GP. Apparently, the dead woman's son had been contacted at school, but Dawson had left before he arrived, and could add nothing further.

I knew Dr. Bruce, or Dr. Brusque as we called him, and arranged to see him early next morning. 'I was treating her for high blood pressure, anxiety, vertigo. Her death was consistent with a fall. Bruising and abrasions, vertebrae fracture and spinal cord damage, but she died only indirectly from the broken neck, as the condition is commonly called. A broken neck by itself is rarely fatal, but in this case the spinal column was compromised, interrupting breathing and heartbeat with fatal results.'

'Could she have been pushed?' I asked. Bruce looked up sharply over his glasses, and, to his credit, thought about it.

'Could have been, but no evidence for it. Her problem with the vestibular system of her inner ear made her a prime candidate for dizzy turns and a fall. At the same time, it takes only the slightest nudge to topple a weak lady down a flight of stairs. There'd be no signs of force or struggle. 'Did he jump or was he pushed?' is usually a question only the victim could answer if there are no witnesses, excluding the pusher, of course, if there is a pusher.'

'Was it determined how long she'd been dead before she was found?'

'Between three and four hours. Rigor mortis was just starting, but it's hard to say how long she was lying there before she succumbed to asphyxia. I would guess death occurred no more than about half an hour after the fall and fracture.'

'Did you know Mrs. Roscoe's son Cyril?'

Bruce looked up again with those careful eyes. 'I met him a couple of times after his mother's death, but he wasn't my patient.' That was it. Bruce wasn't a man to volunteer impressions or opinions, especially outside of his professional practice.

My mind was working overtime. Was his own mother the 'first one' the letter had referred to? The time scale was fine, enough time to push his mother down the stairs, even have breakfast, and get the bus into school. Yes, fine, except maybe Roscoe had absolutely nothing to do with either the accidental death of his mother or the murder of Miriam Torrens. Yet, against all the rules of evidence and procedure, the less I was finding out about Cyril Roscoe the more I felt I might be on to something.

I just had to meet the man in person, face to face. I waited next evening in a shop doorway on Freeman Road, saw him step off the bus exactly on time, and fell in behind him as he walked the short distance to No. 15 Clipper Street. Just as he was putting the key in the lock I said, 'Mr. Roscoe. Could I have a word with you.' He froze but didn't turn, didn't say a word. I came round in front of him, showed my badge, and said, 'We've had a number of break-ins in this area and we're doing house to house enquiries to see if anybody has seen anything suspicious.'

Still no movement, no reply. 'Can I come in for a moment to ask you a few questions, maybe show you a few Photofits?'

'No.'

'It'll only take a few minutes. Like, can you remember if you were here last Thursday evening, or what you were doing, or if you saw anything or anybody out of the ordinary. It could be a big help to us.'

'Nothing.'

'Would you prefer to be asked these questions down at the station?' I asked, raising the ante.

'I had my tea, listened to music, went to bed. Same as every other night.'

'Oh, music. I listen to music too a lot. What kind do you like?'

'Music music. That's all I can tell you.' Next thing the key was turned, he was inside, and the door was closed.

I can hardly tell you, David, how pleased I was with the visit. During it Roscoe kept his head down and didn't look straight at me once, but I *knew* he was looking at me, studying me, assessing the meeting. There was definitely something sinister about the man. I felt him still watching me from behind the ghostly net curtains shrouding the dark windows, and strangely I felt a kind of protective instinct towards Joanne who had to share a workspace each day with this distinctly bizarre individual.

Yet that was all he was, a bizarre individual against whom I had no shred of evidence, no viable reason for suspicion. If I was wondering what to do next, however, the development the following morning removed that problem from my mind. Matthews received another anonymous letter, identical to the first in presentation and delivery, but much more troubling in its message:

I'M READY TO DO ANOTHER ONE. MALE OR FEMALE, IT DOSENT MATTER TO ME. WATCH THIS SPACE.

Again, there was no member of our team who doubted the letter was for real. So serious was the threat, that I was tempted to tell the team about the possible lead I was following, but my case was so flimsy that I knew I would be accused of chasing private shadows at the very time we should be pooling ideas and approaches. I left the meeting, however, with two definite lines to follow.

I found Sergeant Dawson, and, bless him, he remembered not only the name of the neighbour who had found Mrs. Roscoe's body, but also her address. Mrs. Cornthwaite was a widow who lived just down the street in No. 22. She invited me in at once. I told her we were looking into a dodgy insurance company suspected of not paying out on life insurance claims, and that the death of Mrs. Roscoe might fall into our enquiry, but we had been unable to get in touch with her son, who hadn't replied to our letters or to our house calls.

'That's just him,' she said. 'As odd as two left feet. I haven't spoken to him, have scarcely seen him, since poor Dereva died. He never speaks to anybody. Takes after the father, they say. He ups one day and takes off, leaving her and Cyril, who was about two at the time. Never heard of since. I'm sure that house must be in an awful state. Dereva and I were good friends, we both went on bus trips, coach tours you know. Met some nice people.'

I let her ramble on, although it was clear that, like everyone else, she knew little or nothing of interest about Cyril Roscoe beyond his being 'a real odd one'. Just before I left, I threw out a chance question, the last cast on a day when they just weren't biting. 'Did you ever hear Mrs. Roscoe mention a lady called Miriam Torrens?' The line went taut, I'd hooked a big one.

'Miriam? Of course, they were friends. So was I. We met on one of the bus runs, to Peltier I think it was, Miriam and her man, Joseph. Jewish people, very nice. Lived over in Corton. Poor Joseph died, I heard. Yes, I knew Miriam very well, and so did Dereva. Miriam and Joseph were at poor Dereva's funeral. The bus tours sort of petered out after that. These things happen. Things always change for the worse.'

So Cyril Roscoe would have known Mrs. Torrens, where she lived. I can tell you here and now, David, over thirty years later, that I can still remember the quiver of excitement I felt when I got that connection. I had one more thing to do. I rang Joanne at her work and asked if she could somehow get Roscoe to write down the word *doesn't*. She wasn't keen, not liking to talk to him on any pretext, but she agreed to have a go. I called her back at lunch time and she told me she'd done it. An older head would have asked to have it read back over the phone, but I wanted to see for myself, told Joanne I'd be right over, and was on my way.

I parked in the usual place and Joanne appeared. What a clever way she had done it. She had passed Roscoe a large blank fridge magnet, telling him that because he was the best printer in the office, she wanted to read out a message for him to print on the magnet for her: *THIS MILK DOSENT BELONG TO THE SALES STAFF*. She handed me the magnet. There it was, the second big catch of the day, a beautifully misspelt DOSENT in red felt pen. I gave Joanne a big hug and, like a gentleman, came round and opened the car door for her. As she was getting out of the car a shadow appeared on the pavement. I looked up just in time to see Cyril Roscoe sliding through the gap between the open car door and the wall. He wasn't looking at Joanne and me, but I *knew* he had made me, just as certainly as I knew he had been scrutinising me on our first encounter.

I now had enough, David, enough to present to DCI Matthews and the rest of the team. I could see Matthews was torn between tearing a strip off me for my maverick private eye stuff, and commending me for chasing up a long shot, but he shrewdly chose to throw my findings open to the group. The printing on the fridge magnet was compared to the two mailed messages, but bore no resemblance. This was not seen as a setback; a message sent to Police Headquarters was going to come in for close analysis, and the author would have been careful to disguise the lettering. The big question they raised, and one I couldn't answer, was why Roscoe would have waited twelve years between the two killings, and then declare himself *'ready to do another one'* just a couple of weeks after the Miriam Torrens murder. Matthews reminded the team that 'Hennessy's maybe barking up the wrong tree', but organised a stake-out on the Roscoe house just the same. He said we would give it a go for a few nights and maybe by then something 'stronger' would have turned up.

By good fortune No. 18, across the street from Roscoe's house, was vacant and we installed a man on the first floor, with an uninterrupted view of No. 15 and the houses on either side. Two men occupied a car parked down the street, away from the Freeman Road junction, and a hundred yards from the Roscoe house. My duty was to watch the back of the house. Each of the houses had a small back yard with a door through the continuous high wall on to the alleyway that ran the full length of the street. There was a broad area of waste ground across from the alley with a number of scattered derelict red brick square buildings. They looked like old air raid shelters. I was able to park behind one, hidden from observation, but with a clear outlook on to the back yard doors.

Our watch was to be from seven until midnight. The bus service stopped then. It seemed unlikely that he would want to be about on foot after that. Could look suspicious. Police patrols.

I'm going to cut to the chase here, David. First night a blank, nothing. Second night is one I'll never forget. I'd been sitting watching that back door for over three hours when it happened.

I swear, if I'd closed my eyes for a couple of seconds, for a yawn maybe, I'd have missed it. A dark shape seemed to detach itself from the black frame of doorway and kind of flicker indistinctly along the wall. I wasn't sure I was actually seeing something, and I had to shake my head and force my eyes to focus clearly on the dark moving shadow. The shape gradually morphed into the round-shouldered man-figure of Roscoe, making his way down the dimly lit alley. I radioed the car on Freeman Road. 'He's on the move, on foot heading south towards Bauer Road. Unless he turns back on to Clipper Street, he'll be coming out at the junction of Bauer Road and Freeman Road.'

Roscoe did just that, and caught a bus heading into the town centre. Our car dropped a man off two stops down, and he boarded the bus and sat upstairs a few seats behind the target, who was wearing dark trousers, a charcoal grey bomber jacket, and a black woollen beanie hat. Ten minutes later Roscoe got off the bus and walked straight into a bar on the corner of a side street. Our plain clothes man allowed some passengers to board, and hopped off the bus just as it was moving off. He entered the bar. There were only a few customers, and Roscoe wasn't one of them, but just then he appeared from the Gents' toilet and went out through the other exit, and into the side street. I had been kept informed of his movements on the car radio and was just a few yards away when I saw him come out of the side street and dodge his way through the traffic and across the busy main thoroughfare. I honestly don't think he knew he was being tailed, but, whatever his intention, he was making himself hard to shadow, and by the time I had managed to change lanes and direction he was nowhere in sight.

This was a part of Walton I knew well, and with good reason, because it was the district in which Joanne lived. Joanne. Suddenly a chill of fear passed through me, and in a flash I was reliving that moment when Roscoe had passed us in the street outside her work. She had said he was always watching. I knew by instinct what had happened. He had seen her remove the magnet from the fridge and take it with her, and had followed her outside. And I had carelessly allowed him to see us together...

At that instant, David, and for the first time, I was absolutely certain that Roscoe was our man, and that he was on his way to his intended third victim, his work colleague and my girlfriend, Joanne. Her house was just over half a mile further, but the route was through a maze of small side streets with cars parked on both sides, restricting the width to one car, and making progress agonizingly slow. I radioed in Joanne's address, and bullied my way through to her street. It was a row of small, detached bungalows with high straggling privet hedges masking the patches of garden and house fronts.

Can you believe that at the very instant I turned into the top end of the street, I was just in time to see a dark shadow at the far end slip into the gap in the hedge leading to her front door. I wrenched the car up on to the pavement and ran the distance to the entrance. For a split second I saw the lit doorway outlining the dark shape of a man, but even as I reached for the gate latch the light went off and the shape was gone. Whether he had been invited in, or had forced his way inside, I didn't have time to notice; the fact was that I was outside the closed door of a darkened house, and my girlfriend was inside at the mercy of a killer.

The next moments were an agony of indecision – the man in me wanted to rush to the door and bang on it or try to kick it open, or something similar; the trained man in me was telling me that would only alert Roscoe, waste precious seconds, and place Joanne in greater danger; the instinctive solution seeker in me reminded me that I had Joanne's spare key in the glove compartment of the car. Against every impulse and inclination, I turned back through the gate and ran with thumping heart *away* from Joanne's emergency situation.

The car door was lying open, and I found the key right away. In less than a couple of minutes I was back at Joanne's door. The house was quiet and dark. I turned the key in the lock and slowly pushed the door open, hoping for no creaks or squeaks. Nothing. The hallway was in darkness. As I stood listening to my own heart beating, I heard a kind of scuffling from the living room, the second door on the right. I tiptoed down the hall, turned the doorknob as quietly as I could, and then suddenly burst into the room.

I remember afterwards describing the scene that faced me as *hellish*. Remember, David, I was still a young man in my mid-twenties and hadn't the experience of over thirty years' crime scenes behind me. The only light in the room came from the coal fire, which was throwing a reddish glow and creating black shadows round the walls, just as this one is doing. What's missing here now is a white face of evil looking up at me with shock and fear and hatred, drool dribbling down the receding chin into the neck, the eyes black and blank. Roscoe was facing me from the floor. He was sitting straight up on his knees in the centre of the floor, with Joanne held tightly to him from behind. He had his left hand clamped round her mouth. Her legs were stretched out on the floor in front of her. All of this was subliminal. The only thing I could see, really focus on, was the syringe gripped in his right hand, the syringe he was about to plunge into her neck.

The sequence that followed was so sudden that I honestly cannot remember seeing it clearly. Roscoe must have involuntarily relaxed his stranglehold in his surprise, and Joanne drove back her head and shoulders with all her strength to such effect that he lost his balance and sprawled backwards, striking the back of his head on the tiled hearth. Joanne scrambled free of his hold. Things didn't stop there. I don't know whether a loose live coal was already lying on the hearth, or whether his fall knocked one loose, but next thing his mousey hair was on fire, and he was screaming in pain, or in rage, or both. Believe me, I took my time in coming to his aid.

That was the end of the John Nobody case. Roscoe was found guilty of the Miriam Torrens murder and the attempted murder of Joanne, and sentenced to a minimum of thirty years. We didn't even consider charging him with his mother's death. Needless to say, he never said a word before, during or after the trial. He hanged himself in his cell four years later.

You must be wondering, David, why I have told you all this, at such length and detail, especially since it has nothing to do with any proposed memoirs. Apart from its being my first big one, the Roscoe case is so atypical, so unlikely, that it would probably raise a great deal of scepticism, and would be of no real value as a police crime study. How many readers would believe that a detective's girlfriend just happens to suggest out of nowhere the identity of the killer in a baffling murder case? Coincidences like this just don't happen, especially to the advantage of a young detective on his first big case. I know if I were reading this in somebody else's memoirs, I'd enjoy a snigger or two of disbelief.

Then there's the dramatic ending bit, straight from screen fiction. It seems that nine out of ten crime dramas on television nowadays end with the good guy arriving just in the nick of time to thwart the villain and save the innocent victim. Apart from this case, in almost two hundred cases I've never seen that happen in real life. It's too neat, too storyboarded. Why, then, have I chosen to tell you this story 'from the files'? First of all, I think I told it for me more than for your sake. It's like a kind of catharsis or therapy for me. I don't come out of it too well, in truth. Joanne should get the credit. All I did was a little basic police work, and make a careless mistake that put her life in danger. It's good for me to remember that, but I don't get the opportunity too often to self-administer the treatment. Maybe that's why I like the coal fire in the darkness, not just to remember Roscoe's hair on fire, although I do enjoy that, but to remind me of the danger I landed Joanne in, and the fact that the case was cracked in the first place by a coal importer's secretary.'

Just at that moment the door was knocked gently and a trim lady in her sixties came in.

'For heaven's sake, Martin, are you at this nonsense again?' she scolded affectionately, turning on the wall lights. 'People will think we haven't paid our bill and the power's been cut off. Would your guest or you like tea or coffee?'

Martin declined the offer for both of us. The lady smiled in my direction and left.

'Maybe I should have introduced you,' said Hennessy, 'to my wife, Joanne, formerly of Diamond Coal Importers, but even after thirty years of marriage I'm still protective of her. I don't like her meeting strange men, especially spin doctors masquerading as Detective Constables,' and as he turned off the lights and lifted the Smirnoff bottle, that unmistakable Hennessy laugh resonated through the warmly lit room.

## The Boss

When John opened up just before nine o'clock on Saturday morning he saw that the shop phone had a number-withheld message, sent at 8.03am. He immediately guessed, no, he knew, both the identity of the caller and the import of the message. The *Play* confirmed this conviction:

*Hello. Message for Mr. Christie. This is Charlie. Sorry, but I can't make it in today. I think I'm coming down with the flu. I'm going to spend today and tomorrow in bed and try to catch it in time. I'm taking some powders, so hopefully I'll be in on Monday morning. Sorry. Bye.*

Frustration and irritation hit John immediately. Saturday, their busiest day, the one day of the week when he really needed Charlie, the day he tried to do enough business to make up for the commercial doldrums of the rest of the week. He would now have to shuttle between the shop counter and the yard, keeping customers waiting at both ends and, in all probability, discouraging them from using him again. John knew that during the course of the day his irritation would smoulder and finally develop into a helpless anger, but wouldn't mature into rage. He simply wasn't capable of explosive bursts of temper, it wasn't his nature or temperament to give vent to full-blooded rage.

John played the message again to fortify his feelings, '*I can't make it in*' – what he meant was '*don't want to*'. Then the '*hopefully*' should have read '*if I can be bothered*'. And the '*sorry*', twice. How easy to say, such a small word, but how big the bother and potential loss it was supposed to make up for. John's common sense told him he should sack Charlie, get somebody else, but he recoiled from the idea of having to start training a new assistant all over again. The truth was that Charlie was good at the job, the customers liked him, and John needed him. Yes, OK, John liked him too. That was part of his problem, and he knew it – he liked practically everybody.

If Charlie had been reliable, John would have overlooked a whole variety of faults. As it was, he was honest, friendly, good-natured, capable, and presentable, but these qualities counted for nothing if he wasn't here, if he couldn't be depended on to turn up. This latest absence was one of a number, all of them unexpected, last-minute ones that left John in the lurch, but this was the first Saturday non-appearance, and therefore the most serious.

John's business was struggling to stay afloat. In his heart he knew that his small town-centre Builders Suppliers couldn't hope to compete with the huge B&Q or Homebase giants at Bromfield, a mere eight miles away. Just recently, however, he had begun to notice a slight upturn in trade, and had been gratified by the comments of some returning customers who were 'fed up' with having to buy screws in plastic packets, pay with plastic cards, and be given no opportunity for a chat or a haggle. It was customers like these that his business had to court, to nurse; he couldn't afford to lose them through staff shortage or delay.

John believed in nurturing customer loyalty and offering the kind of friendly service that the big stores didn't concern themselves with. In the back yard he handled the timber, bricks, paving and building materials, and the cutting and loading, while Charlie expertly dealt with tools, accessories, and extras at the sales counter in the shop. Together they were a slick enough team; if only Charlie had a better attendance record.

John had a theory about employees' attitude to work in general. It wasn't a new one, by any means, just a rewording of the *'Some are born to lead, but most are born waiting to be led'* thesis. John's variation read, *'Some are born to be employers, most are born to be employees'*. He was a boss by birth, by nature, by inclination, while Charlie was a natural employee, born to take orders, to leave the leadership and planning to the boss. Charlie hadn't the drive nor the vision to be in control.

While John could see the attractions and satisfactions of both groups, he felt he could never be in the second one. There were times, admittedly, when he came close to envying the simpler life of the employee who just worked his hours, lifted his pay, and took his holidays, free of the worries and responsibilities that often beset his employer. He could never know, however, the challenge and the rewards of leading from the front, at the head of his own company, his own creation. John would never swap places, no matter how tough the going might get. A boss instinctively bought in to the work ethic, the worker didn't seriously care if times were tough or things went wrong, provided these things didn't affect him.

Just the same, for all his sense of achievement, there were enough frustrations and problems to raise uncomfortable questions in John's mind from time to time. The overheads were one such factor. Politicians, both local and national, were for ever singing the praises of small businesses, and stressing the need to support them as a vital part of the economy, but where did this verbal support translate into actual financial assistance? Where were the incentives and concessions that would make all the difference? Rates continued to rise every year, and electricity costs were crippling. It irked John to see street traders operating on the public pavements, people who paid no rent or rates or electricity bills to run their businesses, who were probably breaking all kinds of tax and health and safety rules, yet never seemed to be taken to task. It was law-abiding businesses like his that were the soft targets.

He had never been so glad in his life to close up the business, drive home, and get into the shower. The day had been hectic, crazy. John had literally spent the best part of it running, running between shop and yard, running with head stuffed with orders and hands with dockets and money. For eight years he had wished and willed customers to come into his premises; today, for the first time, he hoped the numbers would slow down, to give him a chance to catch up with the people already standing waiting. It was pure adrenaline that kept him going. He was so busy fielding the orders that he simply didn't have time to mope over Charlie's phone message and the last-minute cry-off that had given him no time to find a replacement, any replacement, even if one had been available.

One thing the day's experiences had done was to underline the need, especially at the weekend, for an assistant, whether that person be Charlie or a new employee. Whatever the case, John couldn't have another day like this one.

He slid the pizza from the microwave onto a plate, poured himself a chilled beer from the fridge, and settled into the soft embrace of his armchair to watch the rugby highlights on Channel 2. Oddly enough, to have had such an exhausting day, he didn't feel physically tired. Probably still on auto drive. The tiredness would no doubt hit him later.

A player was receiving treatment on the pitch and the camera switched at random to a section of the capacity crowd. Among the various funny placards and the HELLO MUM greetings, the sign that amused John was the one that read MY BOSS THINKS I'M OFF SICK. He was enjoying the joke when the camera panned around the crowd and in an instant the smile froze on his face. His eye had picked out a familiar figure. Surely that was Charlie on the terraces. John had only a couple of seconds at most before the camera moved on round and the man was out of picture, but he had seen enough of the longish hair and thin black moustache to be *almost* sure. His errant employee had been attending the rugby international when he should have been in bed with the flu, or, more realistically, should have been behind the counter in the Builders Suppliers.

The feelings that this discovery produced in John were a rich brew of dismay, anger, sense of betrayal, and perplexity. Why had the man felt the need to tell him a deliberate lie? Why had he not asked for a day off, and given John time to find a substitute? Was this how he repaid the considerateness that John always tried to show him? Mixed with John's disappointment and feeling of affront was a hint of self-pity – he would like a day off now and again, he would enjoy going to see a rugby international, but nobody cared about that, nobody considered his wants or whims. It went with the job, with the position, he told himself. Nobody expected the boss to have hungers and hankerings outside of the workplace.

What to do now? John's instinct was to keep his powder dry and to fire Charlie as soon as he arrived again for work, whether Monday or later in the week, but cooler counsel had its say. He wasn't totally sure that the man he had glimpsed on the screen was Charlie. It could have been a lookalike. John's enjoyment of the game was killed off, but he watched the rest of the highlights closely in case the same section of crowd was shown again. No luck. A pity he hadn't recorded it.

That forced a decision. He would visit Charlie next day, Sunday morning, ostensibly to enquire about his condition, and to take him his week's pay. He would make sure to have Charlie's pay with him, just in case he was in bed and his flu was for real. John hoped deep within himself that such would be the case. If, however, he found him up and about, fit and fine, he would terminate the employment then and there. Thinking about the bother involved in advertising the job, interviewing people for it, and having to train somebody from scratch, was enough to make him feel slightly depressed.

298 Maye Road. John wasn't familiar at all with the south side of town and had to use his satnav to find it. He was surprised to notice that the built-up part of the road ended at 112 and the houses became separate and increasingly far apart as he left town, so that he had to slow down every so often and check the numbers on individual dwellings, many of them bungalows, to determine his position. He eventually located the number 298 on a piece of board stuck in the front hedge of a modest cottage about half a mile from its nearest neighbour. John checked his watch. It was close on half eleven. He left the car on the roadside in front of the small gate and made his way up the weedy path to the faded green door.

The only response his repeated loud knocking produced was a continuous shrill barking from a yappy dog inside, in time with its scratching sounds on the door. John gave up on the hope that his rapping would be answered. He was holding Charlie's pay packet in his hand but resisted the impulse to put it through the letter box. The dog would probably shred it, and it would only tip Charlie off that he had called.

Better to surprise him with that information when he arrived back at work.

John made his way round the side of the house. There was no sign of Charlie's car. He stood undecided for a moment, and then noticed a large wooden shed about fifty or sixty yards away at the bottom of the cottage's plot of land. Maybe Charlie kept his car in the shed, or was himself working in it. As John drew close he could hear a faint humming coming from the shed, but the hope that his employee was inside was killed when he saw that the door was padlocked on the outside. Still, he was curious about the humming noise, and his curiosity grew when he reached the shed and noticed a distinctly pungent smell in the air. It was unlike any smell he had experienced before, strong and like a mix of other smells, pleasant and unpleasant. It was sweet and spicy, like a blend of hay and celery and wet chicken feathers.

John tried the lock, but it was good. He noticed, though, that the door was curved inwards a little at the top and bottom, not tight against the doorstop, and when he pushed hard near the top, he was able to push open a gap of about an inch. John looked round him. Not surprisingly, nobody in sight. He pulled over a rusty wheelbarrow, placed it along the door, stepped up into it, forced the gap about half an inch wider and jammed his flat hand in to keep it open. He peered in.

John's first impression was that he was looking at night-time into a brightly lit forest floor, a green spread of ferns or some such plants. The light was all downwards on to the plants, while all above was dim darkness. Two other impressions, or sensations, complemented these visuals, a dry heat that made him blink, and an intensification of the smell, which was now not unlike burnt marshmallows, sickly sweet. John knew at once what he was looking at. He had seen a television documentary on the nationwide spread of home cannabis growing and had read of police raids on cannabis factories both locally and across the country.

John drove home with a mind like his shop the day before, a centre of busy activity. So Charlie had a sideline going. There was more to him than the cheery, laid-back shop assistant that the public saw, himself included. What was he to do about this discovery? Part of him looked forward to his next meeting with Charlie, another part dreaded it. He would play things by ear, do or say nothing rash until he had a better grasp of the situation...

'Good morning, Mr. Christie. How's it going?'
'Fine, thanks, Charlie. How are you? Did you manage to get over your flu?'
'Getting there, thanks to Mrs. Cullen.'
'Good. Glad to hear it. Did you manage to see the rugby on Saturday?'
'Rugby? No, not my scene, rugby.'
'You didn't see the highlights on TV?'
'No. No interest.' Charlie sounded genuinely puzzled by these rugby questions, and John decided to cut to the chase.
'Maybe the flu knocked you out completely and you were dead to the world. You were certainly dead to my knocking on your door,

Charlie, when I called on Sunday morning to give you this,' holding up the pay packet. 'Even your dog barking its head off couldn't waken you. And where do you keep your car, by the way?'

Charlie's pallid complexion whitened a shade further. He opened his mouth to speak, but then thought better of it, and leaned an elbow on the counter.

'Didn't know you were into gardening, Charlie.'

'Gardening?' he managed, the word barely audible.

'Yes, gardening. Growing things. Growing plants, for example. Looks like you're a bit of an expert.'

There was a pause of a good half minute, during which Charlie's face had the appearance of a man trying to make a big choice, a major decision. Finally, he sighed, perhaps with relief, and looked John straight in the eye.

'I'm genuinely sorry, Mr. Christie, to have been telling you lies. I only did it to be safe, to protect myself, not through any disrespect to you. You've always been fair to me, and I didn't like having to lie to you. Now that you know the truth, or a bit of it, I won't need to tell you any more lies. That's the truth, for a start.

Yes, I'm growing weed out at the house. Can I tell you how it started? You see, my dad, he died four years ago, got injured working in Keegle Quarry. He damaged his spine badly and went through two big operations, but he lived in pain every day. The doctors said it was damaged nerves, chronic neuropathic pain they called it, and gave him any number of different painkillers, but none of them did the business. A friend told him to try cannabis, and he found it really did give him relief, but it was difficult and expensive to get from the dealers. That's why I started growing it myself at home in a very small way, for medicinal purposes, to ease my dad's suffering.

I'm not making excuses, Mr. Christie, I could and should have stopped once my dad died, but by then I was into the growing, it had become a kind of hobby and I had expanded it and spent a bit of money on equipment and setting things up.

I want you to know this, Mr. Christie I'm not a user myself, never have been, and never will be. The truth is, I've become a fairly big supplier of weed, both for medicinal and recreational purposes. I want to be totally straight with you, and I'll understand if you don't take it too well. You see, I'm really only working for you as a front for my other business. I need to be earning an income, otherwise I would have to sign on the dole. Once you're getting unemployment benefit, or Jobseeker's Allowance as they call it nowadays, you're an open target. The last people I want snooping about are the DWP boys. As long as I'm declaring an income and paying tax, nobody's interested in me.'

'So the days you took off were to look after your 'other business'?'

'Yes, but as few as I could. I didn't like letting you down and making up excuses for being off, but every so often there were things needing to be taken care of.'

'So it wasn't you at the rugby match on Saturday. I thought I saw you on TV in the crowd.'

'No chance. I've never been at a rugby match in my life, and don't intend to be at one in the future.'

There was a silence between the two men until Charlie broke it with, 'So where do we go from here?'

'As a good citizen I should report you to the police or HMRC or somebody, I suppose, but that would do neither of us any good. Any ideas?'

'How about I give you something for your silence, say a lump sum of a few grand, or a few hundred every week? Or maybe I could go on working for you as usual, taking no wages but declaring the income as normal. How would that work for you?'

'No, couldn't do it. Taking a bribe from my employee, or asking him to work every day for nothing? It wouldn't be on.'

Charlie made a couple of false starts, but managed it at the third attempt, 'Well, how about this – and give it a bit of thought. What if you could work a bit on the sly for me? I'm under pressure and a bit of help would be very welcome. You could do a few hours maybe on a Sunday, or the odd evening, and I'd pay you very well. You'd earn the money that way. It would be criminal activity, let's be straight about that, but you'd be very low profile, I'd be the one taking whatever small risk there might be.'

John digested the idea. His first impulse was to dismiss it straight off. The idea of himself working for Charlie was an assault upon his esteem, but his business mind started to explore the possibility, and began to overrule his pride. He had already been considering the idea of closing on Mondays, the slowest day of the week, and that would free up some time for him to help Charlie out. More than anything, though, the notion of easy extra money, tax free, was very appealing.

'Think about it,' said Charlie. 'Why don't you come out one Sunday morning and I'll show you round the operation, give you an idea of how it works and what would be involved?'

John couldn't have said afterwards which had impressed him more, the operation or the operator; one thing he could have said without reservation, both had impressed him mightily. He had gone out the following Sunday as suggested, 'without commitment by either party', and after being formally introduced to the yappy dog, a Yorkshire terrier called Molly, had been taken on 'a tour of the factory', as Charlie put it. The shed was larger than John had thought, 40 feet by 30 feet, he was informed. Charlie pointed out the salient features; the windows boarded up on the outside; the entire interior walls and ceiling clad in black polythene that had been stapled into the wood; the battery of electric lights suspended from above and hanging over the plants, that sat in black plastic pots and covered the entire floor area, with little access paths through them.

'What's the chicken wire for?' John asked.

'Good question. It's what we call the SCROG method of growing, screen of green.

Cannabis plants grow very tall, too tall, so we use the chicken wire to contain them, to hold them back so that they don't burn under the intense heat of the lights.' Charlie spoke in the plural, as though he were representing some corporate association or professional body. 'We use about 2,000 watts daily, running a twelve-hour day. There's a timer on the lighting. Some indoor growers use what are called tents, made from the same black polythene, to isolate the heat.'

As he pointed out the various features and details of the process, Charlie spoke not only with authority and knowledge, but with the pride of the successful entrepreneur. John could hardly square this confident, energetic businessman with the casual, slightly languid shop assistant he saw during the week.

'The big problem, believe it or not, is the smell. You'll know already why it's called skunk cannabis. That's how a lot of growers get caught, the smell gives them away. You hear that low hum? That's from the six-inch extractor ventilator I put in. Here's the beauty of it. It has a carbon filter that draws the smell out of the air. We call it a scrubber. Worth every penny. If it wasn't there, you could smell this place half a mile away. The smell only starts when the plants start flowering, usually during the final four weeks of the crop's three-month growth.'

Charlie went on to give a full tutorial on seeds, seedlings, vegetative stages, harvesting, watering, over-watering, temperature control, powdery white mildew mould, and soil nutrient feeding. He was enjoying the opportunity to share with someone the knowledge and skills that by necessity he had to keep secret. John had never heard him so animated, so articulate.

'Do you not live in fear of getting caught, Charlie?' They were having a beer in the house after a tour that John had found both interesting and enjoyable.

'Well, I suppose that fear is always there whenever you're doing something against the law. Some growers put bars on their widows and even grille contraptions, like a portcullis, over the door, but that's a giveaway in my eyes. That only draws attention, rouses suspicion.'

'So you take no precautions at all?'

'Oh, I take some, Mr. Christie. That's why I asked you to park round at the back of the house. Nosy neighbours, and there aren't too many of them, might wonder who was calling with me. Also, I never do any business from the house, nor do I ever sell directly to the customers on the street. I'm a kind of middle-man, you might say, a supplier to a couple of very big players who take all my stuff. I take it to them, they don't come to me. There's another precaution I take, which affects, or should I say affected, you. I've diverted the electricity supply, illegally of course, to the factory to grow the weed. Now, I'm never at home when the man comes to read my meter, but he always leaves a card to say when he'll call back. Those were the days when I was off work. I had to be at home to hide the evidence. My normal domestic usage isn't affected and shows on the reading as usual.'

'You're a thorough scoundrel, Charlie,' said John with a laugh.

'Yes, a right rotten one. OK, what I'm doing is completely illegal. I mightn't feel like one, and I hope I don't look like one, but in the eyes of the law I'm an out and out criminal. There's something else I should mention. The authorities are not the only people who would be happy to find my factory. Believe me, there's a lot of bad guys, really bad guys, out there, enforcers, dangerous and violent criminals who make a living from raiding and stealing other people's stuff. Most growers are more afraid of them than they are of the police.

You can see what you'd be getting into, Mr. Christie, if you were working for me, but let me put your mind at ease at least a bit, if I can. If you were working for me, it would be on a need-to-know basis. I'd only tell you what you had to learn to look after the weed. You wouldn't be involved at all with selling or distributing, you wouldn't know the buyers, and they wouldn't know about you. If I was raided, provided you weren't here at the time, I wouldn't mention you to anyone, good guys or bad guys. I promise you that on my mother's name. You'd be out of the frame altogether. Think about it, and remember this: I've been growing skunk now for seven years, and nobody seems to suspect a thing.'

How much John had learned in just five months. He was working in the factory every Monday, Sunday afternoons, and an occasional evening if needed. Charlie continued to 'work' for him Tuesday through Saturday, taking no salary but credited as earning his normal pay, while John earned £300 a week in the factory. It was a bizarre but eminently workable arrangement, and they both enjoyed the switching of employer/employee roles. They called themselves The Odd Couple.

John became so used to the smell of the flowering cannabis plants that he never noticed it. He knew now that it was only the female plants that produced the all-important buds, and that after the flowers had been harvested, they needed a week to be dried and two weeks' curing. It was satisfying work, creative and relaxing. He never considered the possible social, physical or mental harmfulness of their crop.

John was in a quandary. The local cricket club had somehow persuaded a travelling South African team to play a one-day match at The Vale Meadows, and some big-name international players were in the visitors' eleven. He was hungry to see the match. Had the Builders Suppliers still been open on Mondays he would definitely have closed for the day to see the game, but this particular Monday was, by chance, an important one in the factory. Charlie and he had earmarked it to separate the Indica and Sativa strains, to remove the male plants to prevent pollination, and to do an overall topping of the screen of green. Yes, tomorrow would be a busy day for both men. As a boss John knew how Charlie would feel if he let him down, but as an employee he felt that for one day he should be allowed a little bit of slack.

He picked up the phone. Which would it be? Chest infection, flu symptoms, or the trusty old vomiting and diarrhoea combo...

## *Valuables*

'Well, at least he doesn't do drugs. That's the only good thing I can say about him. Wait a minute, that's what they should put on *his* headstone: *R.I.P. Carlo Benton. At least he didn't do drugs.*'

The gibe was rewarded with a round of ragged dry laughter, which was better than anything else the past half hour had produced. The sad little funeral ceremony and the interment were over, and Annie lived on only in their memories. The family had come straight to the pub after the burial for sandwiches and a couple of drinks. Needless to say, Carlo had not been there to see his half-sister laid to rest, and the remainder of the family now united once more in maligning everything about him. Any time the family met together it was the custom to vilify Carlo in every possible way, but this time the invective was particularly bitter in the light of his non-appearance at Annie's funeral. In any case, it was easier to abuse their wayward half-brother than to talk about the suffering and passing of poor Annie at the age of thirty-one.

Most, perhaps all, of their criticism was accurate and deserved, but there was an element in its delivery that introduced a less justifiable note, envy. For all their condemnation of Carlo's career, behaviour, lifestyle, they betrayed at moments a resentment that derived from the most basic and personal envy of all, jealousy of appearance. Carlo had the Italianate looks of his mother, darkest-brown eyes, Mediterranean complexion, jet black hair and eyebrows, while his three half-brothers and two half-sisters had, without exception, inherited the mousey hair, pale eyes, pasty skin and weak chin of their mother, Carlo's stepmother. Small wonder they found it difficult to find the humour in his throwaway line, 'I wish I had been born rich instead of good-looking.'

That same note of envy was occasionally present in their castigation of his mother, 'the runaway Romany', 'the gypsy vagrant', 'the travelling tramp'; a well-tuned ear could detect a hint of regret that their own lives were so bereft of romantic adventure and excitement. *The Lovely Benedetta*, as she had been billed on the circus posters, had been a tightrope walker and trapeze artist in a low-grade travelling circus when Harry Benton had found her late one evening at the side of the road near the large area of waste ground that was home for a week to *Giordano's World Famous International Circus*. She was partly drunk and was bleeding from the nose and mouth after a violent argument with a bad-tempered clown. Harry had picked her up in his van, listened to her threatenings and whimperings, taken her to his home to get cleaned up, and had 'comforted' her.

The result of his comforting became clear eight months later when she arrived out of nowhere at Harry's door, heavily pregnant and demanding justice for herself and a home for 'our bambino'. Six weeks later, after the birth of the bambino, the lovely Benedetta disappeared, and Harry was left literally holding the baby.

Word had it that his marriage to Ivy just seven months later was for the sole purpose of securing someone else to hold the baby, and the absence of any signs of affection between the pair thereafter served to confirm this belief. The arrangement was in the nature of a two-sided coin, however. If Harry showed no affection for Ivy, she in turn showed none at all for the baby she had inherited; Carlo grew up under the care of a woman who in every sense was his mother in name only. With almost vengeful haste she produced five children of her own in the extraordinary space of just over four years.

Psychologists and students of human behaviour, especially those interested in the nature vs. nurture debate, could argue at considerable length whether Carlo's later behaviour was the genetic legacy passed down from an irresponsible, rootless mother, or the result of acquired characteristics learned in an arena of unloving parents and hostile siblings. Whatever the case, he learned very quickly at school how people in general are guilty of a basic misunderstanding – they equate attractiveness of face with goodness of behaviour. Carlo's teachers at Primary School were so won over by his fetching features and disarming smile that they initially never suspected him of various little classroom misdemeanours, pilfering, cheating, and the like. The magistrates he eventually came before as his life of crime developed had no such confusion, and branded him *'an utter rascal'*, *'an unprincipled rogue'*, *'a heartless scoundrel'*, *'an accomplished fraudster'*...

The little group of mourners in the pub were expressing similar value judgements, if expressed in distinctly more earthy terms. Had they known where their reprobate half-brother was at that same time, they would no doubt have been surprised, but only a little surprised, and only for a moment or two. They would, quite rightly, have figured that he was up to another one of his moves.

Carlo held the thin, blue-veined hand of his Aunt Martha and looked at the wrinkled, age-spotted skin hanging on her skeletal wrist. She was in the female ward of the hospital's Care of the Elderly Department, the Last Chance Saloon, as it was commonly known. He had gone there, as his relatives would have inferred, with an eye to the main chance, but after a word with the Ward Sister and a minute's futile attempts to communicate with his father's last remaining sister, he knew his visit was a wild goose chase. There was nothing he could do, nothing in it for him.

Carlo looked idly round the ward. It was bizarre how all the elderly patients looked the same, as though age and illness conspired to render them anonymous. The patient in the bed next to Aunt Martha seemed to be the only one who wasn't sleeping. She was propped up against the pillows and was absorbed in a book, which Carlo assumed would be a Bible, but when he sneaked a look over, he found to his surprise and amusement that it was a Karin Slaughter crime novel.

At that same moment an attractive blonde woman of about forty arrived at the old woman's bedside and bent down to kiss her on the forehead, before taking the chair that faced across to Carlo's seat at the other side of Aunt Martha's bed. Carlo, by instinct, rested his forehead in the crook of his hand so that he could peer through the blur of his fingers, but giving the appearance of not looking or listening.

'Hi, Gran. Lovely to see you. How are you?'

'I'm OK, Lola, and feeling better now that you're here. You're not looking so bad yourself, for your age.'

Lola laughed. 'You haven't lost your sense of humour, Gran, and I see you're still reading those dreadful murder stories. Can you not find something nicer than, let me see, *Cold, Cold Heart*?'

'Something lovey-dovey and romantic, no doubt. Look around you, Lola. Hardly the kind of setting for love stories. On that subject, how's your own love-life, or is it none of my business? Not that that would matter. Remember, I haven't changed my opinion, every woman deserves to love and have the love of one good man; my advice is still the same, marry for love, never for any other reason.'

Lola laughed again. 'You never change, Gran, I'm glad to say. No, nobody at the present time, but he's still out there somewhere, I hope. There's still just me and Jack.'

'How is Jack?'

'Fine. Can you believe he's nearly six? Where have the years gone? Millicent's looking after him. Her little girl and Jack play in the back garden.'

Carlo checked the woman's wedding finger. Bare. Mother, possibly widowed, but more likely to be a single parent, or separated. On the look-out for a partner, probably, and ideal for a con. His career was littered with such women, women he had deceived and exploited, but none he had ever considered for a moment as a wife or long-term partner. Carlo never saw a relationship with a woman, sexual, romantic or social, as an end in itself, but always as a means to another end, personal gain. He began sizing this situation up as an opportunity that would justify his visit to the hospital and make up for his disappointment with Aunt Martha. He knew that if the blonde woman looked across she would see an attractive man, in his mid to late thirties, showing love and concern for an old, possibly comatose, woman.

Just at that point the voices from the next bed were lowered a pitch and he sensed more weighty matters were in hand. He knelt closer over the bed and with his lips showing below the fingers began silently muttering 'rhubarb, rhubarb'. A man praying over an elderly lady wouldn't be thought to be eavesdropping.

'No, I'm serious, Lola, not for myself, but for you. Look at all these pipes and tubes and things sticking into me and coming out of me in places I never knew I had. You see, I can't eat. I just can't eat. I'm wearing this dressing gown so that you won't see what's left of your old Gran, but she now weighs in at only six stone.

At eighty-nine I haven't much time left, Lola, and I need to talk to you. Now, I don't want you to cry, I want you to listen. Listen, that's all I want you to do for me. I've my affairs all in order, all written down. The house and all my belongings are to be sold and everything divided equally among Julia, Ronnie and you. Now here's the important bit, Lola, the bit that concerns only you. The really valuable pieces, and you alone know where they are, are just for you. Grans are allowed to have favourites, you know, and the freedom to give special presents to their favourite grandchild, and that's why I showed you the real gems and their hiding place all those years ago when you were just a teenager. Let Julia and Ronnie squabble over the trinkets. You've always been your Gran's blue-eyed girl and my last wish is that you now receive what I told you then would one day be yours. You remember? OK, do what your old Gran wants, and that will make me happy.'

Carlo heard every word and felt the excitement rise in him. What luck. Just when it seemed he was on a loser, the wheel of fortune had turned in his favour. As the woman finally got up to leave, she promised to call at her Gran's house on the way home and pick up 'the special presents' the old girl had mentioned. Carlo was already thinking of a fence he knew who specialised in family heirlooms, especially jewels. He was a man of 'honesty and discretion' who would give him a fair price.

He allowed a few moments after she left and then, with a sorrowing face, kissed Aunt Martha on the cheek and made his way out of the ward. He followed her to the car park. She was parked just a couple of rows behind him. He tailed her red Nissan Micra out of the car park in his worn Toyota Yaris, and kept a couple of cars between them as she headed south.

Carlo disliked this procedure, the element of chance and risk in it. He wasn't in control of things. Just the wrong red light, or a minor hold-up in the traffic flow, and he could easily lose her. Fortunately, the traffic was fairly light, and the two sets of traffic lights presented no problems, but it was a relief nonetheless when she signalled a left turn into a street about three miles from the hospital. Lavender Road. The Micra parked on the left and Carlo pulled in on the other side of the street about fifteen yards behind. He watched as she got out and opened a wooden gate into the small garden of a two-storey redbrick terrace house. Carlo had an uninterrupted view as she opened the door and went inside.

In truth he didn't know exactly how he was going to handle things, but he had full confidence in himself to decide what was the best course of action as the situation arose. The more he thought about it as he sat and watched and waited, the more it seemed best if he continued to follow her until an opportunity presented itself or an idea or plan came to him. Carlo sometimes used the threat of violence, but never violence itself. To wait just until she was coming back out of the house, and then either force her back inside or do a snatch on the doorstep and flee the scene would be far from perfect, and certainly not his style.

The house had been empty for only five days but already it had that fusty, unlived-in smell that older houses brew in their owners' absence. Lola noticed it as soon as she went in. The smell depressed her; it was the smell of age and decay. She noticed too, a thin film of dust on the furniture, and a moistness came into her eyes. Here were the pieces her Gran had loved and tended, keeping everything clean and dusted, and now they seemed to be mocking, undermining, all her life's endeavours. Ashes to ashes, dust to dust. Before she would retrieve the items she had come for, Lola found the spray polish and a duster and set about removing the thin layer from the main articles of furniture in the front room. To have come into the house just to take, to remove, would have felt like a kind of desecration.

When she had finished the task, the fragrance of polish in the air and the gleam of the furniture lifted her mood and she went to the glory hole, to the hiding place of what they had called at the time 'The Treasure Trove'. One of the stairs jutted down from above into the cupboard space beneath the staircase, creating a niche that couldn't be seen but could be felt by extending the arms, bending the elbows, and reaching back into the slanted space. Lola did so now and immediately felt the square edges of the box. She withdrew it carefully and there it was, the same green shoebox her Gran had first shown her twenty-five years ago when she was about fifteen and was spending two weeks of her summer holidays in Lavender Road while her mother recovered from a respiratory illness. She blew off some of the dust, carried the box into the kitchen and wiped it clean with a moistened piece of kitchen roll. Lola was too emotional to open the box and examine the contents right there and then. She took a final look around the downstairs room, opened the front door, and with feelings of gratitude, sorrow, and guilt, carried her treasure down the little garden path.

What was keeping her? Carlo had expected her to be back out of the house in a matter of minutes, but a quarter of an hour was gone and still no sign of her. Surely she didn't have to dig the stuff up, or something like that? His criminal mind wondered if maybe she had made him follow her from the hospital, and had slipped out the back door, but her car still parked outside the house made that unlikely. Just then the front door opened, and she was walking to the car carrying a green box. Whatever the reason for the delay, she had got the jewels. Carlo waited until she had moved off before resuming the careful pursuit. He was more anxious than ever about losing her now that she was in possession of the valuables.

It was as easy as he could have wished. The red car, after a few minutes, swung into a residential area of detached and semi-detached houses and bungalows in what had the appearance of a development constructed in the last twenty years or so. The car finally slowed, signalled, and turned into the driveway of a detached bungalow a few hundred yards from the corner. Carlo stopped and watched as the woman parked down the side of the house and went in through the front door, carrying the box and her handbag. There was a row of these bungalows all in the same style, all with the same low wall dividing them from the pavement, the square of lawn, the garage set back down the side of the house. He eased forward and parked at the kerb right in front of the house, screened from the view of anyone inside by a rhododendron bush tight against the low wall, but able, himself, to see through its broad leaves. Carlo sat back and waited for something to develop.

A short time later, no more than five minutes, the front door opened and a woman and young girl appeared, while the woman he had tailed followed them and stood in the doorway talking to them. Carlo could hear every word.

'Thanks again, Millicent. I'm really grateful. I might well have to take you up again on your babysitting offer, depending on the hospital visiting hours. I forgot to take a note of them. Anyhow, bring Susan down to play with Jack any time you want. He enjoys the company. Bye, Susan, hope you enjoyed it.'

Carlo watched in his wing mirror as Millicent and the little girl left on foot in the direction he had come. They didn't look to their right towards where he was parked about twelve yards away. He sat back and took stock of the scenario. Lola and her son were in the house on their own, and the box of jewels was in there too. The child was a kind of advantage. It would be easier, if things came to such a pitch, to persuade the mother by threatening violence to her son. Carlo wasn't quite sure how to progress the situation and was almost at the point of getting out of his car and knocking on the front door when things took a decided turn in his favour.

Lola came out of the house carrying a waste-paper basket in one hand and a tied, bulging plastic bag in the other. She pulled the door to with the point of her foot and went towards the corner of the house.

A judge about to sentence Carlo had once labelled him '*an artful opportunist*'. He had been so pleased with the compliment that he had almost said, 'Thank you, your Worship.' Had the judge been there at that moment to witness what happened next, he would have complimented himself on the accuracy of his description. In just a few seconds Carlo had slid out of the car, hopped over the low wall, skipped across the ten yards of lawn, and was in through the open door. He pulled it to without shutting it and slipped into the room on his right, hiding himself behind its half open door. All this took place while Lola emptied the rubbish into her bin sitting at the garage. Carlo was in place behind the front room door less than ten seconds when he heard her come back into the house and close the door shut. He held his breath and listened to the kitchen sounds of crockery and cutlery. The words that followed were as welcome to him as a blessing.

'I'm slipping down to the shop for milk, Jack. Be back in a couple of minutes. You behave yourself.' No reply. Chances were the boy was in his room engrossed in some computer game or the like. Then he heard the front door open and close with a click. With a bit of luck, he could locate the box and be out of the house and away, completely unseen. Carlo braced himself for the luck needed to find the box right away, eased himself round the door and into the hall, and found himself face to face with Jack.

As soon as she got back with the milk, she would make herself a pot of strong, fresh coffee and then have a look at the items in the box. It was twenty-five years, or thereabouts, since they had been shown to her, but the impression they had made on a girl in her early teens was indelible.

She had been sitting, that day, in the back garden in Lavender Road when her Gran had arrived out of the house with the box and sat down beside her, opened it, and took out a small bundle of letters tied in a red ribbon, and a couple of old black and white square photographs. She had started to speak earnestly and fondly to her youngest grand-daughter. It was the first time Lola had been spoken to in such a way, had been entrusted with secrets, adult family things she had never seriously thought about before, and afterwards she had felt privileged, and strangely nervous in a new, unaccountable way. Her Gran's words came back to her now from the distance of a quarter of a century as she wandered down the aisles of the large, modern garage shop. She could nearly smell the fragrance of sweet pea and roses that she always associated with this particular memory.

'Lola, I want to tell you about your grandad. I'm talking about your real grandad, not the one you and your brother and sister used to call Grampa. That's your real grandad, there, in the photo, the young, handsome soldier with his back to the tank. His name was David. He was in the 49th Regiment of the British Armoured

*Corps. These photos were taken in 1944 during the Second World War. He was my one true love, and the father of my only child, your mother. I was only eighteen, and three months pregnant with your mum, when I got the news that he had been killed when his tank hit a land mine.*

*We had so many dreams, so many plans, David and I, but you can read about them all in these letters. They're all here, and I want you to inherit them some day. This will be our secret. I haven't told Julia or Ronnie. The only other person who knows the secret is your mum, and I kept it from her for over twenty years until your brother and sister and you were no longer infants. My one big regret is that I didn't tell David I was expecting his child. I didn't want to worry him on my behalf, put pressure on him. I intended to tell him, but I left it too late.*

*Things were very different back then, Lola. An unmarried mother was bad news all round in society's eyes. I married your Grampa two months before your mum was born. He had always wanted me, loved me, I suppose, right from school days. I told him, of course, from the start about my condition, and he accepted it. I'm not saying anything bad about him, he was a good man in his own quiet way, earnest and steady, but I never loved him. I married him for the baby's sake. It was never a happy marriage for either of us, and the fact that we couldn't have children to keep my daughter company didn't help. As you know, he died quietly, the way he had lived, just over seven years ago. He was in his mid-sixties, you maybe remember.*

*You're wondering why I'm telling you this now. Well, it's not often I get the opportunity to talk to you privately, my dear, but also, you're old enough now to understand. Best reason of all is this: I want to tell you, before all the boyfriend stuff starts, to be patient, to choose carefully, to find a man who truly loves you and who you love in return. That's the most valuable thing of all, more valuable than money or career or status or reputation. You owe it to yourself.'*

These words were circulating in Lola's head as she headed towards the chilled counter. Part of her looked forward to reading the love letters her Gran had been sent seventy years ago, another part dreaded it, as if in having them and reading them she was reading her Gran's obituary. She lifted a carton of milk and was moving towards the check-out when a special offer sign caught her eye. It was advertising cooked chicken pieces at a real bargain price. Cooked chicken. Jack loved it and would devour it with almost the same relish as he devoured his favourite food, raw meat.

The blood was pumping out of Carlo's shredded face and splashing on to the tiled floor. He didn't know exactly how he had managed to break free from the snarling, biting jaws and pinning paws of the demon dog, or how he had got the door of the bathroom slammed behind him. The terrible scratching and growling outside the door might have underlined how lucky he had been to find refuge from the Dobermann, had he not caught a look at himself in the bathroom cabinet mirror. The gouged and ripped face that was looking back at him through strips of torn flesh underlined something altogether different. He had lost, for ever, the most precious thing he had ever possessed, the natural good looks that were the only valuables he had ever been honestly entitled to.

## *Crusade*

People were so vulnerable, innocently and stubbornly vulnerable. Every day they just kept on leaving themselves wide open to whatever advantage a predator might choose to take of them. Such creatures of habit. He knew all about their vulnerability. He had studied it, learned from it, knew how to exploit it.

Intentionally or otherwise, the public led repetitive lives, even when free to choose varied and flexible alternatives. Those who worked, the majority, were of course constrained by working hours, the timetables and disciplines of job requirements, but even allowing for this, how easily they set themselves up to be watched, logged, followed: the same route every day to and from work, the same bus, the same train. Even at weekends or during after-work hours, they stuck to a self-imposed routine, the same shopping programme, the same recreational and social activities.

As for the unemployed and the retired, who might have been thought more likely to lead less patterned lives, they exhibited similarly regular habits and behaviour. It was as though people preferred a regulated way of life, the comfort of the familiar, the mindlessness of the mechanical.

Knowing all this, feeding off it, he sometimes wondered why the crime rate wasn't much higher. There were easy targets, potential victims out there for those who took the time and interest to identify them. That was where he would stand out and excel. For him, the actual crime would be just the icing on the cake, the last few yards over the finish line. Indeed, in his plans the crime would be just the means to an end, just part of a larger purpose and design. It was the whole process of the climb, the planning and preparation, the fastidious prosecution of it, that he would enjoy even more than reaching the summit. He would raise rape to a practical science, a professional practice.

He had chosen carefully, pragmatically, but in reality it had been an easy choice. Rape ticked all the boxes. Crimes like robbery or fraud or burglary were never going to make the headlines. He needed an interpersonal offence. He had briefly considered kidnapping or abduction, but had quickly dismissed them. They were complicated businesses and carried too many risks. The big attraction of rape was that, in the public mind, it was second only to murder in the table of serious crimes. The general feeling was that it was a heinous offence that deserved to be front-page news.

He read it up with characteristic thoroughness. What he learned from a number of reports produced by experts, served only to encourage him, to ratify his choice. The serial rapist who attacked strangers, which was what he intended to be, was distinct from the rapist whose victims were known to him, members of family or circle of friends. The rapist who chose his victims at random was said to be impulsive, and therefore likely to leave behind physical evidence that would eventually lead to his conviction in court. He smiled as he read this. No chance in the wide world of such carelessness on his part.

According to the authorities on the subject, the sexual predator was allegedly motivated by deviant impulses, or by the need to express his power over women, to dominate them, humiliate them, either from resentment, anger or hostility towards women in general, or from some sadistic compulsion. Well, none of this had any relevance to himself. He felt no urge to control women, he wasn't driven by any macho-aggressive, hostile masculinity. If these learned reports were not so much nonsense, then he would be different from the rapist stereotype to the extent that all accepted findings and conclusions would be utterly inaccurate and irrelevant. And so much the better. He would be so unlike the established perceptions of the rapist, that the investigators would have no angle on him at all.

Again, it was claimed that sexual offenders in the majority of cases had a childhood background or history of physical or sexual abuse, or of neglect. Way off target again in reference to himself. In fact, the only stuff he read that seemed at all relevant to his own ideas and intentions was the assertion that some sexual attacks were pre-meditated. That would be a glorious understatement in his case. He would choose his targets at random, not specialising in one particular category, but selecting from different age and class groups. He would use only as much violence, or threat of violence, as would be needed to coerce his victims into submission.

He had nothing against women. Why would he want to terrify them beyond simple compliance? The standard rapist figure, the knife-wielding man in a ski mask, was something he could use to this end. It should be enough.

Neither was he interested in or motivated by simple sexual gratification. If that was all he wanted, he could buy it on any street corner in certain districts.

The one statement that amused him most was the belief that a very large majority of rapes went unreported. Not much likelihood of that in his instance. He would sensationalise his offences in every way he could, dress them up with a few touches to attract maximum attention and cause maximum confusion and embarrassment to the hated authorities, especially the police, who would be investigating them. He would lead them a merry dance.

Now that he no longer had any part in the family business, now that his brothers had bought him out of it, this was what he was going to live for. They were mad to think that they could successfully run the business themselves after dad had died, but then there always had been an element of madness from his mother's side of the family. The ironic thing was that his brothers thought he was too unstable, too like his daft cousin Neville, to be in a business partnership. They had called him unbalanced. He knew what that meant. They were balanced all right, sitting balanced on the fence, afraid to lean in the right direction.

Little did they know just how balanced his scales of justice would be. He was going to bring to bear on his enemies the same weight of pressure that they had put on his dad when they had brought a warrant to search his business premises, confiscated his computer, taken away all his manifests and company documents, examined his bank account and tax returns, and then, if that were not enough, searched his home with equal cold-hearted thoroughness. It was now all up to him. He was the really smart one, the one not only with the brains but with the will to stand up and take on the system, to expose to public ridicule the men in authority who had left them without a father. Furthermore, he now had the financial independence that would allow him to devote all his time to this end.

The rage burned in him yet again. The Home Office suits, the border control agency, the customs people, the police, the social services, all had united to prosecute the innocent and protect the guilty. The lorry driver hadn't known there were twenty illegal immigrants stowed away in his vehicle, but as soon as they were discovered, all the combined force of the various authorities was concentrated on his father's freight company, on nothing more than the word of the immigrants. In terror of the smuggling gang behind the operation, the so-called refugees claimed that they had given all their savings to his dad, that he had masterminded it. With the legal powers all ranged against him and his reputation in ruins, his father had succumbed to a heart attack that took his life at the age of only sixty-one He had been another easy target for a law and order system so weak and corrupt that it was able to persecute only the law-abiding, while the lawless and the guilty not only went unpunished, but actually received legal aid and other professional services. This was a moral crusade he intended, a campaign against injustice, inefficiency, and the abuse of power.

His first victim presented by chance, the best way by far in his scheme of things. He had taken to riding the buses in the evenings, choosing the journeys and routes haphazardly, watching his fellow passengers and the people scurrying about on the streets. He enjoyed the feeling of control and advantage he had, especially in the different identities he displayed: sometimes he was the labourer in donkey jacket and beanie hat, sometimes the tradesman in overalls and cloth cap, sometimes the casual dude in baseball cap, denim jacket and jeans, sometimes the smart executive in glasses, suit and sharp shoes.

That Friday evening his bus was passing through the Hawescourt district. It had formerly been the site of the city gasworks, and was now an area of anonymous, new redbrick offices bristling with chrome and glass. It was about eight o'clock and the place was deserted. There were only a few passengers on the bus. The woman a couple of seats in front of him got up, pressed the bell, and alighted. He was immediately interested. She was in her forties, he guessed, and hadn't the appearance of an office worker. This was not a residential district, so he wondered about the purpose of her visit. He got off at the next stop a few hundred yards further and started walking back. He could see her solitary figure in the distance coming in his direction on the other side of the street. She had crossed over. The road stretching between the lines of blank-faced buildings was virtually empty of traffic. The woman was about a hundred yards from the stop where she had alighted when she turned into the tiny forecourt of a small office block, unlocked the front door, and disappeared inside.

He found a deep empty doorway almost opposite and pressed himself into its shadows. The ground floor of the office building flickered into light, and a minute or so later he could see her shape at a first-floor window in the unmistakable posture and movement of someone vacuuming a floor. She was a cleaner. He settled himself in position for a lengthy wait, and traced her progress through the building as the fluorescent lights stuttered on in the various windows. His watch lasted over an hour, and in that time not one pedestrian appeared on the street. The pavements were totally deserted, and none of the buses stopped to set down any more passengers. He took the opportunity to scan the area for CCTV cameras, but detected none.

Finally, the last light downstairs in the office building went out and the woman came out, locked the door, and made her way to the nearest bus stop for her return journey. The service was thin and she had to wait almost fifteen minutes before a bus arrived. He studied her from his hiding place, about sixty yards distant on the opposite side of the street. She was of medium height and build, with short, fairish hair. He would definitely recognise her again. He waited until her bus had disappeared, slid out of the doorway, and crossed over to the office building.

The recce was very promising, in fact, excellent. He hadn't noticed the little alleyway down the far side of the building. Not only was the alley in deep shadow, but a recessed doorway just a few yards down it would allow him full view of her arrival, with no danger at all of being detected. An even better discovery awaited. When he followed the alleyway down the length of the building's side profile, he found that it joined up with a narrow trail that led down directly to the embankment, allowing him a number of alternative routes home, either on foot or by public transport. Perfect.

It was on foot that he made his way to Hawescourt the following Friday evening. He had already been there by day mid-week, and found a different place altogether. Then it was an alive, busy place of call centres and administration offices peopled by young staff with IT backgrounds. Now it was once more empty of life and activity.

His bet was that the cleaner would arrive about the same time every week, maybe even by the same bus, but he took his place in the alleyway about half an hour earlier to give her some leeway. From the darkness of the side doorway, he could angle his view past the front corner of the building and across the alley to take in a fair width of road and pavement on the far side of the street in the direction from which she would arrive.

Sure enough, about twenty minutes or so later, just after a bus had passed on the outward run, she entered his field of vision and crossed the road diagonally, heading directly towards him. He tensed, pulled on the black ski mask, and watched her come closer and closer. She was less than ten yards from him when she went out of view to his right, just past the corner at the front of the building. He heard her feet on the small, paved forecourt area just a few yards round the corner. He slipped out of the doorway, slid along the wall, and, still in darkness, peered round the corner. She had just opened the glass front door and was halfway through it when he clasped his gloved hand round her mouth from behind and in the same movement bustled her inside and closed the door with his foot. It was the work of a couple of seconds.

She gasped a muffled grunt of shock. The ease with which he forced her down the entrance hall made him think for an instant that she had fainted, but it was clear in that first moment when he faced her that she had simply surrendered out of terror. In the half-light coming into the hall from the street he must indeed have been a terrifying figure in the mask and brandishing a thin, glinting knife.

At first the woman seemed to think he was a burglar and tried to tell him there was no money left on the premises, but when he made clear to her what his real purpose was, she sobbed in dread. He hissed his words to her, stretching the sibilants to disguise his voice and to increase the tone of menace, although there was no likelihood at all of her offering any level of resistance. He carried out the rape in the small, carpeted board room on the first floor, which offered a degree of comfort. It went fairly well, all things considered. A pity he couldn't have told her that she was part of a larger plan. She wouldn't have minded so much, would have understood better if she had been able to see the rape in its fuller context. Too dangerous, though. When it was over, he bound her hands and feet together with the cable ties he had brought with him, and left the message he had scrawled in red felt tip pen beside her on the floor, its letters copied from a font that was totally dissimilar to his own style of hand printing. The rhyme was scarily simple:

> *This Is Number One,*
> *I've Only Just Begun.*

In ten minutes he was on the embankment and walking home. On his way he dropped into a mailbox an envelope, addressed to The Daily Record and containing another rhyming message in the same red scrawl:

> *A Wink's As Good As A Nod,*
> *To A Blind PC Plod.*
> *Tell the Boys in Plain Clothes,*
> *I'm Right Under Their Nose.*

That should set the cat among the pigeons.

Next morning, early, he visited his father's grave, on a double errand. Sitting on his knees at the graveside he assured his dad in a low, earnest voice that justice had begun, that those who had humiliated him would soon be humiliated themselves, exposed and ridiculed. Then he lifted out from its niche below the headstone the small, rectangular marble tray that held meshed containers for flowers. He reached into the space below and withdrew a flat plastic box from its hiding place, removed the lid, and placed in it, beside the cable ties and red felt tip pen already there, the ski mask and knife. Finally, he replaced the box and re-seated the marble tray on top of it.

How many times had offenders been caught out by keeping incriminating items on their home property, in house or garage or shed? It wasn't at all likely that he would be a suspect, but he was going to take absolutely no chances, none at all. The more clueless the police were, the more inept they would appear in the public eye, and the more scrutiny they would come under themselves.

The story appeared on the front page of The Daily Record's Monday edition. He had chosen well. Leave it to the gutter press to promote whatever salacious matter it was pretending to deplore. *Rhyming Rapist Strikes in Hawescourt* screamed out the headline, not the lead story of the day, but sound second billing. The report briefly told how a 38 year-old cleaning lady had been raped at knifepoint by a hooded attacker when she turned up for work, and how the '*brutal assault*' had left the victim '*badly traumatised*'. Typical tabloid press exaggeration. The story went on to tell how a crude note written in rhyme had been left at the scene suggesting that further crimes were intended, and then it played its trump card: the rapist had sent to The Daily Record a second rhyming message, taunting the police. The paper was working in close collaboration with the police to assist in *bringing this monster to justice*. The item finished with the usual appeals by the police to the public to report any suspicious activity, and claims that they were following a number of lines of enquiry.

He laughed at this phoney announcement. This was police-speak for an investigation that was at a standstill, that was up against a brick wall.

The first rape was a kind of template for the next two. He knew that to keep the momentum going after such a good start he needed to follow it up fairly quickly, but without compromising his security. His stalking of the student, his careful timings of her movements and timetable, the planning of the attack, and its execution were carried out with the same care and caution as he had given to the cleaning lady.

*Hissing Sid Strikes Again* was the headline this time on the front page of The Daily Record, but now it was the top headline, in two-inch heavy capitals. The newspaper had dubbed him 'Hissing Sid' from the accounts both victims had given to the police of the rapist's whistling kind of speech. The name, he learned, referred to some evil snake character from an idiotic novelty song, but he was happy enough with it; the notion that someone with such a silly title could lead the police up the garden path served to highlight their incompetence.

The report in the paper related how the eighteen-year-old music school student had just opened her upstairs flat door when the figure appeared '*from nowhere*' and bundled her inside, before taping her mouth, threatening her with a knife, and committing the sexual assault. The police view was that this was no random, opportunist attack, but one that suggested premeditation and precision timing. The main focus of the report, however, centred on the rhyming messages which were now the signature of the offender. The one left beside this victim was alarmingly direct. It had been leaked to the newspaper by a disgruntled uniformed officer:

> *Say Hello to Victim Two.*
> *How Many Will I Do?*

It was the rhyming message mailed to The Daily Record, however, which prompted the change of tone and direction in the newspaper's attitude to this second crime:

> *The Police Must Like to Lose,*
> *They're Missing All the Clues,*
> *Leaving Me Safe and Free*
> *To Target Number Three.*

The paper asked what progress the police had made in the three weeks since the Hawescourt rape, what enquiries they were pursuing, if any, how close they were to making an arrest, and what assurances they could give that all was being done that should be done to protect the public from a serial rapist and make the streets safe for innocent women? The thrust of the piece was to put the police on the defensive, to speak out for a worried public who wanted results.

Next day some of the national papers had picked up the story of the rhyming rapist, and the same evening the local TV news broadcast covered it as well. He felt the kind of pride that a man feels when he sees a wrong being put right, knowing that only for him it would have gone unpunished.

He had a strange dream. Normally he paid no attention to dreams, but this one was so strong and vivid that it stayed with him next morning. He was a boy being carried on his dad's shoulders through a forest. He even recognised the place as Pellingham Forest Park, which the family had once visited on a picnic outing. In the dream his dad was smiling and kept asking him if he saw it OK, but he didn't know what it was he was being encouraged to see. Every time his dad turned or reached him higher to assist his view everything was blurred and he could make out nothing, no matter how hard he looked. He woke in a sweat, still aware of the frustration the dream had caused him. With nothing planned for the day ahead, and feeling a kind of urge to get out of town for a bit, he decided he would drive out mid-morning to the place that had been the scene of his dream.

The forest park was farther out of the city than he had remembered, and when he finally got there, he wasn't sure he was in the right place. Unknown to him, the National Trust had discontinued its control and maintenance of the forest, and the consequences were in evidence all around. The large sign had gone, and the car park was under siege by ragweed and brambles. He eased the car past some of these invaders and parked in a relatively clear area of tar macadam in the centre. In contrast to the busy forest park of his boyhood, Pellingham was a deserted, overgrown mockery of its well-groomed, popular past. His visit was over before it had properly started.

He was just about to restart the car when a movement in the driving mirror caught his eye, and his full attention. A lady in a quilted jacket, jeans and walking shoes, a tall lady, in her sixties, he calculated, from her short greyish hair, had walked into the car park and was striding briskly across it towards an opening in the trees, which he took to be a trail or path. It was clear from her confident movement that she was familiar with the place and knew exactly where she was going.

He figured it as best he could. She hadn't arrived by car, so must live nearby. She looked old enough to be retired, and was dressed to suit the terrain. By herself, so possibly widowed or unmarried. He checked his watch. Just short of midday. Taking a brisk walk to sharpen her appetite for lunch. He was tempted to follow her, but argued himself out of it. What he needed to know, needed to find out, was the regularity of this exercise. Something about her manner, her purposeful gait and familiarity with the location, told him it was not an infrequent or one-off activity. He started the car and drove homeward, his mind alive and excited.

The dream. Could it possibly mean something? This was new territory for him, new thinking. He couldn't deny that, had it not been for the dream, he wouldn't now be focusing on another rape, wouldn't have found another potential target so handily. Was this what he had been unable to see in the dream, was this what his dad had been wanting him to see?

How perfect it would be, a different age group, a totally different crime scene, enough to have them tearing their hair out. First thing was to get back out there and discreetly ascertain if the woman was a regular walker with a regular time slot. After that had been firmed up he could get down to the practicalities and finer details of the job.

Eleven o'clock the next morning found him back at Pellingham. He drove past the former main entrance to the car park and passed a couple of houses. Chances were that she lived in one of these. Just about a quarter of a mile beyond the first entrance was a secondary one with wide, fairly deep tyre marks and ruts suggesting that it had been used by industrial vehicles, heavy lorries and such. Ferns and grasses kissed across the track, but he was able to brush the car through them without obstruction. He parked around a slight bend, walked back to the road, and checked that his vehicle couldn't be seen by passers-by. In ten minutes he had walked through the trees to a spot overlooking the car park. Screened by a drift of ferns, he settled down to wait and watch.

At ten to twelve she appeared in what could have been an action replay of the previous morning, the same stride, the same clothes, the same direction. His hunch had been correct. He would have to assume that this was a daily exercise, that he could expect her at this time and place every week, but to narrow the odds he would plan to do the business on a Tuesday or Wednesday, the two days on which he had seen her. With exemplary patience he stayed at the same vantage point until he saw her come back into sight about forty minutes later and go out of the forest park where she had entered it. He waited another quarter of an hour, and then took the path she had taken. His reconnaissance was thorough and rewarding. He found an ideal place for the attack.

His head buzzed with ideas and considerations. To date, he had seen only that woman in Pellingham Forest Park. Nobody else at all had been anywhere near the place at that particular time of day. He would have to take the chance that such would again be the case on the actual day. A man walking by himself in this remote spot might indeed attract attention or suspicion if someone did happen to see him before or after the rape. He would buy a dog, a little dog, a poodle. Nobody would ever think that a man walking a poodle would be in the process of perpetrating a rape. He'd strangle the animal afterwards and dispose of it. He'd have to notify The Daily Record after the rape so that she would be found safe and well. She'd never make it to the road trussed up by cable ties. What a stir when Hissing Sid would detail the whereabouts of his latest victim from a public telephone to a local newspaper, and the police the last to know.

The third rape lit the touchpaper of social outrage and a blaze of public criticism of the police. Gone was any notion of restraint or cooperation with the law in the headlines that took up almost a third of the front page: *Police Snooze On As Rapist Claims Third Victim*. The sub-heading was equally scathing: *Hissing SID 3:0 Missing CID*. The Editorial launched an all-out attack on the incompetence of the Chief Constable and the officers under his command, labelling them too ham-fisted to catch the slippery rapist, and suggesting they would need lessons from Hissing Sid if they were going to be able to wriggle out of blame for their failure to stop him. Public indignation was at an all-time high, the reporter claimed, ignited by the appalling attack on the helpless elderly victim, and inflamed further by the galling accuracy of the rhyming message left at the scene of the violation:

> *Number Three,*
> > *Easy as Can Be.*
> *It's Plain to See,*
> > *You Can't Catch Me.*

After they had received the anonymous hissing tip-off, the newspaper, instead of informing the police at once, had sent some of its people out to Pellingham, professedly to check that it wasn't a hoax, but really to keep The Daily Record in the spotlight. It was these people from the press who had found the victim and the note. As the paper commented, it seemed that the rapist had more faith in The Daily Record than he had in the forces of the Crown. There was certainly no doubt about his contempt for the police, as expressed in the message sent by mail to the paper the day after the offence:

*The Police Must Do More,*
*Than Just Keep the Score.*
*They'll Be Baffled and Sore,*
*When I Do Number Four.*

Bowing to an outcry and pressure that were threatening to depose him, the Chief Constable for the county called a press conference for Friday morning. Flanked on one side by the Assistant Chief Constable and a Chief Superintendent, and on the other by a Chief Inspector and a Detective Inspector, he faced a room filled to over-brimming with reporters, photographers, and TV crews. He was well aware that the high-ranking men seated behind the table were in for a rough ride.

His statement acknowledged the concern felt by the public, their anxiety to see the culprit off the streets and behind bars, and their understandable disappointment that, as yet, nobody had been charged with the appalling offences that had left three women traumatised. He described the perpetrator as a highly dangerous sexual predator who planned his attacks with great care, and covered his tracks so cleverly that the case was one of the most difficult that his hardworking police officers had ever been called on to solve. He invited the Detective Inspector to outline the measures taken to date, but it soon became clear that nothing would be said that was going to appease the mood of criticism and dissatisfaction in the room.

Every known sex offender in three counties had been checked by the task force set up to handle the case, but they had drawn a blank. Apart from a vague description by a resident in the Pellingham area of a small, black car he had seen being driven slowly, there was no witness evidence at all. The description given by the terrified victims was of a tall man dressed in black and wearing a black ski mask. His most distinctive feature was his voice, which all three described as a hiss. They agreed, too, that he had not been excessively violent, and had bound them afterwards without roughness. The Inspector hastily added that this in no way reduced the seriousness of these harrowing experiences or their effect on the unfortunate victims.

The most interesting detail was the one that he did not release: in all three assaults the rapes had not been 'completed'. The rapist had terminated the act prematurely, before climax, which was virtually unknown in such crimes. It led the police psychologists to suspect that although the offences were of a sexual nature, they might not necessarily be sexually motivated. One theory was that these were token or symbolic attacks carried out by a highly disturbed paranoid schizophrenic.

The Chief Inspector's report ended with the profile that had been drawn up of the offender, a white man in his thirties, living on his own, well educated, a car owner, very likely to have served time in prison and to have a grudge against authority. The profiler was not convinced that the offender had himself been subjected to sexual abuse. At this point the Chief Inspector thanked the press, especially The Daily Record, for their support and asked for patience and vigilance until the criminal was brought to justice.

The Chief Constable echoed these sentiments and said he would take a few questions. A hail of them was instantly discharged against defenders who had no ammunition they could use to protect themselves or to return fire. *No, they had no leads at present. No, they had no suspects under question at the present time. No, there was no forensic or DNA evidence. No, they were not going to issue identity cards or impose a curfew. No, Hissing Sid was not running rings round them. Yes, he would make a mistake. Yes, it was possible that there would be further attacks. No, budget cuts were not adversely affecting the investigation. Yes, there was sufficient man power. No, police morale was not at a new low. No, the Chief Constable was not reconsidering his position. No, it was not true that Scotland Yard had been called in to take over the investigation.*

How he enjoyed the whole televised performance, the squirming, sweating discomfort of the county's top police commanders, their hollow, transparent promises, their empty reassurances that fooled nobody. He had to admit that the profile bit wasn't too bad, but did it bring them any closer to catching him? The big question now was whether he should regard this humiliation of the police as the end game, the final act of the show, or should he do one more in the hope that it would topple that blustering clown of a Chief Constable? Maybe, but in the short term he would enjoy the glow of success that had put the spring back in his step. One thing was certain, they would never catch him. He was too well organised, too methodical, too clever, to be taken by a bunch of dolts who knew only how to persecute soft targets like his dad.

*

Stanley Pritchard, like everyone affected by obsessive compulsive personality disorder, saw nothing at all eccentric in his demeanour or behaviour. For him, there was nothing unusual in his concern for orderliness, his perfectionism and excessive attention to detail. He liked to plan activities down to the minute, to adhere to routines in rigid, almost ritual-like manner. The fact that his fixation with endangered species of wildlife, and red squirrels in particular, was just his hobby, not his occupation, led to no diminution at all in intensity or commitment on his part.

Stanley's collection of ten expensive self-operating trail cameras, remote motion-activated camera traps, as some people called them, testified to his dedication. He would choose a location, rise at dawn, and make his way in the half-light to the pre-selected spot and fit the cameras to suitable trees or posts with a strap, confident that the waterproof camouflaged casing would protect the equipment in all weathers and temperatures. Stanley was careful, as always, that his cameras at Pellingham were hidden deep in the forest where there were no trails or paths, safe from the attentions of thieves or vandals. He was also experienced enough to ensure that his LEDs were black; the faint glow from infrared emitters could spook the very shy, nervous red squirrel.

He chose Friday morning to check his cameras. Stanley hadn't checked his pictures for ten days, not wanting to run the risk of scaring the creatures away from this secluded place by repeated visits. The long-life batteries in the cameras lasted for months. He replaced the SD cards in each of the cameras and drove home with ample time to make his usual breakfast, drive to work, and be in his parking space at four minutes to nine. He looked forward to studying the video footage and still photographs that evening.

The evening meal was over, the dishes washed and dried and put away, and he was seated in his armchair at twenty-nine minutes past six, just in time to turn on the TV for the local evening news. Perfect. The main item on the broadcast was a number of attacks on women by some serial rapist who was defying the police's efforts to catch him. Stanley was paying little attention to the piece until he heard Pellingham Forest Park mentioned as the location of the latest attack. Very worrying. The blundering about by investigators could upset the red squirrels so much that they might very well be frightened into looking for a quieter habitat elsewhere. He listened closely to the remainder of the report, which ended with an appeal to the public to assist in tracking down this merciless criminal.

*

The mood at half past eight on Monday morning in the operations room of the Hissing Sid Task Force would have made a morgue look cheery. The investigation was at a dead end, going nowhere, and desperately in need of a lead, any lead, that might help raise morale. The unspoken truth was the team was just waiting for the next rape, in the hope that it might provide them with some evidence or a fresh approach. Just then the Front Desk Sergeant rang up to say there was someone in the lobby asking to see whoever was in charge of the rapist case and claiming he had some information that might be of interest. Might be of interest? At that point the news that Elvis had just entered the building would, by comparison, have stirred no interest at all.

They were clustered round the TV set watching the footage and photos for the second time. When the little fussy man had produced the material and instructed them on the use of the SD card reader through the USB port of the TV set, they had exchanged sceptical glances. This was a nutter or gadget freak or some other kind of time waster. One minute into the pictures and all that changed. What they were watching, in full colour, was bizarre, and undeniably sinister in some indefinable way. The pictures clearly showed a tall spindly man dressed in a black polo neck pullover and black trousers high-stepping along a brambled trail in a peculiar fashion, peering over his shoulder and swinging, in his right hand, a canvas bag in a careless manner that was at odds with his otherwise furtive bearing. The most curious feature of all was the poodle dog dangling at the man's side, the fingers of his left hand hooked through its collar, the lead trailing among the undergrowth and long grasses. The dog was wriggling and obviously distressed.

'He's like some kind of spider checking its web,' one of the detectives said softly, and nobody thought the remark ill-considered.

'Bring up that close-up again,' said a Detective Sergeant. 'I'm positive I've seen that face before somewhere. Recently. I'm sure of it. I'll trawl back through recent stuff, and it'll maybe come to me.'

'If he's our man,' said the DI, ' then this is him on his way to the crime. He's off the beaten track but seems to know where he's going all right. It's the right date, and about an hour before the victim says she was attacked.' Pritchard's cameras automatically recorded on screen the date and time when they were activated. 'So, this individual was at or near the scene when the crime was committed, but even if we do identify him, we're still going to need to connect him with the crime. As it is, all we have on him now is cruelty to a small dog. I don't imagine he's going to hiss a confession of three rapes for us.'

'Munton,' the DS suddenly said. 'William Munton. The suspect we investigated for smuggling illegal immigrants. This dog lover here is one of his sons. That's where I saw him before. I'll have his name in my notebook. There were three sons. I had a brief word with all three of them when we called down to their freight yard.'

That exquisite moment of excitement when the break arrives that will crack a case electrified the room. The DI allowed the buzz for a moment or two, they deserved it, but then discussed strategy. All they knew for sure was that the suspect fitted the time and place. Their instincts told them this was Hissing Sid the rapist, but without harder evidence they were unlikely to be granted a search warrant.

'We'll not put him on his guard. He's good enough at covering his tracks as it is. We need round-the-clock surveillance and an in-depth look at everything about him: address, vehicle, criminal record, if any, medical record, marital status, education, interests, relationships, contacts, what he has for breakfast. We've been accused of dragging our heels on this long enough, now it's time to go on the front foot.'

The discovery that Desmond Munton, the youngest of the three sons, drove a black Mazda which fitted with the witness evidence, only served to confirm what they already knew, that he had been in Pellingham the day of the third rape. They set up a twenty-four-hour stake-out on his house and put to work their top team of tailing experts. An examination of the contents of his bin uncovered nothing suspicious or incriminating.

The whole matter of the dream intrigued him. Was his dad observing his revenge, assisting him in it, applauding as he played merry hell with his father's tormentors? He liked the notion that his efforts were receiving approval from beyond the grave. The grave. He would make an extra visit and pay tribute to his dad by leaving a token of appreciation for his inspiration in the third rape. He had dumped the dog in a rubbish skip, otherwise he could have left the collar or lead. No, what he would add to the felt markers, gaffer tape, ski mask, knife and cable ties in the cemetery cache, would be a cutting from The Daily Record's front-page coverage of the police press conference. It would serve as memorabilia of perfect crimes and imperfect policing.

The burial ground was its usual deserted place as he knelt before the gravestone and spoke aloud to his father his solemn words of grief and gratitude. He carefully lifted out the marble tray, opened the plastic box, and was in the very act of dedicating the newspaper report, when two police officers stepped out from behind the large yew tree immediately behind him.

*

Stanley Pritchard's fears were justified. All the hullaballoo in the forest had scared off the red squirrels. At just about the same time as the handcuffs were being snapped on Hissing Sid, Stanley was unstrapping his cameras from their hidden locations deep in Pellingham Forest Park and comforting himself with the news he had just heard. Otters had been seen in the small lake at Vincent Peak. Yes, they would be ideal alternative subjects for his camera traps.

## *Medium Rare*

'You know I love you, Diane. Whatever you think, right or wrong, good or bad, you know I love you.' His candlelit face confirmed the earnestness of the words. She dropped her eyes and gently withdrew the hand his fingers had imprisoned on the table.

He waved away a hovering waiter. 'Yes, I know it's only six weeks, but, six weeks or six years, we are meant for each other, Diane. I believe in fate bringing people together. That's why we met. We were destined to meet at the bereavement counselling meetings, I've never been more sure of anything.'

She kept her eyes lowered, but her tone was firm. 'Please don't rush things, Derek. I feel I shouldn't be here with you like this, so soon after the accident. It feels wrong. Bill has been dead only four months. The inquest isn't even over, and here I am with you as if he'd never existed. And your poor wife, her months of suffering. It just seems wrong. I feel guilt or shame or something. I keep wondering how Bill would feel about all this.'

'He doesn't blame you at all, he wants you to be happy.'

She looked up sharply. 'Don't say things like that.'

He hesitated, feeling the rebuke, but continued. 'I know he approves, I know you are not to feel you are doing something wrong.'

Diane turned away. 'How can you say that? Every day I'm surrounded by his things, his books, his clothes, his fishing rods, everything. I've made my mind up, I'm going to put the house up for sale. For me it's like a scrapbook of Bill's life. I feel too guilty even to invite you home, Derek, and you're saying I should feel I'm doing nothing wrong. And how can you have forgotten Alison so quickly?' In the soft light, the anguish showed in her delicate, well-bred face.

Suddenly he folded the menus flat and trapped both her hands on the table. 'Diane, there's something you have to hear, you must please listen.' His voice was hoarse. 'When I said I know that Bill approves, I meant it literally. I know, yes, know, that both Bill and Alison give their blessing to our relationship.'

Diane's mouth opened in surprise, but before she could say anything he was rushing on. 'You see, I've been in touch with them, or they've been in touch with me. They've spoken to me, not directly, but through a medium. I've been to a spiritualist, Diane, a medium, a genuine man, a good man. Please believe me, both Alison and Bill are happy, and they want us to be happy together.

No, wait, please, it's true. I'm not a fool, Diane, I'm not being conned, it's not just some phoney telling me the things I want to hear. This man is real. He's told me things that nobody knew but Alison and me. It's amazing. You'll see for yourself, you'll believe too. Bill will speak to you, I promise, he'll speak to you, just as Alison spoke to me.'

The emotion overtook him, and he wiped an eye with his napkin, freeing a hand, but she was too dazed to withdraw it. They sat in silence, Diane unable to reply.

'You must go and see this spiritualist, for your own sake, no matter about me, about us. Go with me, or go by yourself, but please go, for your own peace of mind.'

Diane freed her other hand and laced her fingers together, her expression uncomfortable. 'I'm sorry, Derek, but I just don't believe in these things. I never have. I've always avoided fortune tellers and palm readers and horoscopes, all that kind of stuff. I can't take any of it seriously. I'm surprised you do.'

'I didn't, not until a week ago, but there's fate again. Can I tell you what happened? It was last Tuesday evening. I was driving home, and there happened to be one of those chat or call-in programmes on the radio, you know the kind of thing.

Well, the subject was the spirit world, contacting the dead, something I'd never seriously thought about in my life before. I was only half listening, thinking about other things, but then a detective came on and he spoke about this spiritualist who had helped them solve two murders, two crimes where they had no clues and no suspects. It was amazing. The detective was totally convinced, and he said that all his police colleagues, hard cynics, every one of them, were convinced as well.

At the end of the programme anybody interested or wanting further information was invited to phone in. I couldn't get it out of my mind, Diane, and the next day I called the radio station and they were permitted to give out the spiritualist's number. I rang him, and the following evening I went to a meeting. He doesn't like the term séance. It wasn't anything like I'd imagined, it was just a group of ordinary people wanting, for different reasons, to get in touch with someone who had passed over. There, you see, I'm using their terms already.'

Derek gave a short laugh at his own expense, but his mood was totally serious. 'I felt right away that this was real, that there was nothing fake about it. There's something humble and caring about the man, and he doesn't make great claims about himself. He admitted from the start that there might be people there he couldn't help, and that he might be contacted by people on the other side who had no connection with anybody in the room.

Suddenly, Diane, and the shock of it nearly stopped my heart, he was talking about me, and Alison's cancer, and how I had to keep watering her flower boxes, and the new wooden flooring we had been talking about just before she went into hospital. He mentioned other things, little things, things nobody but Alison and I knew about. It was incredible. He said it was a woman speaking to him, and I knew it was Alison, there was nobody else it could have been, no other way he could have known those things.

She told me she was happy, and that I was close to happiness, and I wasn't to worry. She said the person who was going to make me happy was not to be anxious, that it was all right. Diane, the tears were rolling down my face, and other people in the room were crying too.'

'How much was it?' asked Diane, trying to control a voice that was trembling and noticeably softened.

'That's another thing. There's no actual charge. People give according to their means and to their own feelings of gratitude. I don't mind telling you that I gave him fifty quid, and I would have doubled that if I had had it with me. But there's no use me telling you all this, Diane. The only way you'll believe me is if you go yourself...'

\*

'If you're expecting a crystal ball, spooky voices and flickering lights, you're going to be disappointed.'

They were in one of the side chambers of the Town Hall, its ornate mouldings, trompe-l'œil ceiling of drifting clouds, panelled walls and gilt-framed portraits at odds with the fire extinguishers, EXIT signs, and panic doors of the modern public building. The speaker was a middle-aged man in casual clothes. His only remarkable feature was a full head of steel-grey hair. The audience was a cluster of anxious looking people, mostly women, the youngest in her thirties.

Diane was disappointed. 'He doesn't look too impressive; I imagined a spiritualist would have looked a bit more... spiritual. Where's the table we're meant to sit round?'

'There isn't one. It's not like that. It's not a carnival sideshow,' Derek said defensively.

The speaker was continuing. 'You don't need to sit in darkness, or hold hands, or close your eyes. I'm going to reduce the lighting to help you relax and think about the one you would like to hear from. Remember, I am just a medium, a means to receive and transmit messages. All I can do is tell you what I hear, if anything.'

The lighting dimmed and the people involuntarily shuffled their plastic chairs into a half circle. Diane noticed a woman shiver, as though a chill had passed through her. For a few moments there was silence. The man didn't have his eyes closed, but seemed to be listening intently. When he spoke it was softly, in the manner of an interpreter keeping pace with a foreign speaker.

'Is there someone present who wants to hear from Sean, someone who is worried, unhappy... unhappy that she was not on speaking terms with Sean, someone who wanted to patch things up with him but feels she left it too late?'

As the words were being spoken in that odd mimetic manner the woman immediately in front of Derek stiffened and put her hand up to her mouth. She looked like she had been given an electric shock.

'She has left her red setter, Rory, with a neighbour,' the voice continued smoothly. 'She wears bright clothes, but her heart is sad.'

The woman started to sob. 'Sean, Sean, I'm sorry, Sean, it was all my fault. I haven't enjoyed a single minute since that day. I should have said I was sorry, I should have, I should have...' Her voice trailed off in grief.

'You are not to worry. It is worry that has given you the ulcer. Sean loves you, you are still his little sister, the little sister with the pigtails. He is happy. There is nothing to forgive. Sean knows you love him. He asks if you can remember the name of the little yellow duck he won for you at the fairground.'

'Sukie, it was Sukie,' the woman sobbed, her love for her brother shining through the blotchiness of her face, her heart open with tenderness. One or two people in the audience were visibly moved by her flood of emotion.

'Is Diane here?' the medium suddenly asked, and Derek sat forward in his chair, the muscles in his jaw tensing. 'I need to speak to Diane. Is Diane here with us today?'

'Yes.' It was Derek who answered. Diane looked too stunned to speak for herself. The medium was unperturbed. 'Diane, Bill is here. Why are you worrying about him? He knows you are anxious, but you are to forget about the accident and remember him with love. He suffered no pain. The blood you saw on the road was just rusty water from the lorry's radiator. He wants you to know he is happy. He wants you now to take the happiness that is being offered by someone who loves you.'

Diane suddenly got up, overturning her chair, and rushed out through the side door. Derek found her in the lobby, trembling. He put his arms round her and she let her head sink on his shoulder. He gently stroked her hair.

'I'm sorry, Derek, I'm sorry, I just couldn't listen anymore. It's so frightening, so strange. I'm so confused.'

'Ssshh, ssshh, of course you're confused. That's just how I felt when Alison spoke to me. It's hard taking in what's happened... Sssshh, I know, I know...'

*

'Yessir, here's to me,' and the medium raised his glass to himself. Without the grey wig he looked even more nondescript. 'We're home and dry on this one.'

'Derek' didn't join in the toast, but he was equally satisfied. 'Friday evening's the clincher. It's her birthday and I'm going to celebrate it in style. Wining, dining, and then the sparkler. She's a class lady, Leonard, so it'll be the real thing, a five grand diamond, none of your Zircon stuff for my Diane.'

'Listen to you,' said Leonard. 'There's my little team away back in the train, happy with their sandwiches and the fifty quid in their pocket, and you're splashing out five big ones on a rock. I could get you one for a coupla hundred.'

'Derek' smiled. 'Don't spoil the ship for a ha'p'orth of tar, Lennie, old son. Remember that, when I've got my hands on dear old Bill's two hundred grand life insurance.'

'The sooner the better,' grumbled Lennie. 'I'm sick of this town. It's about time we moved on. Anyhow, if you want to be the big spender, I'll have another pint.'

Derek was on a high. The champagne, the meal, the surprise birthday cake, and then the presentation of the ring with the proposal. His face glowed as he refilled their glasses. 'To us, darling, to our lives together. I'll never order another medium rare without thinking how much I owe to a rare medium.' He was pleased with the inversion. Suddenly his voice was husky. 'Seeing you wearing that ring makes me the happiest man in the world, and I can say that now without any other feelings to spoil it.'

Diane smiled and didn't reply, but stretched wide her left hand in that universal signal of a woman newly engaged.

'You'll have to excuse me, darling, but I can't hold my champagne.' He laughed, and headed for the Gents to phone Leonard and confirm the triumph. It was the last time he ever saw his fiancée.

'For the first time in my whole career I nearly laughed out loud and gave the game away. I had to run out to get my face straight,' 'Diane' giggled. She was in bed with Anita, her lover. 'You should have seen the antics of that medium, in touch with the dead husband I had invented. And that ridiculous creature sobbing 'Sean, Sean'. The whole thing was hilarious. Pure 'amateur night' stuff. Wonder if I'll get as much fun the next time I decide to be bereaved?'

'It's a lovely ring.' Anita cuddled up close. She laughed. 'The things men will do for money.'

Noel Spence

# About the Publisher

L.R. Price Publications is dedicated to publishing books by undiscovered, talented authors.

We use a mixture of traditional and modern publishing methods to bring our authors' words to the wider world.

We print, publish, distribute and market books in a variety of formats including paper and hard back, electronic books e- books, digital audio books and online.

If you are an author interested in getting your book published; or a book retailer interested in selling our books, please contact us.

www.lrpricepublications.com

L.R. Price Publications

Ltd, 27 Old Gloucester

Street, London, WC1N

3AX. (0203) 051 9572

publishing@lrprice.com

Printed in Great Britain
by Amazon

87167261R00203